A Lifetime Again

By
Rosanne L. Higgins

To all of the inmates of the Erie County Poorhouse, Hospital and Insane Asylum.

Thank you for sharing your stories. Rest in peace.

Prologue

May 28, 1870

Approaching the institution from Main Street, Martha still wasn't used to the massive complex that had replaced the single brick building that had served as the county poorhouse in Black Rock, the building where she had spent the first year of her new life in America more than three decades earlier. It was to the insane asylum that Martha was headed this morning.

The Erie County Poorhouse, located just outside the city limits in Buffalo Plains, had a separate building to house the insane. The three-story limestone building radiated an unsettling sense of permanence. Despite repeated complaints and suggestions from both the keepers and the physicians, there was no separate hospital on site for the insane patients. Because those patients were often disruptive to both the staff and the other patients, the Keeper of the Insane Asylum transferred only those inmates who were seriously ill or injured to the hospital ward. Medicine was making rapid progress, but the condition of insanity, both its causes and its cures, remained elusive. So many people had been brought low by the harsh realities of urban life;

the new building served as an omen for this terrible plague, which would reach epidemic proportions in the decades to come.

Martha was the only female physician in the city of Buffalo, although soon she hoped there would be more. When she graduated from medical school in 1852, most people, even those seen by her esteemed brother-in-law Dr. Michael Nolan, were wary of a female physician. The poorhouse was always in need of doctors willing to work for little or no compensation, and so she found a place to practice medicine there. Many of the inmates of the asylum experienced physical ailments in addition to whatever affliction of the brain they suffered, and Martha did what she could to alleviate both.

The matron of the asylum gave Martha a quick smile when she entered. "Good morning, Mrs. Quinn." Henrietta Boswell had been assigned the unpleasant duties of the matron of the lunatic asylum, as it was known to the other inmates of the poorhouse, since the Keeper's wife had run off earlier in the winter. Mrs. Boswell was a widow and was glad of the position and the small salary that went with it, and was it anyone's business that she was the Keeper's sister? She did not think so. Like most of the poorhouse staff, Mrs. Boswell couldn't quite bring herself to address a woman as doctor, and always referred to Martha as Mrs. Quinn. "Mr. Leonard said to send you straight to the women's ward," she said, continuing to scrutinize the daily chore list in her hand.

The second floor housed the patients considered not to be a danger to themselves or to others. It was they who did the bulk of the chores around the asylum and the poorhouse, everything from laundry and cooking to ditch-digging and tree-trimming. The women's ward contained fourteen cells and the men's ward eighteen, each intended to house a single patient. It seemed lately that there were two or three inmates sharing a cell, particularly in the women's ward. Martha hoped that the other occupants of her patient's quarters were off about their chores so she wouldn't have to crawl over them to perform her examination. Three people sharing a room only five feet by seven, and only one bed among them, invited trouble of all kinds, not the least of which was the easy spread of disease.

"Thank ye, Mrs. Boswell." Martha had long since given up the fight of being addressed by her proper title at the poorhouse and continued without further comment toward the large oak staircase.

Mason Leonard, Keeper of the Insane Asylum, would not be there to meet her, she knew. She would be directed to the new patient by whoever was assigned to tend the ward that day. It would likely be a poorhouse inmate who worked in exchange for his keep and a small wage. Martha had learned long ago to disregard whatever details of patient conditions the attendants had to offer. In most cases, the individuals assigned to the wards did not understand the medical terminology associated with various conditions, and sometimes the attendants simply made things up. Martha would learn what she could from the patient directly.

"Good day to ye, Mrs. Sutton." Martha was relieved to see Rose Sutton was currently in charge of the ward. She was kind to the inmates and accomplished the tasks required of her without complaint. "I understand we have…" Martha's comment was cut off by a strangled shriek, followed by a series of methodic thumping noises from the floor above.

Rose looked up and shook her head before addressing the doctor. "We've got a screamer upstairs, arrived last night. Poor soul's been at it all morning."

Martha knew that the inmates considered by the Keeper to be dangerous were kept in locked cells on the third floor. The sounds directly above her were all too familiar. The patient causing the ruckus was shackled to the bed and trying to break free by slamming the headboard against the wall. After eighteen years of seeing patients with a primary diagnosis of insanity, Martha was still both shocked and saddened by the cruelty or, at the very least, ignorance that was applied to the treatment of the so-called diseases of the brain. They had come to understand that, in cases of true insanity, it was the brain rather than the mind that was ill. It was the liberal use of insanity as a diagnosis that troubled her. She grew frustrated by the number of patients committed to the asylum who could have easily been cured by kindness and compassion alone.

That was the case for many women, particularly, who had been consumed with grief over the loss of a child or husband, and had become unreachable to the outside world. Others, prostitutes mostly, could endure no more of the apathy, violence and heartbreak of the vocation that misfortune had forced upon them. Martha would not let herself think about those few women whom she suspected ended up in the asylum because they ran afoul of the wrong person, a cruel and controlling father or husband, perhaps, who would not suffer insubordination from a woman. It had happened more than once, if the patients were to be believed.

"I'll have a look upstairs when I'm done here," Martha told her. She made it a point to take a tour of the third floor whenever she was attending at the insane asylum. Sometimes the patients there became less dangerous when their pain was relieved or they simply had an opportunity to tell their story to someone willing to listen. Martha was not always able to help them, but she felt she must always try. "Now, let us see to Miss Potter's headache."

Prior to her commitment to the asylum, Linda Potter could be found often wandering the Canal District, intemperate and begging for money or drink. Martha had never learned what had driven this young woman to such a pitiful existence. Miss Potter's belligerent disregard for the constable had resulted in her commitment with a diagnosis of periodic mania, although her disposition had improved considerably when forced to give up the drink. Martha opened the door of the small room to find Linda face down with the covers pulled up over her head. Gently, she placed a hand on the woman's back as she spoke. "What troubles ye this mornin', Miss Potter?"

She rolled slowly over and peeked out from under the wool blanket, worn thin from its years of service. "It's my head," she groaned and retreated back under the blanket.

Her face was drawn in agony, eyes mere slits as she tried to focus her attention on Dr. Quinn. Emotional outbursts aside, Linda was otherwise usually healthy and had been assigned to work in the laundry. Unlike some of the other inmates, she was not inclined to feign illness to get out of her chores. "I'm going to pull the drapes open to have a better look at ye. Ye may keep yer eyes closed if it eases yer pain." Martha moved toward the window as she continued to speak. "Can ye sit up for me?"

With some effort, Linda sat up and cracked her eyes only the tiniest fraction more, immediately shielding them from the early morning sunlight streaming in from the window across from her cot. Martha noted she was pale, but only just a bit. A hand across her forehead revealed no fever. More than anything, the woman looked tired - not so much from working, more like the fatigue that comes from severe, relentless pain. "How long has yer head been hurtin' ye, Miss Potter?"

"It started yesterday, in the laundry." The words hurt coming out, and Linda closed her eyes.

Any other doctor would either have left her to her bed or sent her back to work. After all, what could be done for a headache but a hot compress with a bit of lavender or peppermint? However, Miss Potter looked to be in severe pain. Surprisingly, it was not uncommon among the inmates of both the poorhouse and the asylum to suffer severe headaches. Martha held up her left hand, extending the first and second digits. "Just answer a few more questions and we'll be done. Can ye see how many fingers I'm holding up?"

"Two," Linda mumbled.

"Did ye feel a bit wobbly when ye sat up?" Martha noted the ever so slight nod of the head that indicated that the answer was yes as she went to draw the drapes again. The light from the open door would be enough to finish the examination. "Are ye able to eat?" This time a twitch followed by a groan suggested the answer was no. "Are ye able to move yer bowels with no trouble?" Linda answered in the affirmative. Martha took out the stethoscope from her bag. "Can ye manage a few deep breaths for me?"

Other than a severe headache, there were no other obvious symptoms. Many factors could have contributed to Miss Potter's discomfort, ranging from a simple change in the weather to the timing of her courses. A few more questions eliminated the simpler explanations leaving no obvious source of the symptoms. Martha would generate a list of possibilities later that afternoon, starting with the stifling conditions in the cellar laundry where Linda Potter normally spent her days, and continue the inquiry tomorrow.

"Just ye stay abed and we'll see if another day's rest doesn't give ye some relief," Martha told her. "I'll be back tomorrow to check on ye." Throughout the brief examination of Linda Potter, the pounding of the headboard against the wall could still be heard above them. After a few brief instructions to Mrs. Sutton to keep the window in Miss Potter's cell open and to see that she gets a bit of beef tea at suppertime, Martha made her way upstairs.

She was surprised to see the Keeper, Mason Leonard, deep in conversation with the attendant in front of the cell from which all of the noise was coming. Leonard was less than pleased by the intrusion and gestured for Martha to follow him back down the stairs as he walked toward her. "Dr. Quinn, I think you must have been misinformed. The patient for which I summoned you is down in the women's ward. I'm on my way there now. Allow me to escort you."

"I thank ye, Mr. Leonard, but that won't be necessary." She made to step around him, but he moved as well, preventing her from reaching the door. Martha wasn't surprised. This was not the first time Mason Leonard had tried to prevent her from entering a cell on this ward. Her eyes shifted to the attendant, a rather stout man they simply called Kraus, and noticed he held his left hand slightly behind him. She smiled. Did he actually think she would make a grab for the key he held on to so tightly? "I've already seen Miss Potter. I've instructed the attendant to keep her in bed for the rest of today and I'll return and check on her again tomorrow."

"Well, I was hoping she would be back to work this afternoon. We can't afford to get behind in the laundry and at present I've got nobody who can replace her," Leonard complained. He normally wouldn't have summoned a physician for a simple headache, but there were so few able-bodied inmates and many of the daily chores were not being regularly performed.

"Mr. Leonard, she cannot be expected to work amongst the boiling cauldrons and the poor woman can scarcely open her eyes." Martha shifted her weight to look around the portly Keeper. "I might be of some help here if ye will allow me."

"You are sure that you have done all you can for Miss Potter?" The question had less to do with the patient's wellbeing and more to do with the fact that Leonard would prefer that Martha go back down to her rather than examine the patient behind the locked door. Dr. Quinn simply did not understand that these patients suffered from chronic insanity. They came to the asylum having failed to be cured elsewhere. Leonard needed Dr. Quinn to treat the other inmates, but he was determined to keep her from interfering with the dangerous ones that were clearly beyond the experience of a female physician.

Martha considered her next move carefully. The banging had stopped, the patient likely exhausted from the effort of protest. She would be safe for now. It might be a wiser choice for Martha not to try and force her way in and instead come back at another time when Leonard was occupied elsewhere and one of the more agreeable attendants was on duty. "Aye, I'm sure. As it happens, I recall I'm due elsewhere, so I must leave this patient in your expert care, sir."

That last comment earned her a relieved smile. "Yes, well, we wouldn't want to keep you from your responsibilities elsewhere. Thank you, Dr. Quinn."

Martha took care not to react to the rare expression of gratitude, and made a mental note to stop by the asylum just before supper, after Leonard had left for the day and while the night attendant was on duty.

* * *

Spring, 2016

Maude awoke startled. The room was still dark and she knew where she was, but she also knew where she had just been. Finally, she groped around on the nightstand for her notebook and pen. The body next to her began to stir.

"Hey, what's goin' on?" Don switched on the light on his side of the bed. Seeing the notebook, he sat up and rubbed the sleep from his eyes. "It finally happened again, didn't it?"

"Yeah."

"You okay?"

"Yeah, I'm okay."

"Wanna tell me about it?

"No, let me write it all down first. Go back to sleep."

Part One

Chapter One

Spring, 2016

Maude always entered the museum through the front door rather than the entrance closest to the parking lot, although she had to walk all the way around the building. Coming in through the main entrance she got to see the sign, *The Erie County Poorhouse Memorial Museum and Research Library.* The project was the result of two decades of research which started with her doctoral dissertation and ended with the poorhouse cemetery excavation not far from where the museum now stood. She still could not believe an actual museum stood in memory of all those people who had lived and died there and that it was now being used by researchers all over the world.

Equal to the thrill of reading those nine words on the small plaque outside of the building was the short cruise by the display cases on the main floor on her way back to the library. The first case held the earliest of the inmate ledgers, its binding long deteriorated, the pages yellowed and frayed. Maude had chosen that ledger herself and insisted that it be open to the first page, dated January 8th of 1829. She never walked by without stopping to acknowledge the Pixley family: a man, his wife and seven children. The Pixleys were the first family taken in at the Erie County Poorhouse, and each of their names was listed in the ledger. For Maude the story of the institution began with them. Mr. Pixley came to the poorhouse in the hopes of keeping his family together, only to have it torn apart by policies that favored miserly efficiency over compassionate aide.

Closer scrutiny of the Pixley case revealed that while the parents and younger children stayed in the poorhouse until May of that year, the older children had left in January and February, likely bound out as laborers by the Poormaster. This was a common practice that served two purposes in the minds of the administrators: it reduced the cost of care and removed the children from the unwholesome atmosphere of the poorhouse. It also tore families apart and often subjected children to abuse and neglect far worse than they would have experienced in the institution. There was other information listed with the nine people that made up this unfortunate family, their ages, places of birth and the reason they sought relief at the poorhouse (destitution), but it remains unknown if Mr. and Mrs. Pixley were ever reunited with their older children after they departed the poorhouse.

If she were being honest with herself, Maude would admit that she focused on that particular family in the hopes that she would have some sort of dream or vision that would reveal the fate of the older children. Maude's experiences with the inmates of the Erie County Poorhouse crossed over into the supernatural. A few years ago, she had experienced visions when she was working with a particular skeleton from the poorhouse cemetery that revealed the brutal physical abuse the deceased woman had received at the hands of her husband during her life. That was hard enough to grasp, but not long after that a series of dreams of Buffalo during the cholera epidemic in the mid-nineteenth century revealed that Maude had actually been an inmate of the poorhouse in a former life. Talk about your revelations! She was an anthropologist, not a psychologist, and could not even begin to understand how to interpret such a bizarre set of experiences.

A study of the inmates of the poorhouse had started as a project in graduate school two decades before, and, if the spirit guides and spiritualist advisors were to be believed, had turned into a life's work meant to help her understand...what? Maude still wasn't sure. One thing had become certain, though: whatever was happening to her couldn't be accessed on demand. What was the use of having a window into the past if it couldn't be opened at will?

Other social scientists would commit treason for the ability to see into the past. Yet, Maude could not seem to focus this ability to answer questions of historic relevance. Every time she came to the museum to collect data for a paper or to gather historic details for her latest novel she passed by the display case that held the Pixley's brief story, making a point to read each name to herself, each record of their short time in the poorhouse. Yet all she knew was the basic information written in the ledger. There had been no dreams or visions. (And a good thing, too. How would she explain it if she were to collapse suddenly in front of the display case?) Whatever was to be learned in this manner came without warning or provocation. The rest of the time, she had to settle for good old-fashioned research for the answers to her questions.

"Hi, Dr. Travers. What can I do for you today?"

Maude looked up from the display case, briefly disappointed that the voice coming to her attention belonged to a real live person and not some shadowy figure from nineteenth-century Buffalo. "Hi, Paul. I'm still working on the hospital records."

The tall, lanky undergrad from the sociology department rose from his desk and motioned for Maude to follow him back to the library. They passed several large display boards depicting the excavation of the poorhouse cemetery. The exhibit served as a timeline of the project starting with pictures of the field site, and the team of students carefully maneuvering trowels through the bane of every archaeologist and gardener in Western New York: wet clay. The images captured the best and the worst of the weather that season, alternating between sunny skies, and water-filled graves. Who knew you could have the hottest and the wettest season at the same time? The final images consisted of cleaned skeletons in the lab, laid out in anatomical position with students hunched over them using calipers, osteometric boards and digital cameras to document individual identifying factors like age, sex and ancestry. It was one of the many impressive exhibits Maude helped put together to tell the story of the people who had come through the Erie County Poorhouse.

The library was rectangular, divided at the end by a counter separating the work area from the collections which could only be accessed with the help of Paul or one of the other work study students. The work area consisted of two large oak tables sufficient for several researchers to work at one time, a microfilm reader, and another table upon which sat a desktop computer, scanner and printer. On the walls were images of the Erie County Poorhouse, Hospital and Insane Asylum from the late nineteenth and early twentieth centuries. This was Maude's favorite room and she always took a minute to notice each of the buildings that made up the huge complex. The real story of life at the poorhouse was told in the cabbage fields, the barns, the laundry, and the other out-buildings where inmates toiled each day to keep the institution running. Those pictures inspired Maude the novelist. She could almost hear the dull thud of the hoe as it cut through the soil, its user methodically making his way down each row, content to be out in the sunshine and away from the overcrowded and stuffy men's dormitory filled with those who could not manage the work. The pictures helped inspire her works of fiction, but today she was there to continue working on a scholarly paper.

"The usual spot?" Paul asked as he carried the oversized ledger to the far corner of the work area.

"Of course!" Maude smiled, embarrassed to be so predictable. She always worked in the same corner, just under the picture of the huge limestone building that had served first as the insane asylum and then as the hospital. It was another attempt to draw out whatever spiritual energy might be associated with the original photograph in the hopes that the close proximity of the hospital ledger with the actual hospital might reveal something more about the patients she was studying. Silently chastising herself, again, for trying to outsmart the spirits, she took a seat.

Paul placed the ledger gently in the cradle on the table. "Let me know if you need anything else."

"Sure thing. Thanks, Paul." Maude pulled out her laptop and found where she had left off in the ledger. Then she was lost in the rhythm of clattering keys and turning pages. Reluctantly, Maude kept her phone out on the table just in case she was needed at the shop. The Antique Lamp Company and Gift Emporium, which she now referred to as her day job, was a business venture Maude had shared with her husband for the last twelve years. She ran the retail end and Don was responsible for acquisitions and repair. With the help of a part-time employee, Maude was able to sneak away for a few hours in the morning to do some work at the museum. She had left a fulltime career in anthropology more than a decade before, but still liked to dabble in research and so held an adjunct position at the university.

Maude was so engrossed in the details of the ledger that she nearly missed the vibration of the phone on the table. The caller ID indicated it was from work, so she quickly glanced around to confirm she was the only person in the library before answering the phone. "Hey, Christine. What's up?"

"I just wanted to give you the heads up that Mrs. Houston will be in later today." Christine answered.

"She'll want to deal with you, so I was hoping you'd be here by noon."

Maude looked at her watch and then at the ledger. It was already eleven o'clock. Where had the morning gone? There were a few more cases still to transcribe before she would be finished with the page. "I should be there. I'm just about finished here." Maude clicked on the save icon, making sure her latest entries were not lost in cyberspace. "Did she say what time she'd be in?" Mrs. Houston was renovating one of her properties on Chapin Parkway and had dropped off a few wall sconces for repair. Maude remembered she had her eye on a brass Victorian parlor lamp, which would add a healthy sum to the day's sales receipts.

"No, she just said 'later today', but the last time she was here she came in around noon and was less than pleased to find me here instead of you."

Christine had become friendly with Maude and Don when she worked for Trinkets and Treasures, the antique shop next door to theirs. A perpetual graduate student of history, she and Maude had a love of Buffalo's past in common. When her former employers retired and closed their shop, Christine came to work at The Antique Lamp Company and Gift Emporium. Longtime customers like Mrs. Houston had grown accustomed to dealing with Maude, and were reluctant to do business with a stranger. When they came in and found Christine behind the counter, it was like going into your local bar only to be told your favorite waitress no longer worked there.

Maude knew Mrs. Houston's tastes, but beyond that, Maude knew Alexandra Houston. She knew Mrs.

Houston, Sr. had just moved into a nursing home, which was why the property on Chapin needed remodeling. She knew that Mr. Houston had not been much help in settling his mother in her new home or in hiring the contractors for the renovation of the old one. She knew that John Houston was attending his first year of medical school in Boston, and that Alexandra hoped her son would finally break up with that dreadful woman he had been seeing since his undergraduate days in Buffalo. Mrs. Houston wanted to deal with Maude because she had become a trusted friend, in the way some longtime business acquaintances do.

"She certainly has her hands full these days." It was all Maude could think of to excuse the woman's less than pleasant reaction to seeing Christine in the shop. "Don't worry, I'll finish up now and head over. I'll make sure I'm there before noon.

Maude quickly typed the last few details of the case she was working on and closed out her computer with that sense of guilt that always came when work interrupted her research and she had to leave a page of the ledger unfinished. She pushed the feeling from her mind and glanced at the clock on the wall, then turned to the next page in the ledger just to get a sense of what she would be dealing with next time. Some of the patient records were very straightforward with few details beyond a diagnosis and dates of entry and discharge. Others were very detailed, with descriptions of treatment or symptoms taking up half of the page. Sure enough, there was an entry near the bottom of the page with several lines of physician comments. The handwriting was difficult to read; nineteenth-century doctor handwriting was worse than that of modern day doctors. At a glance, Maude could make out only a few words. The words *violent* and *shackles* jumped out at her. Deciding she would decipher the comments when she had more time, Maude quickly looked at the diagnosis: *Insanity*. Against her better judgment, Maude's eyes wandered over to the patient's name. She did not have time to get wrapped up in another interesting case, particularly when she wasn't done transcribing the records on the previous page. Still, it was hard to resist. An insanity diagnosis, particularly in a female patient, always demanded further scrutiny. "Holy crap! You've got to be kidding me!" Maude looked at the patient's name again, sure she had misread it.

Paul came running in from the main floor of the museum. "What's wrong?"

Maude hadn't realized she'd raised her voice. "Oh! Sorry, Paul, I just recognized one of the names in the ledger. It always takes me by surprise." Not wanting to encourage further discussion, she glanced at the name one more time and then quickly closed the ledger. "I've got to get to work. I guess I'll have to finish this up tonight. Can you please leave Brian a note that I will be in after hours?"

"Sure, but I know he will be in late today, so you may end up seeing him yourself, depending on what time you get here." Paul scribbled a note and left it on the Director's desk. Dr. Brian Jameson had been the project director of the poorhouse cemetery excavation and was one of the key figures in helping to make the memorial museum and research library a reality. He was the natural choice for Director, a position he juggled with his faculty position. Brian had given Maude a key to the building and permission to work whenever it was convenient.

"I doubt it. I won't be back until tonight. Would you leave the ledger out on the counter?" Maude slipped her laptop into its case and was off before he could answer.

The short ride downtown was consumed with thoughts of hospital records and the patient she couldn't believe was real. Surely, there had to be some meaning in discovering one of the individuals from her dreams among the patients listed, and with an insanity diagnosis, no less. After her work on the cemetery collection was finished, Maude tried her hand at writing fiction, determined to tell the story she had learned from the skeletal remains of a woman who had been abused by her husband in life. At first, she thought she wasn't any good at storytelling, but soon Maude realized that it was just that particular story causing her trouble; another equally interesting story was waiting for her to write it.

After she and Don had made the decision to sell their house and renovate the apartment above their shop, Maude began to have vivid dreams of nineteenth-century Buffalo during the second major cholera epidemic in 1849. Using her dreams as inspiration, Maude began a new work of fiction. However, things got even more bizarre when she began to realize that her nocturnal imaginings were reflections of the actual past. Period newspaper reports confirmed the existence of people and places about which she had dreamt. When she consulted a genealogist, Maude found out that Martha Sloane, a medical student and former poorhouse inmate, had actually lived in the very building where Maude had worked for the past decade and in which she was now living. In an attempt to try to understand what was happening to her, Maude met with a psychic medium in Lily Dale, New York. Lily Dale is one of the oldest modern spiritualist communities in the United States, and had also figured into Maude's unusual dreams. If her new friend Charlotte Lambert was to be believed, Maude had actually been Martha Sloane in a former life.

She was still trying to make sense of that, which in part explained the attempts to jump-start spirit communication through contact with the poorhouse inmate and hospital ledgers. What was this connection she had with Martha Sloane and the Erie County Poorhouse? After all of the research she had done and all the long discussions over tea with her spiritualist friend, Maude still wasn't sure what it all meant. She had been seriously considering dropping the whole thing and refocusing on her business and family. After all, Glen would be off to college in two years, and Billy just after him. Maude had given up a career as a professor so she wouldn't miss these important years with her sons, and yet she found she was back again in the library with her nose in those ledgers.

The poorhouse cemetery project, which had drawn Maude back in to academia, had finished a few years earlier. Since then, she had written a few scholarly works and one historical fiction novel in addition to establishing the museum. Recently, she had promised herself that when this analysis of the hospital records was finished, she would take a break from the poorhouse project and spend more time with Don and the boys. That was before this morning, when Felicity Taylor showed up in the hospital records.

Felicity Taylor was a child from Maude's dreams who had lost her mother during the cholera epidemic, and was spared the conditions at the orphan asylum when she was taken in by Martha Sloane and her family. Martha feared a deaf child would be more than the women at the orphan home could handle. Felicity spent the summer months at the home of Michael and Ciara Nolan, Martha's sister and brother-in-law. When the epidemic had run its course and the travel bans in and out of Buffalo had been lifted, Felicity had traveled to Batavia to live with her uncle and his family. She was just a small child in 1849. The woman listed in the hospital records was 25 at the time of her admission in 1870, so the age was about right. She could be the Felicity Taylor of Maude's dreams.

Could Felicity Taylor's story be the subject of her next novel? Maude had been keeping notes on various aspects of Buffalo's early history which she thought would be interesting to include in her next book, but as yet no story had emerged from this collection of details. Perhaps Felicity's name appearing in the ledger was divine intervention. Charlotte had always told her that Spirit was always willing to give direction, but that we had to pay attention or we were likely to miss the subtle hints.

Maude would need to examine the hospital ledger further to be sure it really was the person of her dreams, although it was entirely possible that no detail in that lengthy record would confirm her suspicion. The hospital entry was the only indication she had that Felicity Taylor might have been a real person. The record had to be meaningful, didn't it? Maude had kept a journal during those months she was having vivid dreams from the past. She would review the journal, scrutinize every detail documented about the child of her dreams and compare that against the woman in the records in the hopes that Felicity's story and its reason for emerging now would become clear.

Maude was so distracted by her thoughts that she missed the side street that allowed her access to the alley behind her shop, so as she circled around the block she tried to push the poorhouse inmates to the recesses of her mind and focus on the workday ahead.

It was a surprise to find that Don had replaced Christine when she entered the building. "What are you doing here?" Maude found as she was getting older that switching mental gears was not as easy as it used to be, and since Don had no place in her current stream of thought, her question sounded a bit more abrupt than she intended.

"How lovely it is to see you, too, my dear." Don kissed her soundly on the mouth, not at all put off by her less than enthusiastic inquiry. "I came to surprise you for lunch, although I suspect something has got you distracted because you have yet to notice the enticing aroma of fine Mexican cuisine!"

Maude smiled and sniffed the air with appreciation. "Mmm, that place on Allen, right?" The heavenly bouquet of cilantro was the tip-off.

"Ah, now there is my wife! You have the olfactory receptors of a bloodhound." Don smiled, leading Maude to the office where two plastic bags with large Styrofoam containers sat.

"Did Christine tell you that Mrs. Houston would be in soon?" Hungry though she was, Maude was reluctant to get started on lunch if she would have to stop mid-fajita to help her longtime client.

"She did, and I called Mrs. H. myself to get a sense of when she would be coming in. You have plenty of time, so dig in."

Maude became suspicious. Don seldom showed up in the shop during business hours and now he was here, with lunch from one of her favorite restaurants, and he had made sure they wouldn't be interrupted. "What's going on?"

Don smiled. He had not expected his attempt to butter her up with Mexican food to go unnoticed. "You first. You can usually detect the smell of nachos a block away. Something must be on your mind if you missed this." He gestured towards the two bags that were responsible for the delightful aroma wafting about the back of the shop.

Maude was hardly surprised that her husband had noticed she was distracted. He had an uncanny sense of her moods, but there were still a few details to figure out before she would discuss her discovery in the library. "Not so fast, buddy. Why are you here in the middle of the day with bribery food?"

"Okay, you got me. I have to cancel our plans again tonight." Don assumed he would be in trouble for breaking date night for the third week in a row. The first time was work-related; the second time he had a friend in the hospital. But this time, he knew his excuse would not meet with acceptance or approval. "Gil has box seats tonight for the Sabres game. Say you forgive me?" He looked at her with comical desperation in his eyes and was prepared to argue that he and Gil had been friends since childhood, and how often does a guy get to share box seats with his best friend? "Wait a minute, you're relieved! Did you forget about tonight?" Don might have missed the brief expression of surprise that transitioned to relief on his wife's face had he looked away for just a second.

Maude laughed out loud. "Yes, I did, which is the only reason you are forgiven. Gil gets to sit in the company's box at least three or four times every season." She made a quick decision to tell Don about her discovery after all. "I was just finishing up at the library this morning when I found a familiar name in the records."

"Familiar on the earthly plain, or familiar in the netherworld?" Don walked over to the desk and began to arrange the containers so they could eat. He had a feeling this was a conversation that would go better with food.

"Well, both, I guess. Do you remember the deaf child from my dreams?"

"Felicity Taylor?"

"Yeah." Maude should not have been surprised that Don knew the child's name. She had based her novel on those dreams, and he had read several drafts of it during the editing process. Also, Don had the ability to remember seemingly irrelevant details. "I found her name in the hospital records in 1870."

"Are you sure it's her? How old would she have been?"

"The woman in the record was twenty-five, so the age is about right. I didn't read the entire case. I found it just as I was leaving, so I don't know where she was from or any of the details of her case beyond the fact that she was considered insane."

Don munched on a few tortilla chips before he continued. "So, you were planning on going back to the library tonight to take another look?"

"Well, since you are going to the hockey game, I guess I will. Of course, I would have reconsidered once I remembered it was date night, you know…if you hadn't made other plans."

Now it was Don's turn to laugh out loud. A few months ago they had established date night, thinking that they needed to set aside a particular night to make sure they spent quality time together. They agreed to spend one evening a week outside of home and work doing something together, but in truth, they seldom stuck to it. More often than not, either something unforeseen came up, or they were just too tired to go out. "You know, maybe we should just give up on date night and reinstate cocktail hour?"

"We never gave up cocktail hour." Maude and Don always had a drink after work while they threw dinner together and shared the details of their day. With the boys active in sports and after school clubs, that hour after work, before their sons came home, was really their quality time together.

"See? We had it right all along."

Maude raised her water bottle in agreement. "If it ain't broke, don't fix it!"

They sat in companionable silence for a while eating lunch. Don picked up the final tortilla chip and swirled it around the Styrofoam container to be sure he got the last of the guacamole and salsa. "So, you found Felicity Taylor?"

Maude looked up, her mouth full of steak and onions, and nodded. She took the time to swallow her food and wipe her mouth with a napkin before she answered the larger question he was really asking. "You know, Don, I have been wondering for a while now if anything else was going to happen. It's been over a year since I had those weird dreams. I did what I thought I was supposed to do. I wrote a book, and here it sits, waiting to be discovered." She gestured over to her computer. "I had no delusions that I would become some sort of famous author, but I do find myself wondering what the point of it all was. Who was I writing it for?" She did not provide a pause long enough for him to answer, even if he thought he knew. "I was really getting comfortable with the idea of letting all of this go when I am done with this paper, and now she shows up!"

"So you think you found Felicity in the records because you were thinking of leaving your poorhouse research behind?" Don sounded like one of those therapists who had just asked "*How do you feel about that?*" and she had to resist the urge to throw her plastic fork at him.

Still, it was a fair question. "I don't know. In general, I have a tendency to overthink things, but when it comes to this project, that tendency becomes an obsession. What does it all mean? Why am I the person experiencing all of this? I'm actually sick of trying to figure it out." Maude closed the empty Styrofoam container and placed it back in the bag, motioning for Don to hand over his. "I only started this project with the hospital records to give me an excuse to keep going to the museum in the hopes that I would get some kind of sign."

"Be careful what you wish for." He smiled and then casually glanced at his watch. Mrs. Houston would be there in the next ten minutes or so. "So, go back to the library tonight and see what happens. You don't expect any visions or anything dangerous, do you?" Don had been with her when she was working with the skeleton. What she saw was so visceral when she touched that old woman's broken bones, Maude seemed to feel the pain that poor woman had experienced during each blow from her husband's fist. As a result, Don had not been at all comfortable with his wife working on that particular skeleton when she was alone.

Maude shook her head. "I doubt it. What happened with Mrs. Kaiser seemed related specifically to the trauma she had experienced. I actually had to touch the bone to see how it happened." Through the analysis of an old journal and an artifact from the cemetery excavation, Maude had learned the identity of the woman whose bones told such a sad tale. Maude referred to Mrs. Kaiser like an elderly next-door neighbor rather than as burial #116, which was how she was recorded in the archaeological record.

"Well, then, just continue working. I'll be with you later tonight if you have any weird dreams. Keep a journal like you did before." Don kissed his wife on the top of the head and left the office, continuing toward the back door.

"Coward!" Maude called after him. She knew Don had timed his apology lunch to be over well in advance of Mrs. Houston's arrival.

He turned to his wife and raised his hands in surrender, "You know she only likes to deal with you," and then he was out the door.

Chapter Two

On her second visit to the museum that day, Maude had to sacrifice her principles and use the back door because the front entrance was locked remotely by the computer at the reception desk. She punched in the numbers on the keypad to disable the security system and used the key Brian had given her to enter through the back. It became necessary to fumble around in the dark for a few minutes before she found the light switch which couldn't be reached without closing the metal door. *Who the bloody hell designed this?* That thought wandered through her mind as she placed the computer bag on the ground with care and continued to grope the wall in search of the elusive switch.

The building had served many purposes before it had been modified into the poorhouse museum, and prior to the remodel the door had opened up into one large space. Now the door opened to a hall, on the right of which was the library while on the left was a mausoleum that contained the individuals whose burials had been excavated during the salvage project a few years ago. The space was configured perfectly such that the face of the mausoleum formed the back wall of the main exhibit room and served as a sort of monument.

The names of the individuals from the hospital mortality ledger who had been buried in the poorhouse cemetery were hand stenciled on that wall. For each individual, their age at death, country of origin, occupation, and cause of death were recorded. It was uncertain if those names actually matched up with the individuals whose earthly remains were housed in the mausoleum. Only a few hundred of the thousands of individuals who died and were buried in the poorhouse cemetery had been removed from it, but it gave people a sense of who these individuals were as a whole.

They may have died as paupers, but in life they had worked as stonemasons, carpenters, jewelers, shop owners and in other vital trades or services that kept the burgeoning city in business. Some had come from across the ocean, some from across the country. A few were old when they passed, but many were not. Maude and the rest of the committee thought it was important for museumgoers and researchers to understand this assemblage that had been labeled "the poor" particularly since it had been impossible to identify the individuals excavated from unmarked graves.

The mausoleum door was locked and on a separate security code. That climate-controlled room was to be the final resting place for the individuals whose eternal slumber had been disturbed. Anyone interested in studying their bones could have access to the data that had been collected as part of the original project, but not to the bodies themselves. The researchers had been very thorough and measured every long bone, foramina and suture. There had also been x-rays, photos and scanning from a variety of equipment that measured everything from bone density to chemical composition. The powers that be had agreed that the poorhouse cemetery had the potential to contribute a previously unknown and important chapter to Buffalo's history, so the research team had been given a year to learn what they could about each individual. While they did not learn any names, the team determined how many were male or female, and approximately how old they were at the time of death. They learned how many individuals suffered from nutritional deficiency or infectious disease. They observed pathological conditions in the bones caused by trauma, disease, or just overuse. Each skeleton had revealed parts of its life, and some even told of its death.

The florescent lights in the back hall took their time to flicker on and Maude made her way down the dark hall to the door of the library, accessible by a second key on the ring that she held in her hand. She entered and her attention was immediately drawn to her usual spot under the picture of the insane asylum because a single strip of florescent lighting remained on right above it, casting an eerie glow upon the imposing stone edifice, while the rest of the museum remained dark. "We'll leave the light on for you!" Maude chuckled uneasily, not referencing the old Motel 6 commercial, but rather a meme she had seen posted on Facebook that read *Spiritualism: We'll leave the light on for you!*

It was a bit creepy that the only light on in the whole building was just above the picture of the insane asylum and, standing alone in the dark, Maude's mind immediately leapt to the supernatural. "Like I said, overthinking becomes obsession. Get a grip, Maudie. Paul just forgot to shut the lights off in the back." Having scolded herself out loud, she turned on the rest of the lights in the library just as the hallway flickered to life.

The hospital ledger was out on the counter so Maude wasted no more time pondering the meaning of the lights and went to retrieve it. There was a note on top. *Paul told me you would be in tonight. Sorry I missed you. Hope all is well. B.* It was from Brian. She had not expected to run into him, although Paul suggested she might. The museum closed at 3 o'clock, but she knew Brian would not be there much past five. He was a devoted husband and father and Maude could think of nothing that would keep him on campus past the dinner hour, short of an emergency. She scribbled back a quick reply, took the ledger and set it on the table.

"Okay, I have five more entries on the previous page, so I'd better get those done before I get to Felicity." Maude spoke aloud in the direction of the ledger as if by hearing the words it would prevent her from reading Felicity Taylor's entry out of order. She was hopelessly compulsive about collecting the data line by line, in chronological order. She felt guilty enough having left the library that morning with the ledger page only partially transcribed. It would actually be more stressful to skip ahead to the next page than it would be just to finish what she had started earlier that day.

The five entries took more time than Maude had anticipated. Although they were relatively brief, there was something about each case that demanded further investigation. The first two records were children with

prolapsed anus as the diagnosis. There had been
fourteen of those cases between October and
December of that year, these two made sixteen. What
was that all about? Maude sorted the data on her
computer so that she could review all sixteen cases. She
counted ten boys and six girls, all under age five with
the exception of one boy, who was nine. Three of the
cases had been labeled as severe. For the older boy, the
physician had recorded that this was the second time
the child had been admitted with a prolapsed anus.
Yikes! Maude couldn't imagine what would cause that to
happen twice. The average length of stay at the hospital
for those patients was about two weeks.

Her first thought was that perhaps all of the young
children had been the victims of sexual abuse - a shiver
ran down her spine at the thought - but there was no
indication from where they had come. Not all patients
at the poorhouse hospital were inmates; in fact, few
were. The Erie County Poorhouse Hospital served the
general public, regardless of ability to pay, as did
Buffalo General Hospital and Buffalo Hospital of the
Sisters of Charity. Place of residence, unfortunately, was
not recorded in the ledger. In fact, there was little
additional information with which to determine the
cause of such a condition during this finite period of
time. Perhaps there was an outbreak of dysentery or
cholera and severe diarrhea was responsible for the
prolapses... or parasites maybe. Maude transcribed all
of this into her spiral notebook with the intention of
consulting a pediatrician.

Two of the remaining entries on the page were a
mother and daughter who had recently arrived from

Germany and were very sick with ship fever. Maude knew that ship fever, or typhus fever, was common among steerage passengers who often shared their accommodations with louse-infested rats. What was interesting about these two people was that the physician had noted they had come with three hundred other passengers from Boden, Germany, and that they had all been paupers before they left their homeland. Maude had seen the same reference to other passengers from that ship in the hospital records. "Give me your tired, your poor, your huddled masses...," she mumbled as she turned again, with pencil in hand, to a blank, white page in her notebook. After adding the details of the Boden paupers, Maude wrote the name Abby and underlined it several times. Abby Stevens was a genealogist Maude had met the previous year when she was trying to sort out fact from fiction in her dreams of nineteenth-century Buffalo. An entire boat of paupers from Germany was right up Abby's alley. If anyone could find out more about these people, she could.

Maude had all but forgotten about Felicity Taylor, so engrossed was she in the final case on the page. A woman had been admitted to the insane asylum two years previous, but the record Maude was reading reported the birth of a child. Maude filled a whole page in the spiral notebook about Anna Griffin, Irish, age 25, delivered of a stillborn son after four hours in travail. It was not the first pregnancy or delivery Maude had recorded among women who had been at the insane asylum for more than nine months. Just how were women who had been diagnosed with chronic insanity, and were largely restrained, ending up pregnant? Another quick sort of the data revealed no pattern among these patients either, with the exception that all twelve of the women had been classified as intemperate. "Perhaps they were easily wooed to bed for a wee dram." Maude wondered aloud. With a final note to consult some other published sources in the hopes of learning more about promiscuity or rape in nineteenth-century asylums, Maude moved on.

With a sigh of relief, she reached the end of the page. Glancing at the clock at the bottom of the computer screen, she was surprised to see that it was already 8:30. There were no windows in the building, so she had no way to mark the passage of time, not that she would have noticed as the sun went down. When Maude was working, it was unlikely that she would notice if the fire alarm went off. She turned the page and glanced down towards Felicity's case. "I really should continue on in order," she reminded herself. Still, there were thirty entries before Felicity's record, and it would take nearly an hour to transcribe all of them, maybe. That was assuming every record was straightforward, which had not been the case with the last five.

It would do no good to take a quick glance at Felicity's case and then continue because Maude would be preoccupied and get little else done. On the flip side, if she were just to skip to the bottom, the nagging thought that she hadn't collected the previous records would cloud her thoughts as well. "Well, I guess I just have to keep at it," she said with a chuckle, knowing that at this point she would have driven Don mad. He always read the last page of a book first, so he would have come in and immediately got into Felicity's record, and damn the rest until he was ready to go back and finish them.

It was 9:45 by the time Maude had made it to Felicity's case. The first few entries were straightforward and included her case number, name, age, and date of admission, which was May 27, 1870. Other details included nativity (recorded as American), and her occupation. Women who worked in the home were recorded as domestics. Her diagnosis was listed as insanity, but according to the ledger she did not stay at the hospital very long because her date of discharge was May 29, 1870.

The comments were very detailed in comparison to the rest of the entries on the page, and Maude reached for her magnifying glass to begin the tedious process of comparing letters with the handwriting above and below to try to make out the words. *Patient brought from Laona by Dpty. Constable...,* "I think that's an h, yeah, definitely an h." *...having been arrested.* "Is that an r?" *Refuses to answer questions.* She could not make out the next two words and raised the magnifying glass to make the individual letters larger in the hopes of deciphering the loops and whirls. "Lively? No, Likely..." *Likely incurable.*

Maude sat back and yawned. It was just after 10:00 and the hockey game would be over soon. She should finish up and get home. After a few stretches produced a satisfying crackle of her vertebral column, she read the passage she had transcribed into the database.

```
Patient  brought  from  Laona  by  Dpty.
Constable,  having  been  arrested  for
refusing  to  leave  her  home,  which  had
gone  to  foreclosure  after  death  of
uncle.  Refuses  to  answer  questions.
Violent  nature,  struggles  against
shackles.  Otherwise  appears  in  good
health.  Likely  incurable.
```

Maude had brought along her dream journals, which she had studied closely earlier, but had found no indication that Felicity had lived in Laona. Felicity had gone to live with her aunt and uncle in Batavia when she left the Nolan farm. Still, she felt certain that she was reading about the same person. Her uncle evidently had died, but what of her aunt? There couldn't have been any financial support if the house was foreclosed upon and she was removed from it forcibly.

How distressing the whole situation must have been. "No wonder she was belligerent. I'd be in no hurry to leave my home, particularly if there was no place else to go," Maude mumbled to herself as she quickly wrote down her immediate observations and questions. "Did they realize she was deaf?" Her words were barely audible as she added them to her list of questions. Fifteen minutes later her hand was stiff but she had filled several pages in the spiral notebook and had laid the framework to find out more about Felicity Taylor.

Unable to stifle a series of yawns, Maude decided it was definitely time to call it a night. She returned the ledger to the counter and began to pack up her things when she noticed the light beginning to flicker over the picture of the asylum. "What?" She asked it, just in case it was the work of Spirit. "What more can I do right now? If there is something I need to know you will have to freaking tell me!"

Wondering if yelling at a picture hanging on the wall was somehow crossing a line, Maude sat back down and took several deep breaths. Her eyes grew heavy as she simply stared at the picture hoping it would sprout lips and tell her what she needed to know. The ringing of her phone broke her concentration and she fumbled in her bag to grab it.

"Hey, are you planning on coming home?"

"Yeah, Don, I'm leaving now. Are you home yet or are you stopping for a beer?" Post-game traffic was always a problem and the wise man always found a bar until it had thinned out.

"Maudie, it's nearly two o'clock. I did stop for a drink, but I've been home for hours. I fell asleep on the couch waiting for you."

"What?" Maude glanced up at the clock above the door. Don was right. It had not even been eleven o'clock when she was packing up her things and now it was over three hours later. Where had the time gone?

"Is everything okay?"

Maude ran a hand through her hair and took a deep breath that she hoped he couldn't hear. "Yeah, everything's fine. I was just busy and didn't notice the time." Realizing she wasn't fooling him, she added, "I might have dozed off for a while."

"Want me to come and get you?"

"No, thanks; I'm leaving now." Maude paused for a minute and then added, "Wait up for me, will ya?"

"Sure. Drive safely."

Maude looked at the picture of the asylum - the lights had stopped flickering - and then at the clock. Had she really lost three hours? Had she dreamed? No, she had not. "What the hell?" she asked the picture. "You've got my attention, but I'm gonna need more than flickering lights to make sense of this."

Chapter Three

Don woke to find the other side of the bed empty. They had been up much of the night discussing Maude's findings in the museum's library and he was surprised she was awake so early on a Saturday morning. He searched for a pair of slippers under the bed and made his way to the kitchen to find his wife staring at the screen of her laptop with a cup of coffee in her hand. "What are you doing up so early? Did you have a dream?"

"No." Maude made no attempt to hide the disappointment in her voice.

Barefoot and still in a tank top and an old pair of her husband's boxers of which she'd taken possession for sleeping, Maude had not even combed her hair. These were the signs that sleep had eluded her during the remaining hours of the night. Don had found her like this many mornings in the beginning of her academic career and was still a bit ashamed to admit that he was very attracted to his wife, disheveled and exhausted though she was. He glanced at the clock on the stove. It was just after seven. "Any chance I can talk you into coming back to bed?"

Maude smiled, put the coffee cup down and walked toward him. "Maybe."

Their lingering kiss was rudely interrupted by what sounded like a herd of wildebeest coming down from the third floor. All too often moments like this were interrupted by the boisterous entrance of one or both of their sons and the couple reacted, as they always did, without irritation. "Did you two knuckleheads fall asleep in front of the Xbox again?" Don asked the two boys as they turned up in the kitchen.

Glen gave a noncommittal shrug and opened the refrigerator. "We have to be at the Mission by eight."

"Oh, yeah, I forgot about that." Maude had signed up her sons at the Buffalo City Mission to fulfill the volunteer hours required for school each year. Both of the boys found that they really enjoyed working there and had agreed to continue on one Saturday each month.

"I'll drive you there and we can grab some breakfast along the way," their father informed them, "but plan on walking home because your mom and I are going out for the day." The City Mission was just a few streets over on Tupper, so it would be an easy ten-minute walk home.

The boys nodded in agreement, but Maude looked puzzled. "Where are we going?" She asked.

"On a date. Go lie down while I run the guys over to the Mission. When you get up, we're going out." He kissed her soundly on the mouth and then reached for his keys. Maude didn't see the need to remind him that he was still in his pajamas. He was only dropping the boys off and wouldn't be leaving the car. Besides, it had become a habit for both of them to put off the transition to street clothes for as long as possible on weekends.

After Don and the boys left, Maude went obediently to the bedroom and, strangely enough, fell asleep within minutes. It was just about eleven o'clock when she woke. Sitting up in bed, she closed her eyes and tried to remember her dreams. "Nothing, damn it!" She padded back out to the kitchen to find her husband, now fully dressed, with his nose buried in the newspaper. "So, a date?"

"Oh, good. You're up. Any luck this time?" Her expression told him the answer was no. He motioned to the chair opposite his and rose to pour her a cup of coffee. "I thought we'd pick up a few bagel sandwiches and maybe drop by Canalside for a little breakfast picnic. After that, we can rent some kayaks and troll around the grain elevators. What do you think?"

"What about the shop?" Christine typically worked on Saturdays, but there was always some sort of maintenance or repair project in their nearly two-hundred-year old building that kept Maude and Don busy on the weekend.

"It's too nice a day to spend working. Besides, you need to relax and get your mind out of the insane asylum."

It was indeed a beautiful spring day and the sun warmed their faces as they crossed Commercial Street and walked over the bridge to the Central Wharf. During the mid-nineteenth century, the Central Wharf was a bustling center where canal and lake traffic merged, as people and goods made their way east or west. The area had undergone a major revitalization recently, and was a common destination for city dwellers and tourists alike to spend an afternoon biking, kayaking or just strolling along the shops.

Maude and Don wasted no time, after their foil-wrapped breakfast, renting kayaks and spent a lovely afternoon paddling around what had once been known as Big Buffalo Creek, now known as the Buffalo River. They made their way along the river and around the grain elevators. Prior to this ingenious invention perfected by Joseph Dart, surplus grain traveled from the Midwest on ships large enough to withstand the tempestuous weather the Great Lakes could wreak. Upon its arrival in Buffalo, the grain would be unloaded by hand, an arduous chore taken on largely by Irish immigrants. They reloaded it onto the smaller canal boats in order to continue its journey along the Erie Canal to the east coast. With the invention of the grain elevator, ships could be unloaded by steam-powered conveyor belt, at the rate of 1,000 bushels per hour, thus making Buffalo the largest grain port in the world.

Paddling along a bend in the river, Maude's attention was drawn across a narrow stretch of land separating the river from the larger body of Lake Erie, toward one of the lakeside bars which had changed hands recently and was closed for renovations. Although she could not see the actual bar, she felt compelled to look out toward it anyway, squinting for better focus. A large wake rocked the kayak and she looked around to find its source, but saw nobody on the water, not even Don, who had previously been paddling just behind her.

Bringing her attention back toward the lakeside bar, she could not believe her own eyes. Instead of the brick and iron skeletons of Buffalo's industrial past that had just been in her line of sight, she now saw almost nothing. Instead, there were only two sets of railroad tracks that merged at the bend in Big Buffalo Creek. The details were so vivid, but impossible because those particular tracks were long gone. It was such a quick flashback, but it brought a sense of foreboding that made her stop paddling and stare up at the spot where she was sure the railroad tracks had been.

Don paddled up behind her. "Ready to call it a day?"

Maude blinked and looked again to find that the vision had passed and she was once again looking at the modern landscape. "Yeah, I'm ready." She paddled alongside Don, but glanced behind her one last time. "Hey, you know that place by the marina that's under renovation?" He nodded and she continued speaking. "Wouldn't it be just over there?" She pointed across the industrial ghost town on the narrow stretch of land between the river and the lake.

Don looked behind him, considering the question. "Yeah, that looks about right. Why?"

"Oh, I don't know. I was thinking when it finally opens maybe we could give date night one more try." Her smile was strained and she knew it did not fool him.

"Sure, but I don't think they will be reopening any time soon." He noticed she hadn't taken her attention away from that spot. "Everything okay?"

"Yeah."

Now that he was focused in that direction, the spot just out of their line of sight on the shore of the lake held his fascination too. Don continued to look in the direction of the marina as if he was trying to remember something important, but couldn't quite put his finger on it. The wind came up behind him and he felt a chill run down his spine. With a shiver, he turned his attention back to Maude. "C'mon, let's head back."

"Good idea." Maude decided it was too nice a day for overthinking and paddled away. By now, there were other kayaks, water bikes and motor boats around them and it became necessary to pay close attention to the traffic on the river as they made their way along. As Maude approached the Commercial Slip, which had been the access point into the canal system, she experienced another flashback, this time at the spot where the bridge crossed Canal Street. The distillery of Jay Pettibone and Company loomed off to the right. "What the hell?" she mumbled. How could she possibly know what businesses crowded around the Commercial Slip back in the day? The intricacies of the Erie Canal district in Buffalo had never been something about which Maude knew much, so it surprised her that she would zero in on such an unusual detail.

"Did you say something?" Don asked her as they paddled up to the Central Wharf to return their kayaks.

"No, just talking to myself."

Don climbed out and secured his vessel before turning to help his wife. Maude reached for his hand and allowed herself to be hoisted topside. She stumbled as she took a step forward, unaccustomed to solid land after hours on the river. She grabbed for the arm that had reached to steady her, but it was not the bare, tanned upper limb of her husband. It was a wet shirt-sleeve of rough calico. She could hear the shouts of the men on the docks and the sounds of the nightlife not far off. The air around her smelled of horse manure, rotting river debris and dead fish. Startled, Maude looked up expecting to see the bustle of the nineteenth-century Canal District late in the evening when the hardworking folks blew off steam after a long day, but instead it was Don again, and the few people waiting in line for kayaks.

Like the glimpse of the railroad tracks and Mr. Pettibones' distillery, it happened so quickly she wasn't sure it actually *had* happened. This was different, though, because she had experienced more than just a visual hallucination; other inner and outer senses had contributed to the scene. Maude had felt a distinct sense of conflicting emotions: fear and hope all in the same heartbeat. Even the air was different when she had exited the river. Instead of the touristy aromas of cotton candy and sunscreen, the decaying stench of the docks and the people and animals who worked them was evident.

Don pulled Maude firmly to her feet. "I've got you." Maude stopped and took a minute to collect herself. She resisted the unsettling urge to embrace Don and hold on for dear life, which did not go unnoticed. "Hey, are you okay? You look like you've seen a ghost." He realized the truth of those words as they exited his mouth. "Let's sit down for a minute."

Maude allowed herself to be led to a bench near the river. They had stopped briefly along the way to purchase two bottles of water and she took the time to open hers and take a long drink before she spoke. "Just now, when we were getting out of the boats, I felt like that happened before, like I had that same moment by the Commercial Slip, but not during our time." She looked up at him and noting no alarming reaction, continued. "I remember that feeling of being off balance on the dock. It was late at night, and I had such horrible feeling that nothing would ever be the same again. I wasn't alone; there were other people there, but I'm not sure who."

Before Don could comment, she quickly pulled out her phone and clicked her way to an old map of Buffalo's waterfront. "I'll be damned." She looked at the map for a while and had almost forgotten that Don was sitting beside her until he gently moved her hand to see what was holding her attention. "When we were paddling around out there, somehow I was drawn to that spot at the bend in the river. When I looked out in the direction of the lake, the modern landscape was gone. I could only see railroad tracks." She showed him the map on her phone. "...Tracks which were evidently part of the Buffalo Creek Railroad merging together and following the bend in the creek. Not the river, Don. In my head, it was Big Buffalo Creek, the old name. Oh, and it may surprise you to know that I've never even heard of that railroad company. What the hell is going on? How did I see things that did not exist in my lifetime?"

"Maude, it's all part of the city's history. You must have learned about it at some point in your research." Seeing her skepticism, he added, "Maybe you learned about it in school or on a fieldtrip or something. The brain stores a lot of information, so at some point in your life you must have learned about those things."

"I don't know. That's pretty obscure for the New York State social studies curriculum. Besides, I actually saw the tracks." Don looked surprised and so she pointed to the phone again. "I could actually see where these tracks on the map merged by the bend in the creek!"

Don paused for a minute, more to give his wife the opportunity to calm down than because he wasn't sure how to respond. "Could you have come across this information inadvertently when you were looking into something else?" She started to shake her head, but he continued speaking anyway. "My point is, it's not unusual that you would know these things, especially given how much research you have done recently about the city's early history."

Maude was quiet for a while. It was pointless to argue, especially since she knew Don was just playing devil's advocate. If Maude thought these experiences were meaningful, Don did too. "What about that place out by the lake? Why was I drawn to that spot? You can't even see the bar from the water, yet I knew it was there. Don, I have a bad feeling about that place."

"Well, then, I guess we won't be going there for date night, will we?" He couldn't resist a mischievous smile, although he knew humor would not be well received at this point in time.

"Don, this is not a joke. I'm having hallucinations, or flashbacks, or something. It all seemed so real just now. Everything was different. The air smelled different; the arm that reached out to grab me was not yours." She thrust her phone into his hand. "If you pull up a city directory from the nineteenth century, I'll bet you will find that Jay Pettibone and Company had a distillery on the corner of Lloyd and Canal Streets."

"I'll take your word for it." Don gently pushed the phone away. "How long did all of this last?"

"Seconds, I think. The minute my feet hit the dock and I lost my balance, I could hear the bustle of the nightlife around the Canal District. I could actually smell that rotting river flotsam and horse manure. Don, there are no horses here. It was so real, but when I looked up, you were there along with all those annoyed-looking tourists waiting for our boats."

Don looked around. There were few people left on the boardwalk and none of them within earshot in case the conversation got weird, or rather, weirder. "So, the railroad tracks, the distillery and the Slip...were they all part of one specific...experience? I mean if they were Martha's memories, were all of those things part of a single memory?"

The startled look on her face indicated that Maude had not even considered Martha Sloane in her reckoning of these experiences. "Um...I don't know, but I think so. You think what I experienced were Martha's memories?"

"C'mon, Maudie, you gotta admit if you experienced something here, it was likely related to her, or you when you were her...well, you know what I mean."

"I don't know, Don, that is a pretty big assumption. I mean, what proof do we really have that I was Martha Sloane in another life?" He looked as if he were about to speak, but wisely allowed her to continue. "All we have is the word of a ghost and the opinion of a little old lady from Lily Dale, who freely admits she does not understand what is happening to me!"

"I don't think it's a big assumption. Just hear me out." Don leaned back on the bench, rearranging himself so that he was facing her and continued. "Maude, you have been trying for months to trigger more dreams about the past, not so you can better understand why this is all happening to you, but to give you more insight into your research. And who would blame you for trying? I know I would do it, too. The thing is, in doing that you have managed, purposely, I think, not to deal with the whole past life thing."

Maude considered this for a moment. "So you think what happened here today was meant to force me to deal with my past life, assuming I believe I actually had one? If that's so, how do you explain finding Felicity's name in the hospital ledger?"

"Honey, I can't explain any of this, but I doubt there is someone up in the heavens pulling the strings."

"Damn it, it feels like someone is pulling the strings!" Frustrated, Maude stood and began to pace in front of the bench. "Look, I just want to live my current life with you and the boys. I would be happy to still dabble in writing and research, but I don't want to feel like I'm on some sort of quest, the purpose of which has yet to be discovered."

"Maude, if you really don't want anything to do with the past, why are you trying to encourage communication with it?" He could tell she was becoming more agitated, but continued his thought anyway. "If you really don't want anything to do with Martha Sloane, then walk away. But if you are going to tap into whatever ability you have to understand the past, you have to be prepared to accept what information comes to light as a result of it, especially if it's not what you were hoping for."

"Easier said than done, I'm afraid." Maude heaved a sigh of exasperation and sat back down on the bench. "Okay, let's just say I accept all that has been revealed thus far. I was Martha Sloane, and I have access to some of her memories. Why? Better yet, now what?"

Don smiled, "I know you will smack me if I tell you to try not to think about what it all means, but you should try not to think about what it all means." He leaned back, but not in time to avoid the outstretched hand that knocked the baseball cap off his head. "Seriously, though, if you insist on asking these questions, why not direct them to your girlfriend in the cave?"

"Ha, ha, very funny." Maude knew that Don was referring to her spirit guide whom she had identified as the result of a meditation exercise Charlotte Lambert had related to her. Or it could just have been another weird dream. If one chose to believe in such things, Maude's spirit guide, it turned out, was a *Homo erectus* woman, an early human ancestor who had lived more than a million years ago. "Shall I just stroll up to the fire and see what she has to say?" The first and only experience Maude had with her spirit guide scared the daylights out of her, and really had not provided any real understanding of her unusual experiences, except that the woman revealed that Maude had been chosen to tell the stories of the poorhouse inmates. This task she had undertaken, but the journey had yet to reveal its significance in the greater scheme of things.

"I'm not kidding. Why don't you try that meditation again and see what happens?"

An audible rumbling of her stomach indicated that the time to ponder had past and the time to eat was upon them. "I'll think about it, I promise, but we really should get back. The boys will want dinner soon."

* * *

Few thoughts were spared for Martha Sloane and the Canal District when Maude got home. They had all been in the mood for beef on weck and ordered sandwiches from their favorite bar and grill a few blocks away. The dinner conversation hovered around the boys' morning at the City Mission, and their afternoon spent with two girls from Nardin Academy who had also been volunteering that morning.

"Ha! Now I understand why you two continued to volunteer at the Mission when your required hours were completed." Don continued to laugh as the boys made no effort to deny that they had met these girls in the fall and had been working up to asking them out.

"So, where do these young ladies live?" Maude asked cautiously, realizing that if each of them had a girlfriend, there would be considerably more chauffeuring involved since neither of the boys had his driver's license yet.

"Sue lives in Grand Island and Mandy lives in Clarence," Glen told them.

"Lovely," she mumbled, and met Don's rolled eyes with her own. Of course, neither girl lived remotely close to their downtown apartment. That was one of the disadvantages of attending private school in the city of Buffalo. Students came from all over the surrounding suburbs, so after school socializing was often a logistical nightmare for working parents.

After a day spent on the river and an evening spent trying to figure out how her sons could fit girlfriends who lived on opposite sides of the city into their already tight schedules, Maude was exhausted. She had managed to keep nineteenth-century Buffalo and all its characters, real or imagined, off her mind until her head hit the pillow and then she found herself wondering, again, about what had happened earlier in the day by the river. It was too late and she was too tired to begin the meditation that Charlotte had taught her, which involved imagining a long hallway with a series of doors. *Why couldn't you just chant 'Spirit Guide, Spirit Guide, Emergency! Come right away!' It worked for Elizabeth Montgomery in Bewitched,* she thought. Lying in bed, she closed her eyes and took several deep breaths. She let her mind wander back to Canalside and could feel the motion of the boat floating on the surface of the river. As her mind continued toward sleep, the rhythm changed and her body was rocked gently by the motion of a horse drawn carriage as it carried her down Main Street.

Maude awoke startled. The room was still dark, but she knew where she was. She also knew where she had just been. Finally! She groped around on the nightstand for her notebook and pen. The body next to her began to stir. "Hey, what's goin' on?" Don switched on the light on his side of the bed. Seeing the notebook, he sat up and rubbed the sleep from his eyes. "It finally happened again, didn't it?"

"Yeah."

"You okay?"

"Yeah, I'm okay."

"Wanna tell me about it?

"No. Let me write it all down first. Go back to sleep."

Chapter Four

May 28, 1870

Martha pulled her trap into the livery on Main Street just a few blocks away from the Nolan's Dry Goods Emporium. The city's premiere dry goods store had been owned and operated by Daniel Nolan and his wife until about twenty years earlier. When Daniel passed, the shop transferred into the hands of Martha's husband, Johnny Quinn. As a young lad, Johnny had come from the poorhouse with Martha and her older sisters. They had all lived together with the Nolans until Martha's oldest sister Ciara married Daniel's son, Dr. Michael Nolan. Johnny Quinn had taken a liking to Daniel Nolan from the beginning and lent a hand where he could in the shop when he was a boy. Johnny and Martha had raised their only son in the rooms above the shop and had welcomed numerous extended family members over the years.

The plot of land on which Nolan's Dry Goods Emporium stood, which once boasted a small stable, chicken coop and kitchen garden, had reduced in size when property values soared in response to the increasing demand for property on or near Main Street.

The Quinns now lived as many city dwellers did. They purchased their food, rather than raising or growing it, and rented out space in the livery for the few horses they still owned, plus Martha's trap and a wagon.

"Ye're a wee bit late today," her husband said as he helped her down, handing off the horse to a stableboy. Johnny had been just outside the stable, waiting for Martha as he always did at the end of each day. He could see her horse making its way down Main Street from their second floor sitting room and even during the cold winter months, Johnny enjoyed the leisurely stroll to the livery at the end of the day to meet his wife.

In years past, with two other adults and four growing children about the upper two floors of the shop, their stroll home along Main Street was the only quiet time they had. Martha and Johnny had shared their home with Bruns Friedlander and his family. Bruns moved in to the floors above Nolan's Dry Goods Emporium in 1849, after the death of Daniel Nolan senior, to help Johnny run the business. He was just fourteen years old at the time. In the blink of an eye he was a grown man with a wife and children. The Friedlanders would have found a home of their own to accommodate their growing brood, had Bruns not been killed in the War Between the States. His widow Gertrude and their three sons remained in the living quarters above Nolan's Dry Goods Emporium.

"Aye, the widow MacTavish's new daughter took her time coming into the world," Martha told him as she folded her arm through his and steered him toward the street.

"Are mother and child both well?" Johnny always hated to ask that question, but he knew he must. The poorhouse took in many young women in need of a safe place to give birth. Some, like Bernice MacTavish, were young widows, but many of these women were unwed. Over the years, Johnny had heard too many stories of kitchen maids or prostitutes turned away by their employers when they fell pregnant. So often, these women came to the poorhouse sick and malnourished, with little hope of giving birth to a healthy babe. Johnny knew that Martha needed to share her joy when both mother and child survived the birth or, more often, her frustration and sorrow when one or both did not.

Martha nodded. "Aye, both are well. The babe is a good size and likely to survive if the woman will keep her to the breast." More than half of the infants born in the poorhouse hospital did not survive their first year. Infectious fevers and flux were ever-present threats to the survival of the youngest inmates. Beyond that, the poorhouse matron insisted on bottle-feeding all of the infants born there, even those whose mothers survived the birth, although Martha had explained to her several times the virtues of breast-feeding when it was possible. Poorly washed bottles and spoiled cow's milk often claimed the lives of infants that fevers had not.

"Somethin' else is on yer mind, then?" Johnny had taken notice of the absence of a smile on her face when she delivered the good news.

Martha had come to treasure this walk with her husband, an oasis of time when she could shed the worries of her day. Slowly, as they made their way home, he would draw out of her concerns over particular patients or frustration over the ignorance she faced every day from the keepers or the matrons. By the time they reached home, she'd found a shelf in the storage closet of her mind to place her concerns until they could be dealt with in one way or another. "I was called to the asylum early this morning. Miss Potter had a dreadful headache."

"I'm surprised ye were called over for somethin' as simple as a headache. Do ye think it is more serious?"

Martha was surprised to realize that she hadn't given Linda Potter's head any thought since she left the asylum. The hospital department of the poorhouse had kept her busy all afternoon. She treated two of the kitchen girls for severe burns, stitched up the leg of one of the men who had accidentally lacerated it with a garden spade, and checked on all of the chronic patients before attending the very long and complicated birth of Mrs. MacTavish's daughter. Throughout it all, it was the patient on the third floor that was on her mind. "Aye, maybe. I'll see her again tomorrow. There was a dreadful racket coming from the third floor. When I went to offer assistance Mr. Leonard seemed determined to keep me away."

"That's hardly unusual," Johnny reminded her.

"Aye, but I just got the feelin' this woman needed me." Martha and those who loved her had accepted long ago that she had the second sight and so Johnny knew never to second-guess her "feelings" because she was seldom wrong. If she told him not to take a certain road when he traveled, he listened, because the one time he didn't, a tree limb fell into the road and nearly killed the team of horses pulling the wagon. More times than she could count, Martha had foreseen a complicated birth or surgery before it happened, or diagnosed a tumor simply by laying hands on the patient. It was not a skill she honed or made a fuss about; it was just part of who she was. Over the years, however, she had learned to hide her ability from people like Mason Leonard, who was already skeptical and even fearful of a woman physician.

"Ye wanted to go back after supper, did ye not?" Johnny knew that if Martha was determined to see a patient, she would, even if she had to sneak around in the dead of night.

"I did, but poor Mrs. MacTavish needed me. I'll go straight there tomorrow morning before Leonard gets in and the night attendant is still on duty."

"Just ye stay clear of old Kraus." Johnny had heard tell many a tale of the attendant on the third floor of the lunatic asylum, and not just from his wife. Kraus had been chosen by Leonard himself because of his ability to subdue even the most aggressive patients. He was Leonard's man and if Leonard did not want Martha to see that patient, Kraus would restrain her physically if necessary.

"Ach, I'm no' so foolish as to ruffle his feathers, or Mr. Leonard's for that matter." In nearly two decades as a physician, Martha had dealt with a handful of Keepers of both the poorhouse and the insane asylum. Many were glad to have her, but more than a few resisted and resented help from a female doctor. Martha knew with men like Leonard she had to tread carefully lest she be forbidden to practice medicine there for the duration of his tenure as Keeper.

"If need be, I'll have Michael check on her." Martha knew the only reason Mason Leonard did not want her involved with patients on the third floor was because she was a woman. Michael Nolan's decades of dedicated service to the Erie County Poorhouse had earned him the respect of the keepers and matrons there. Martha would send word to her brother-in-law if she couldn't see the third floor patient herself in the morning.

"The lads will be off come the mornin'," Johnny told her in an effort to change the subject.

"Aye, they'll be well pleased to get on the road, I should think."

The lads her husband was referring to were their only son Robert and Bruns' eldest son Walter. Robert and Walter were only boys when Bruns had gone off to fight with the Union Army. They received word early on in the war that Bruns had been killed. During those years and until recently, Johnny had taken over Bruns' responsibilities, spending four months out of the year traveling up and down the east coast between Canada, New York City, and Boston procuring the fancy silks, laces and other luxury goods that the well-to-do residents of Buffalo had come to expect from Nolan's Dry Goods Emporium. Last year it was time to pass the job on to his son, now nineteen years old, and Walter, who was fifteen. This season they would take on the full responsibility without Johnny's help.

"To be sure the two of them will enjoy the time away. It was a long winter." What Johnny really meant was that it was a long winter to be cooped up in such a small living space with so many people. Martha and

Johnny could hardly expect Gertrude to raise three boys on her own, and so the Friedlander family had remained. Johnny had seen that old Doc Hackstein's place on Linwood Avenue was for sale and he hoped to raise the issue with Martha, for it would be a lovely place for them. But that was a conversation for another evening.

When the couple arrived home, they were greeted with the usual chaos of Gertrude and the boys settling around the supper table. The relative silence immediately followed, when everyone applied himself with purpose to full plates of sausages, boiled potatoes and red cabbage. This scenario always made Martha smile. It never lasted long, though. After a few mouthfuls conversation resumed and voices were raised as the younger boys presumed volume added weight to their words.

"Rudolph, there is no reason to shout at your brother. He is seated right next to you," Gertrude scolded. "Frederick, let your brother finish speaking. It is rude to interrupt!"

Martha smiled again, thinking of similar dinner conversations between her nephews Ian and young Daniel when they were young. Frederick, 9, and Rudolph, 8, argued as much as they had. They also got up to as much trouble, too. Martha understood the boys were disappointed to be left out of the big adventure that Robert and Walter would begin tomorrow, and judging by the lack of conviction in their mother's voice, she knew it, too.

"I have need of a trip to the butcher tomorrow. The child who engages in polite conversation and finishes all of his supper may accompany me, I think," Gertrude offered. This comment immediately got the attention of both of her younger sons, who sat up straighter and methodically consumed their meals. There were two advantages to going with their mother to Behringer's Butcher Shop on Elm Street. First, it was owned by their Uncle Henry and Aunt Ellie, and the boys would get to see their four cousins, Charles, Robyn, Samuel and wee Gwynneth. Even better than that, the butcher shop was full of interesting things, like pig snouts and feet, as well as entire rabbits and geese hanging upside down in the window. If they were on their very best behavior, Uncle Henry would let each of them take the meat cleaver and cut the foot off a rabbit. That was always fun, even if ma wouldn't let them take it home.

A part of Walter ached to go with them to see his cousins, although he would not say so aloud. He loved Uncle Henry's shop as much as his younger brothers and, was it not for the fact that the man had sons of his own, Walter would have aspired one day to help in the running of it. Another thing he would not divulge was that he was a bit nervous to be setting out on the road to New York City with Robert. This journey marked him for a man whose responsibility it was to take care of his mother and his brothers. It was a burden for which he was not certain he was prepared. Anything could go wrong on the road, even with a loaded rifle clearly displayed on the bench of the wagon.

Johnny caught the apprehension on the boy's face. "The two of ye are all set for tomorrow?" He directed the question at his own son, hoping Walter would take comfort from Robert's enthusiastic and confident answer.

"We are!" Robert made no effort to hide the wide grin spreading across his face. "We'll leave at first light, right, Walter?" The young man nodded in agreement.

"Good. Now, mind the wagon at the docks. Don't turn yer back on it or it'll be gone," Johnny reminded them. "No sleeping rough; keep to the inns along the way," he continued. "Don't forget to pay the innkeepers a wee bit extra to keep an eye on it when ye stop for the night."

It wasn't the first time or even the tenth time they had heard these instructions, but Robert nodded in acknowledgment. "Aye, Da, we know: check the wagon every night after supper and again in the mornin' before we move on." Before his father could respond he continued, "...and send word when we're on our way home."

"Mind ye stay out of the pubs." Johnny didn't bother trying to hide his smirk, which was met by similar expressions by the two young men, but looks of disapproval from their mothers.

Martha was pleased that her son took this new responsibility seriously and was at ease with it. "Well, it promises to be a journey to remember," Martha added.

"Did ye see Ciara today?" Johnny asked her. It was not unusual to come across Martha's sister at the poorhouse, as she had once again taken on the role of advocate for the poor children of Buffalo now that her own children were grown. There were a number of orphanages in the city, and yet so many children still found their way to the poorhouse.

"Aye, just for a minute," Martha told him. Today they only had a few minutes to visit before each woman had to return to the business at hand. Ciara had been there to reunite Mrs. Schlatt with her daughter, who had been transferred to the Buffalo Orphan Asylum a few weeks ago when her recently widowed mother was admitted to the poorhouse. Ciara hated the idea of separating children from their families, as was often the case when they sought refuge there. It seemed almost like a punishment, and often was reason enough to keep women like Mrs. Schlatt from seeking assistance there. At the same time, the poorhouse was no place for children - so many people brought low by disease, drink, old age or apathy. The institution was three times the size it had been when Ciara and her sisters had lived there, and the negative influences grew in proportion to the population.

There was constant pressure on the Keeper of the Poor to remove the children to a more favorable environment. Often, however, children separated from their families would find themselves in more dire circumstances if bound out as laborers, which was often their fate. The situation required constant vigilance from Ciara Nolan and a few of her friends, who did their best to help those they could. Fortunately, Ciara was able to find a position for Mrs. Schlatt as a housekeeper. Using her charm and her will in equal proportions, Ciara managed to convince the new employer to allow Mrs. Schlatt's daughter, Matilda, to share the small room offered along with the position.

"Nothin's changed at home, then?" She met his eye and shook her head, answering the question he did not want to ask in front of the others. Daniel had not changed his mind. Johnny had hoped that Ciara might talk her son Daniel into traveling with the boys. The trip would certainly do him good and he knew it would put Gertrude's mind at ease if he had agreed. If there were any details of Martha's conversation with her eldest sister, he would hear of them later.

Chapter Five

Young Daniel Nolan was greeted with the usual moos, whinnies and grunts as he entered the barn. They would all be hungry for their breakfasts, so he wasted no time dispensing sweet feed and hay to the four-legged creatures that provided milk, meat, and transportation for his family. The fourth stall to the right was empty. "Da must 'ave been called out last night," he said to the bay mare in the next stall as she poked her head out to greet him. It was not out of the ordinary to see no occupant in the fourth stall come morning when Daniel started his chores. Beau, the dependable chestnut gelding who normally resided there, was his father's mount of choice when he was called away at night. The old horse had seen the doctor through croup, cholera and everything in-between. Although Michael Nolan was the Dean of Medicine at the University of Buffalo, he still saw patients at all hours of the day or night, as he had since Daniel was a boy.

The bay mare turned her head toward the barn door in response to the sound of hoofbeats coming up the drive. Daniel followed her and observed his father dismounting just outside the barn door. The mare blew out a snort and then turned to tuck into her oats. "Ah, ye thought ye might get his share, did ye? Not a chance, my girl, not a chance. Beau never misses a meal and well ye know it!"

"The old boy will be needin' a good rub down before his oats." Michael entered the barn bleary-eyed and a bit wobbly after the hard ride home, the winded gelding trailing behind him. "We both did our fair share last night."

"Go and have yer own. Ma will be waitin' for ye. I'll see to old Beau."

Michael smiled as he led the horse to the crossties and removed his bridle. "Ach, I'm no' so old that I can't put away my own horse." Michael removed a saddle and took the thick cloth off the hook by the stall door.

For a few minutes Michael was silent while he rubbed the back and withers of his sweat-stained mount. Finally, he mentioned casually, "I ran into Charles Malone at the University yesterday."

"Do ye mean to tell me the man's still alive? He must be near eighty years old!" Daniel was only half kidding. He knew well his old mentor was still alive, but he also knew what likely transpired between the attorney and his father.

"Aye well, not quite, but close enough, I suppose. Still has a keen mind, does Charles Malone." Michael continued with the cloth, gently rubbing behind the ears and down Beau's face. "He asked about ye."

"Aye, and what did he ask?" Daniel replied warily.

"He says ye were as fine a lawyer as ever he's worked with, and he'd have ye back whenever ye had a mind to return." What he really asked, indirectly, was why Daniel had thrown away a promising career, and why had his father let him, but there was no need to reveal that.

"Da, I'm not a lawyer anymore." Both Daniel's tone and the resolute expression on his face said clearly that this was not a topic open for discussion.

"Aye, so ye've said." Michael ran a hand down the horse's neck and chest. Confident Beau was cooled down enough to be put away, he led the horse into his stall and then walked out toward the house without another word.

Daniel headed towards the back of the barn to retrieve a wheelbarrow and a pitchfork to muck out the stalls, trying, as he vigorously removed the soiled bedding, to push the past out of his mind. He had been a lawyer once. He studied under the great Charles Malone and so impressed the man, was offered a position in Malone's law firm when he graduated. Then came the War Between the States. He and his older brother Ian were eager, as all young men were, to charge into battle in defense of a cause they considered just. The hardest thing Daniel ever had to do was return home without his only brother.

Michael's brief conversation with Daniel had left him pondering his own life on the way up to the house. He was almost ashamed to admit, even to himself, how easy his life had been. Raised by loving parents who provided him a comfortable place to live, he hadn't known the hardships of growing up on the frontier. It seemed Michael became a doctor, a husband and a father in the blink of an eye. It was a blessing to grow old with Ciara and to watch his sons become men. In a medical career spanning over three decades, he'd known many men who hadn't been so fortunate. He hadn't known war either, as the men who had come to Buffalo before and after him had. It nearly killed him to see his sons go off to fight without him, but he was not a young man and what would Ciara have done if he had left, too? It was cruel, he thought, to have lived so long in health and happiness only to have war sneak up and take the life of his eldest son. Ian's death was devastating enough, but he and Ciara had not counted on losing so much of Daniel, too.

Ciara was putting porridge on the table when Michael opened the back door, still lost in his thoughts. "Ye've Ian on yer mind, I expect." In answer to his questioning look, she added as she took his coat, "I watched ye walk up, makin' a careful study of the stones on the path as ye went. It could only be Ian, and Daniel, I should think, for ye seldom think of one without the other."

"Aye, just so. I mentioned to Daniel just now that Malone would have him back should he take an interest in the law again."

"'Tis not the first time ye've relayed such a message to him, and was his answer the same?"

"Aye, it was. He's been home these three years now. I thought he might be ready."

"Michael, I wonder sometimes if he'll ever be ready." She went to the pantry to retrieve some butter before continuing. "Ian was his only brother and the two of them seldom apart for more than a day or two, even as grown men. I fear he will never stop blaming himself." Tears welled up in her eyes, as they always did when she thought of her youngest son without his older brother.

Michael gave her hand a squeeze. It was all the support he could offer for fear of breaking down himself. "He's a young man yet. I pray that in time he will be able to continue on as he was before that blasted war."

Their conversation came to an abrupt stop when the door opened and Charlie Edwards shuffled in. "I see the lad got an early start with the chores again," he said and took the chair across from Michael. Charlie Edwards had worked for the Nolans maintaining the farm and the livestock for more than thirty years, and, while he welcomed Daniel's help, he did not take kindly to being put out to pasture. In his younger days, Charlie had been one of Ciara's protectors in the poorhouse and saved her life when she was viciously attacked by one of the other inmates. When she left there to marry Michael, Ciara could not leave behind those who had become her family in that wretched place. Karin Friedlander, a widow who had helped Ciara take care of the children's ward, as well as her two protectors Charlie and Alex Hanley, came with her to keep the house and manage the farm while she took on the responsibility of the newly established Buffalo Orphan Asylum.

That was a long time ago and so much had happened since. Old Alex had passed more than twenty years earlier, and Karin a decade after that. She had lived as Charlie's wife for nineteen years and together they raised her son, Bruns, and Ellie, a babe she took in as her own who had been born at the poor farm. What benevolent god would finally bless the couple with a babe of their own only to have both mother and infant die in childbed? They had all pondered that question often over the last ten years. When Karin passed, Bruns and Ellie were both married with families of their own. Charlie was welcome in both of their homes, but he had chosen to stay in the cottage on the Nolan's small farm, where he had lived with his beloved Karin.

Ciara placed a steaming bowl of porridge in front of the old man. "Aye, well, there'll be plenty more to do when ye've finished yer breakfast. Now eat up before it goes cold." Ciara and Michael knew that the early morning chores had become a problem for Charlie over the long, cold winter. He'd had a wonky leg most of his life, the result of a debilitating injury that had left him no choice but to seek refuge in the poorhouse when he was a young man. In recent years the pain it caused him was evident when the seasons changed. She knew right now that Daniel was working like the devil to get the stalls mucked out before Charlie came down, leaving the easier chores for him. There was plenty of tack to clean and repair, tools to be sharpened and a few other tasks that could be accomplished sitting down. Charlie might grumble, but he would appreciate it at the end of the day when his legs could still get him to the supper table.

"A bit of hard work will do the lad good just now," Michael added.

Their somber expressions had not escaped Charlie's attention when he entered the kitchen. "What's amiss, then?"

"Nothing new," Michael told him.

"The lad needs time, is all." ...and the love of a good woman, but somehow Charlie couldn't bring himself to say that last part out loud. He had known despair during his time at the poorhouse. A severe compound fracture of the leg had cost him his livelihood, and worse, his first love. It took years before he was whole again. Karin had been patient through that time, a gift for which Charlie had never thanked her.

"Aye." It was all Michael could say. Although he grieved Ian's death every day, Daniel's loss was different. The brothers were born a year and a half apart and had been constant companions. Even as young men, there was no end to the mischief they got up to together. During the war, they belonged to the 116th Regiment New York Volunteer Infantry and had fought side by side. Daniel had been near death himself from typhoid fever when Ian was shot and killed during the pursuit of General Early's forces who had been chased out by Union soldiers after the skirmish at Fort Stevens in Maryland. It was more than a week before Daniel learned of his brother's death.

When the war ended, Ian remained in an unmarked grave near where the field hospital had stood in Maryland, but it took Daniel nearly two years to make it back to Buffalo. He'd sent word to his parents that he was offered a position in a Pennsylvania law firm owned by one of the men of the 116th and that the pay was too good to pass up. The truth was he couldn't face his family, and ended up working odd jobs, whatever needed doing that put a few coins in his pocket. When something or someone reminded him of that fateful skirmish in July of 1864, he moved on.

It was never far from his mind, though. He had been quarantined at Fort Monroe in Virginia, delirious with fever, when the rest of the regiment was ordered to help the 6th Corps in pursuit of the rebel invaders of Fort Stevens. Ian had always had Daniel's back. In the schoolyard, in the pubs, and on the battlefield the eldest Nolan son kept his brother out of harm's way. Daniel could not look his mother in the eye and tell her that he had failed to do the same, so he stayed away.

The war had been over for almost two years, and all Ciara had were letters from Daniel filled with reasons he could not return to Buffalo. Finally, she sent Michael and Johnny to Pennsylvania to bring her boy home. By then Daniel was tired of drifting and went with his father and his uncle willingly. Once home, he could not bring himself to take up the life he had before the war, the life of which Ian had been so much a part. He stayed close to home, mostly, and only ventured elsewhere in the city when there was need of supplies or his mother had an errand that needed running.

"I do wonder, though, if bein' here isn't doin' more harm than good," Michael confessed. "Here he can't help but see Ian at every turn. I've often thought he might be better off at the shop."

"Maybe so, but they're already burstin' at the seams," Charlie added. Although they would welcome Daniel, and gladly, there was no room for him above Nolan's Dry Goods Emporium.

"'Tis no different for any of us," Ciara reminded them, "and would any one of us take kindly to the suggestion that we move?"

Before Michael could respond, Charlie stood to leave, seeking to give the couple a chance to finish the conversation upon which he had intruded. When the door was closed behind him, Michael spoke, making an effort not to sound defensive. "I don't mean to tell the lad he must go."

"Aye, I know." Ciara sat down to her own porridge, which had gone cold. "Michael, ye don't know what it is to lose a brother or sister."

Ciara's words were meant to comfort not accuse, but there it was, the very thing he was mulling over on the way up to the house earlier. He did not know loss the way the others did. Certainly, both of his parents were gone, but they had lived to see him married with a family of his own. He had no experience to draw on to see his son through this storm. "No, I don't, and if I could take this burden from Daniel, I would, and gladly." Michael reached across the table for her hand. "I don't know how to help him, Ciara."

She placed her other hand over his and gently squeezed. "There is nothing we can do to remove the burden he carries. All we can do is love him and give him enough space to put it down himself." Wise words, but easier said than done.

* * *

As Charlie headed back down to the barn his eyes were drawn, as they often were, to what once was the northwest corner of the property, at North and Ellicott

Streets. The small plot had been a gift to Ciara's middle sister Patricia, and Rolland when they married. The couple built a cozy cottage and lived there until about three years ago with their daughter, wee Mary Karin. Wee Mary Karin was now a woman of twenty, married with a child of her own, living in Albany near her father's family. The year their daughter married, Rolland had been offered the position of Headmaster of the Heathcote School on Pearl Street. The city was growing by leaps and bounds, and the small plot in the northwest corner caught a fair price when Rolland and Patricia sold it and moved closer to the school. The little house was barely recognizable there had been so many additions to it.

Somehow, over the years, the quiet little farm had become enveloped by the city. Charlie wondered, if things had been different when Daniel came home, whether Michael and Ciara would have sold up and moved on. Michael hadn't much use for the nearby hospital on High Street. When he saw patients in hospital, it was either at the poorhouse or at the Catholic hospital on St. Louis Place. He and Ciara had started out their lives together with a ready-made family, and so a farm seemed a wise option. Now, just about all of the members of that unusual extended family had found their way in the world, or out of it, and there was no real reason for Ciara and Michael to stay where they were, with the city sprouting up around them.

Charlie had considered finally taking his step-daughter up on her many invitations to come and live with her family on Elm Street, but then Daniel had come home. The lad reminded Charlie of himself at that age, broken and adrift. Had it not been for Ciara, Charlie might have lived his entire life at the poorhouse, lonely and without hope. She had given him a home and a purpose and he would stay there until her son found peace again. With that mental affirmation, Charlie continued on to the barn to see what chores yet needed doing. After all, a man must earn his keep.

Chapter Six

It was still dark when Martha finally gave up and opened her eyes. The soft grunts of Johnny snoring beside her indicated that there would yet be a few hours before the night gave way to dawn. There were often evenings when the weight of a particular patient on her mind kept Martha from a full night's rest. If she stayed abed, the shifting gears of her thoughts would wake Johnny eventually, but if she got up, surely someone else would hear. The living space above the shop had been overcrowded nearly from the day she married Johnny and moved in, and any late night prowling seldom went unnoticed by one or more of the other occupants.

Having long given up on sleep, Martha weighed the risk of waking one of Gertrude's boys who shared the room at the top of the stairs. If she could make it past them, there were a few medical journals in her office that would help to pass the hours until dawn.

"Ye'll never make it past the first stair." The voice whispering beside her roused Martha out of her thoughts and she turned toward the sound of it. Although it was dark, she could see the smile of satisfaction on Johnny's face at having read her mind yet again.

"I'll never know how ye do that," she said as he pulled her in.

"Aye, so ye won't. Now that ye've got the both of us up, I aim to keep ye in bed for a while longer." He kissed her slowly, and then with purpose, driving all thoughts of the patient on the third floor away.

Having spent the remaining hours of the night in her husband's embrace, Martha was sleepy but content as she left for the asylum in the morning. She got an early start in the hopes of sneaking up to the third floor while Mrs. Boswell was occupied supervising the kitchen staff. Pleased to find the reception area empty, she hurried up the stairs. There were voices raised in argument as she climbed the stairs.

"Sir, I must insist that you let me in to see this patient immediately!" It was a woman's voice, and was unfamiliar to Martha.

"I'm that sorry, ma'am, but Mr. Leonard gave strict orders that nobody be admitted to this room, save for himself, of course." That voice Martha did recognize. It was Edward Morrissey, the night attendant.

"Good mornin' to ye, Mr. Morrissey." Martha gave the man her best smile as she approached.

"Good mornin' to ye, Dr. Quinn." Martha had saved Edward's leg from the necessity of amputation a few years back, and so he always used her professional title when they spoke. "May I present Mrs. Awalte, from, ah…Where is it ye said ye were from, ma'am?" Both Mr. Morrissey and the doctor turned to find the woman staring at Martha.

Mrs. Awalte ignored the question, but issued one of her own. "You are a physician?"

Martha extended her hand toward Mrs. Awalte, who still hadn't relieved the doctor of her scrutiny. "My name is Dr. Martha Quinn. I am a physician here. What, may I ask, is yer business with this patient?"

The woman looked as if she had made up her mind about Martha and offered a confident bow. "Dr. Quinn, my name is Alva Awalte, and I am a healer here in Buffalo." She looked at the attendant and then back at Martha. "I wonder if I might have a moment of your time."

Martha knew she must move quickly if she wanted to see this patient before Mr. Leonard arrived or Kraus came on duty, but the woman looked as if she had something important to say. She looked at Mr. Morrissey, who seemed relieved to be excluded from the conversation, and smiled. "Go and have yer breakfast. Yer patient will be safe enough behind a locked door while ye do."

Edward Morrissey was more than happy to oblige, but Mrs. Awalte waited until he was well down the stairs before she continued. "Dr. Quinn, there is precious little time until that imbecile of a Keeper returns and removes us both, for he not only has no respect for women, he fears people like us." She gave Martha a quick but penetrating stare before she continued. "Now, that woman shackled to her cot is as sane as you or I, and I intend to remove her from this wretched place. May I count on your assistance?"

"Ye'll pardon me for sayin' so, Mrs. Awalte, but I've only just met ye, and ye'll have to explain how ye've come to understand the condition of the patient in that room when none but the Keeper himself has spoken to her."

Mrs. Awalte blew out a sigh of frustration. "The woman is called Felicity Taylor. She lived in Laona with her uncle until his death last month. She has always been considered an outsider where she lived. You see, she is deaf, but she also possesses special gifts."

Martha stood there speechless. She recognized the name, of course, but did not know which part of the woman's statement to react to first. *Felicity Taylor here in the asylum? How did this woman know about her special gifts?*

"Dr. Quinn, there are so few of us whose abilities are genuine. Let us not play games, for this woman's fate is now in our hands. Would you let her remain in shackles?"

Wee Felicity, in shackles! The thought made Martha's blood turn cold. "May I ask how ye've come to know this woman?"

"As I said, there are so few of us, and those who fear us would have our numbers dwindle, so we must watch out for each other. A number of years ago, her aunt wrote to me. Felicity did not make friends easily in Batavia, not because she was deaf, but because she could hear people's thoughts. It was how she was able to communicate in those early years, before she learned sign language. Her Aunt Taylor made the mistake of telling the schoolmaster, in the hopes that it would make it easier for the child to learn in common school, but instead, it made him fearful of her. His fear spread to the students and even their parents. The Taylors moved to Laona at my suggestion, where people were known to be more tolerant of such things. Still they kept the child out of common school." She stopped for a moment and looked toward the locked door. "I met her a few times; she was such a sweet child. But make no mistake, her gifts were powerful."

Martha grew pale. She knew well Felicity's special gift. They had considered it a blessing to have a way to communicate with her, as had her aunt and uncle. That blessing had turned into a curse. "Did she go to the school for the deaf?"

"She did, and took up a teaching position there when she graduated. She only left to keep the house for her uncle when her aunt became ill. Mrs. Taylor had written me shortly before her death and asked me to keep in touch with Miss Taylor when she came back to Laona. She feared for her niece's safety, for the new constable showed no kindness toward the Free Thinkers and he and Justice Pennyworth were thick as thieves. The Justice of the Peace accepts Constable Schaeffer's recommendation for commitment to the asylum without question." Mrs. Awalte cleared her throat as if she had just swallowed something vile before continuing. "Rumors circulated when Felicity came home that she had been in an asylum, but her uncle managed to keep her safe when he was alive." Her expression darkened as she explained how the constable had forcibly removed Felicity from her home and transferred her to the insane asylum. "So you see, Dr. Quinn, we must free her from this place."

The two women were silent while Martha took in all she had been told. Finally, she spoke. "I knew her as a child. She had lost her da during winter, and then her ma to cholera that following summer. I knew the orphanage could not manage a deaf child so we took her in. I traveled with her to Batavia myself, when we found she had kin willin' to take her. We exchanged letters, Mrs. Taylor and I, for a time. I haven't heard from any of them in years. I had no idea that they moved to Chautauqua County."

"Will you help me?"

Martha did not hesitate. "Aye, I will. Let us go now, before we are seen. We need to find Michael."

The two women made their way out of the asylum undetected. "Ye are goin' to a great deal of trouble for a woman ye hardly know," Martha mentioned casually on their way to the University. "May I ask why?"

"I made a promise to her aunt." That was all that Alva offered by way of explanation.

"If ye don't mind my askin', how was it that Mrs. Taylor wrote to ye in the first place?"

"Many people were entertained by the Fox Sisters, who have the ability to speak to the dead. Do you remember them?" Martha nodded and Alva went on. "For some years now, there have been many other people traveling about the country claiming to have special gifts. Well, after the novelty wore off, what was left was healthy skepticism, but with some there was also fear and suspicion. Chautauqua County became a gathering place for the Free Thinkers. It was a safe place for us until Constable Schaeffer arrived. Men like him, with a little bit of power, are dangerous when they let their fear get a hold of them. We watch out for each other now." Alva was silent for a moment, as if trying to remember something. "I really do not recall how

Mrs. Taylor knew to contact me, but she made sure Felicity knew how to reach me. I received a letter last week from her. She knew things would go bad once she was behind on the rent. By the time I got to Laona, Felicity had already been committed. It took me the better part of a day to discover that she had never been to the Chautauqua asylum, but was sent by the Justice of the Peace to Buffalo Plains. I came here yesterday afternoon, but could not get past the matron downstairs."

Martha smiled as she realized that Mrs. Awalte had come this morning with the same intention, to try and talk poor Edward into letting her in to see the patient. "Aye, Mrs. Boswell is the Keeper's sister and much pleased with her current position."

"Do forgive me, I hadn't thought to ask earlier, but who is it we are going to fetch, and how will he be of help to us?" Alva Awalte was not accustomed to asking men she did not know for help. She trusted very few men and would need to know more before she would confide in a total stranger.

"Michael Nolan is my brother-in-law and my mentor. Mr. Leonard will release Miss Taylor upon Michael's recommendation."

"I know Dr. Nolan by reputation only. I understand him to be respectful of women, at least. Will he help us, do you think?"

"He will, and not just because he once offered Felicity a home. I have solicited his help often on behalf of patients in that asylum. He has saved many a poor soul from a life in shackles, I daresay."

That wasn't enough for Alva Awalte to place her confidence in the man. She knew all too well of men who were resentful or, worse yet, fearful of women who possessed talents or skills that they did not. They were a dangerous lot. She would see for herself whether he was a man of honor. She could always tell. "Does he know of your gifts?"

"Mrs. Awalte, ye've mentioned several times about these gifts, which ye assume I possess, and I wonder if ye'd be more specific, please."

Alva Awalte was silent for a moment, again taking Martha's measure, and again deciding favorably to confide in her. "I mentioned before that I am a healer." Martha nodded and Alva continued. "I was not trained at university, or by other healers." She hesitated again, searching for the right words this time. "When I was a child, back in Germany, I had dreams of an Indian woman, although I did not know she was an Indian until I came here and saw those people for myself. She told me I was meant to be a healer and gave me access, in my dreams, to all that the vegetable kingdom has to offer to cure the maladies of mankind. I have learned over the years that I have the ability to access her knowledge when I have need of it." She looked directly at Martha and added, "You see, I am a clairvoyant healer with an extensive knowledge of Medical Botany. I am able to put myself in a trance and access the healing knowledge of my spirit guide." Alva took a moment to evaluate Martha's reaction to this statement before she continued. "As you might assume, my skills are not valued by the medical establishment, and yet I have a substantial practice here in the city. This is because I have an insight into illness that medical doctors do not. I can cure what you cannot." After another penetrating stare, she added, "It would surprise you, I think, to learn who some of my clients are."

Martha was not sure what she meant by the term trance, and asked. "Oh, I didn't know ye could do that."

"Dr. Quinn, I suspect that you have similar gifts."

It was not something Martha had ever really discussed with other people and, frankly, it was a bit disconcerting to be doing so with a stranger. Ciara had told her when she was a child about the gift of second sight, and that it was a blessing. It was part of who she was, like her dark hair and her green eyes. She did not talk about those either; there was no need to. True, the gift of second sight was a bit different, but Martha had learned long ago not to share that particular detail about herself with people outside of her family. She understood exactly what Alva meant when she spoke of suspicion and fear going unchecked. Martha walked a fine line with Mason Leonard as it was. Should he become aware of her abilities, the least of his reaction would be to forbid her to practice medicine at the poorhouse. She would not let herself think of what the worst of his reaction might be. There had been whispered rumors for months that Leonard's wife had left him to join a group of Free Thinkers in the area of Cassadaga Lake, near Laona. The very people who possessed such gifts as Mrs. Awalte was speaking of could be found among the Free Thinkers. The last thing Martha wanted was for Mason Leonard to connect her to those people.

Her reticence was evident on Martha's face and Alva watched her struggling with it. "You are wise not to discuss such things with strangers. You understand, perhaps, my reservations about your Dr. Nolan." Martha nodded and the older woman continued. "I have put my trust in you. Please understand that if you choose to return that trust it will not be betrayed."

Martha could not think of a response to that and chose instead to focus on the issue at hand. "Let us worry about poor Felicity. Perhaps when she is safe there will be time to talk of other things."

The trap turned from Main Street on to Virginia and Martha pulled up behind the large brick building on the corner. As the Dean of Medicine, Michael had a large office on the ground floor. His secretary, Miss Sturgis, recognized Martha and immediately went to the operating theater to fetch the Dean.

"Dr. Quinn, what brings ye here today?" Michael always addressed his sister-in-law by her professional title, but usually dispensed with a more formal greeting unless there were colleagues present.

"Good day to ye, Dr. Nolan. Allow me to present Mrs. Awalte. Mrs. Awalte, may I present Dr. Nolan, Dean of Medicine."

Dr. Nolan made a brief bow in the direction of Alva Awalte. "I am pleased to make your acquaintance, Mrs. Awalte."

"The pleasure is mine, sir." Alva's tone was sincere, but reserved. Men of Dr. Nolan's stature didn't rise to important positions by interfering in what most would think were the follies of women, but perhaps this one might.

"How may I be of assistance to ye this day?" Michael asked.

"We are in need of yer help at the asylum. One of our own has been committed."

Michael understood her to be referring to a patient or an inmate they had formed a relationship with, someone they had helped in the past, rather than a friend or family member. "Aye, who is it?"

"Felicity Taylor. She was admitted not two days ago," Martha told him.

"Felicity! Are ye sure?"

Martha explained briefly how Mr. Leonard had not allowed her in to see the new patient on the third floor and what she had learned from Mrs. Awalte that morning. After a glance at his pocket watch and a few brief words to Miss Sturgis, the three of them were off.

Alva Awalte had to admit that it had been a wise decision to involve Dr. Nolan. He had walked into the asylum with the full weight of his position behind him and in less than an hour had seen to the discharge of Felicity Taylor and the treatment of two other patients on the third floor, who, unbeknownst to the Keeper, had terrible cases of *tinea capitus*, ringworm of the scalp.

Felicity had recognized all of them, although none of her rescuers would have recognized her on the street. She was tall and thin for want of a good meal, which she certainly hadn't gotten in the poorhouse asylum. Her thick brown hair hung unkempt about her face. She had been given back the dress in which she had arrived, which was of good quality, and Martha had done her best to help the woman tidy up before they left. Still, she wore the trauma of the last few days clearly on her face.

"She'll stay with us of course." It was Michael's answer to the unspoken question as they exited the asylum.

Tears were streaming down Felicity's face as Michael helped her into the carriage. Her hands began moving in rapid gestures and Michael recognized it as sign language, although she spoke the words as well. "You have saved me again."

Chapter Seven

Maude sat at the counter in her shop and looked at the last of her notes from her bedside journal. It was nearly full and she would need a new one soon. She had dreamed of Martha Quinn and her family for the past three nights. The vivid details were startling, even in the light of day. Another story was unfolding, but she didn't know what might happen next, or why it was now being revealed. She had created a list of the people in her dreams with the intent of identifying who had actually lived in Buffalo in the spring of 1870, and who was entirely a figment of her imagination. Tapping the tip of her pencil on the notepad, Maude pondered the addition of one more name. If she had really graduated from medical school, Martha Sloane could be found in the university archives. She might also be mentioned in some of the poorhouse records if she had been a physician at the asylum. Still, there was something weird about looking up your past life in the historic records, assuming one believed in past lives in the first place.

Her thoughts were interrupted by the jingling of the bell above the door announcing a potential customer. "Good morning, how can I help you today?"

The man's smile made Maude wary, like he seemed pleased to be delivering bad news. "Maude Travers?" She nodded. "I'm Lester, Lester Northrup."

Maude did her best not to flinch as she recognized the name. Lester Northrup was the ne'er-do-well brother of Phillip Northrup, the man who had previously owned the building in which she and Don worked and currently lived. They had almost lost their business last year when Phil decided to sell the building to Lester so that Lester and his wife Dawn could run an antique business similar to the one Maude and Don had spent over a decade building. Luckily, they put together an offer that Lester could not match and were able to purchase the building themselves. She put on her warmest smile and walked out from behind the counter with her hand extended to shake his. "You're Phil's brother, right? What brings you here today?"

It took a minute for him to respond. He was looking at Maude as if he recognized her, although they had never met. "Yes, I am." He made no mention of his efforts last year to usurp her business, much to Maude's relief. "I just wanted to pop in to introduce myself and to let you know that I am your new neighbor." The confused look on her face was just the reaction he had hoped for and, with a fiendish smile, he dropped the bomb. "I just signed the lease on the building next door."

Maude smiled, careful not to give him the satisfaction of seeing the shock that she was feeling. "Oh really, what do you intend to do with it?" He looked familiar. Had they met before? She did not care to ask.

"Open an antique shop, of course. We tried to buy Trinkets and Treasures, but David and Tom wouldn't sell." He casually picked up a vintage pocket watch and glanced at the price before he continued. "I did manage to purchase most of their inventory at auction, along with some jewelry and lamps I found at an estate sale, so I won't be starting from scratch."

"Congratulations." What else could she say to a person whom she had never met, but detested nonetheless, and who had just announced he would open a business similar to hers right next door. By mutual unspoken agreement, Trinkets and Treasures did not sell vintage lighting or jewelry and The Antique Lamp Company and Gift Emporium did not sell furniture or books. They had often referred clients to each other over the years and had become good friends. Maude doubted she would maintain such a supportive business relationship with Lester and his wife.

"Thanks. Well, I've got contractors to meet, so I gotta run. You can expect me to drop in over the next few days. I'll want to pick your brain." With that, he turned and left.

"Well, I don't know about you, but I'll be keeping the back door locked," Christine said as she joined Maude from the back room. "No sense making it easy for him to pop in."

"Oh, did you hear that?" Maude was a bit surprised to see Christine because she wasn't due for another half hour.

"I most certainly did. Can you believe that jerk actually cornered me in the alley and asked if I was interested in working for him?" Christine stowed her purse under the counter before she continued. "When I told him no, he asked me out on a date! What a jerk!"

"He asked you out? I thought he was married!"

"Not any more. Gold digger Dawn took off right after the deal for this place fell through. He's got no business running an antique shop. I give him six months before he's broke again."

"Oh, it will be longer than that. You know Phil must be bankrolling him if he was able to purchase David and Tom's inventory," Maude told her. "I wonder how long it took him to talk big brother into setting him up in the shop next door."

"Well, I know that Phil had approached the boys shortly after you bought this building last year, but they refused at least two of his offers." Christine always referred to her former employers as "the boys" because they acted more like school chums than businessmen. "I wonder if they know who ended up buying all of their stuff."

"I doubt it. A check would have been issued from the auction company. As long as it was in the range they were expecting, they probably wouldn't have asked any questions." Maude suggested. "Let's not tell them. It might irritate them to know Lester outsmarted them."

"As much as we would like to think so, they didn't refuse to sell Northrup the business out of loyalty to you and Don...well, not entirely anyway. It's more likely that there was simply less paperwork involved with just closing and auctioning off the inventory." Christine smiled as she remembered her bosses fondly. "You know, neither of them ever needed the money.

They were a couple of rich boys who had been friends since prep school. This was always just a hobby for them." Laughing, she added, "Maybe it will give them some satisfaction to know that Lester probably spent way too much of his brother's money at that auction!"

"I know it gives me some satisfaction," Maude agreed with a smirk. "I think you're right, by the way, about keeping the back door locked. I don't want him anywhere near my office."

"Too bad we can't keep the front door locked, too!"

Maude told Don before dinner that night about Lester Northrup and then listened while he expressed his disbelief, outrage and concerns. In the end, they agreed to be cordial but cautious whenever Lester darkened their doorstep.

"Okay, that's enough of him," Don said, declaring that particular discussion over and done. "What's going on with your dreams?" He had been out of town for the last two days at estate sales in Syracuse and they hadn't had much time to talk.

Maude took a liberal sip from her wine glass before answering. "Well, Höhle has been keeping me busy in your absence. I've been dreaming every night."

"I'm afraid to ask, but who is Höhle?"

Maude chuckled in an attempt to hide her uneasiness. "Well, if I have a cave woman for a spirit guide, I thought she should have a name. *Höhle* is a German word for cave." He seemed confused at her choice of names and she became a bit defensive in an attempt to explain. "Well, the word for guide is *führer*, so I wasn't going with that. If she doesn't like it, she can damn well tell me what her name is!"

"Spoken like someone who has not slept well in a few days."

"Well, yes, there's that. I have these vivid dreams, and then I have to write it all down so I don't miss any details." Maude finished her wine and turned to pour another glass before she continued. "Actually, giving her a name is my way of accepting that this is real, that she is communicating with me and that I am receptive to the message."

"Okay, I get that. So, what's the plan?"

"I have made a list of the people who have been appearing in my dreams with the intention of trying to look for them in the historic record. Last time, I found people by chance, so I'm curious to see what I find if I go looking for some of them." Maude reached for her bag and grabbed her notebook to show him.

Don gave the list a quick look and placed it back in her bag. "I see you left someone out."

Trust him to zero in on the very issue she had been considering all day. "Well, I'm not sure I want to start digging into Martha Quinn's life."

"I can see your point. Have you called Charlotte to see what she has to say?" Don asked.

Maude was quite sure that her friend from Lily Dale was entirely sick of being pestered with questions about weird dreams and spirit guides who live in caves. "No, I'm afraid if she sees my name on the caller ID she won't pick up!"

Don laughed. "You know that's not true."

Maude nodded in agreement. "I know. Truthfully, I'm afraid of what she might say."

This time Don laughed even louder. "Coward!"

"Easy for you to say! I thought I'd start with Alva Awalte. She seems like an interesting woman, and she's supposedly connected to the Spiritualist community. She claims to be a clairvoyant healer. There might be something about her in the Lily Dale library."

Don examined the stack of mail he had brought in earlier. "She does sound interest..." He stopped speaking and opened an envelope with an official looking return address. "Son-of-a-bitch! We got a summons!"

"What? What for?" Maude came around so that she could read over his shoulder but all she could see were the words *crumbling façade*.

"The bricks on the side of the building need to be repointed," Don told her. "I was planning on waiting until the boys were done with school so they could help."

"Did someone complain? How bad is it?" Maude tried to picture any part of the building façade that looked so bad as to draw attention, but couldn't.

"It's back toward the alley. You can't see it from the street, but if you are looking for damage, it's easy to see." Don folded the summons back up and slipped it back into the envelope. "I'll call the city inspector tomorrow and ask if it can wait until the end of June. They're usually pretty good about cutting people slack as long as the job gets done in a reasonable amount of time."

Maude took four plates from the cupboard and motioned for Don to grab the flatware to accompany it.

"Do you think they'll tell you who complained?" she asked as she set the table for dinner.

"They are not supposed to, but it depends on who answers the phone."

The arrival of Billy and Glen essentially ended the conversation. Maude was glad to have the discussion around the dinner table focus on their plans to take their newfound girlfriends to the movies. Still, her mind wandered, as they chattered on about who should pay for the tickets and popcorn, back to the list she had made earlier. She decided to send an e-mail after dinner asking Abby Stevens to see what she could find out about the people on her list. After some more consideration, she added Martha Quinn to that list. Delegating the research into Martha's life to Abby gave Maude the ability to ask a few simple questions regarding her findings with less risk that she might find out something better left in the past.

As Maude lay in bed later that night, her thoughts crisscrossed between the unexpected appearance of Lester Northrup on her doorstep and the list of names from her dreams she had generated for further research. As she drifted off to sleep her mind conjured an image of Mason Leonard sitting at his desk in the asylum not at all pleased with whatever had recently transpired. Wanting to know more, Maude allowed herself to relax deeper into sleep, seemingly unaware that in her semiconscious state she was able to do what she had previously thought was impossible. With that single image of Mason Leonard sitting at his desk, she had been able to conjure up the past. Would she recall that in the morning?

Chapter Eight

Mason Leonard's chair protested with a loud creak as he shifted his weight and leaned back against it. It wasn't the first time Martha Quinn had solicited the help of her brother-in-law to override his authority. He simply could not seem to get either of them to understand the danger in which they placed themselves by removing that woman from his care. It took more than a pleasant home and a few good meals to treat the violent ones, and Justice Pennyworth had assured him that this woman was not only very dangerous, but likely incurable. He reached into the open drawer of his desk and pulled out the letter from the Justice of the Peace that had accompanied the woman and read it once again.

> To Mr. Mason P. Leonard
> Keeper of the Asylum
> Erie County Poorhouse
> Buffalo Plains
>
> May 25, 1870
>
> Dear Mr. Leonard,
>
> I entrust to your care this poor woman whom God has forgotten. She had found a

home among the Free Thinkers, as many cursed with her injured mind do, but so engrossed with their Godless pursuits as they are, she did not receive the care that might have freed her from the evil daemons, whom I fear reside now permanently within her. Sadly, our own asylum is ill-equipped to manage such a violent patient on a permanent basis. I fear she will not be the last case I encounter, as the Free Thinkers are entirely unable to manage these tortured souls and Constable Schaeffer feels they pose a direct threat to the wellbeing of our citizenry. I am confident that under your care this woman will pose neither a danger to the public nor to herself. I will leave it to your discretion whether or not to transfer her as incurable to the state asylum in Ovid.

Your Humble Servant,
Horace W. Pennyworth
Justice of the Peace

"Well, I can't say it surprises me," Leonard said to himself out loud, placing the letter back in the desk drawer. He had some experience with those so-called Free Thinkers, after all. What did they call themselves now? Spiritualists? They had lured his wife away with promises of teaching her how to communicate with the dead. It had saddened him deeply to lose their son so young, but he was not so foolish as to believe that it was possible to speak with him on the other side. He was fairly certain that Martha Quinn had encouraged this folly. She went out of her way to speak to his wife. At one point, he actually had to tell her to leave the poor woman in peace.

The Spiritualists were charlatans and he told his wife so. Leonard was certain his beloved Pamela was not the only simple-minded soul to fall victim to their ruse. They were a dangerous lot, breaking up God-fearing homes and going on about the enfranchisement of women. There was even a woman among them who planned to run for the Presidency of the United States! He could see how the fragile sensibilities of the fairer sex could be taken in, but what man in his right mind would be a part of it?

Leonard had often wondered if he had somehow missed the signs of his own wife's descent into insanity. What else could have explained her flight away from their happy home and toward such a band of outcasts? Could she be one of the very people whom Justice Pennyworth described, living among the Spiritualists in the hopes of salvation, only to be cast adrift as they pursued their own godless agenda? It was easy to see how that might push an already feeble person over the edge.

The thought of his wife in shackles, far away at the new state asylum in Ovid with the rest of the chronically insane, left him panic-stricken. He could not bear to have her under anyone's care but his own and would do what he must to protect her and assure himself that, if the worst should happen, she would come to Buffalo and not Ovid. Leonard wasted no time pulling out paper and pen.

To Mr. Horace W. Pennyworth
Justice of the Peace
Hamlet of Laona

May 29, 1870

Justice Pennyworth,

You have my profound gratitude, sir, for entrusting this patient into my expert care.

I, too, share your concerns regarding the dangerous influence the Spiritualists seem able to exert over many of our fragile-minded citizens. Be assured that we here at the Buffalo Plains asylum are able to offer accommodations to any patients you deem fit to transfer and can offer a level of security unattainable at any other asylum.

Sincerely,
Mason J. Leonard

Leonard sealed the letter, hoping it would insure that any patients transferred from Chautauqua County came to him first. If Pamela were among them, he would be able to see to her care himself. Perhaps a few months on the third floor would help her to see how happy they had once been together. Any others could be transferred to Ovid as incurable. It was pointless, after all, to treat them here if there was no hope for a cure and they would ultimately be transferred there anyway.

* * *

The joyful reunion, as Felicity made her way back to the Nolan farm, gave Martha little time to consider her unusual meeting with Alva Awalte. She was grateful that Felicity had learned to read lips because neither she nor Michael knew sign language. And, although her voice sounded awkward and constrained, Felicity could also speak. They spent the short carriage ride bringing her up to date on the rest of the family, including the deaths of Ian and Karin, which brought Felicity great sadness. Felicity made no mention of her aunt and uncle, nor the circumstances under which she found herself in the insane asylum. There was no need to press for those details as both Michael and Martha knew they would be offered when she was ready.

Ciara came out of the house, and, as the carriage drew closer, became more curious about the expressions of delight on their faces than why her husband and sister had come with a guest in the middle of the day.

"Ciara, my love, we've brought ye an old friend," Michael announced as he pulled up in front of the house.

Ciara smiled at the woman, who looked the worse for wear but was nevertheless beaming back and making no effort to hide the tears streaming down her face. It was her eyes that Ciara recognized, and her smile. "Dear God, can it be wee Felicity?"

Forgetting for a moment that she was a grown woman, Felicity jumped down from the carriage and ran into Ciara's outstretched arms. "It is you! Hush now, child." Ciara held her at arm's length to get a good look at the woman she had become. It did not escape her that there was a story to be told, and it would not be a pleasant one. "Ye're home now, lass, and all will be right soon enough." Ciara looked at Michael, who just tilted his head toward Martha, crediting her with Felicity's reappearance. Then she shifted her attention to her sister. "Martha, show Felicity to yer old chamber so she can clean up a wee bit, and then go down and fetch Daniel and Charlie for tea."

Once the two women were out of sight, Ciara turned to Michael. "What's happened? But for being a grown woman, the poor soul looks as forlorn as the day I first met her."

Michael remembered the grubby-faced orphan that Martha had brought home so long ago, and couldn't for the life of him understand how she had ended up in the insane asylum, shackled to her bed. "Well, we've not yet heard the details from Felicity, but Martha found her on the third floor of the asylum, and old Kraus on the other side of the door. Mind, Martha didn't know it was her until this mornin', when another woman came to try and have her released." Ciara looked confused, but Michael continued to tell her the little he knew.

"I'm that sorry to hear she has found herself without kin yet again," Ciara said and Michael nodded in agreement. "Aye, well, she's a home here so long as she needs one."

Martha left Felicity to settle in and her sister and brother-in-law to discuss the new addition to their household as she wandered down to the barn.

"Auntie! What brings ye here in the middle of the day?" Daniel carefully placed the bale of hay he had been about to throw down on the floor of the loft and climbed down to greet Martha.

"Daniel, come and give yer auntie a kiss. I've wonderful news."

The exchange between them brought Charlie out of the far stall, pitchfork in hand. "We'd be pleased for some wonderful news," he said as he approached and kissed Martha on the cheek.

"I've brought Felicity home!" Her proclamation initially brought expressions of confusion, then a spark of recognition that quickly turned to delight.

"Wee Felicity? What brings her back to Buffalo after all this time?" Charlie asked.

"Well, her tale is not a joyful one, to be sure. Were it not for Michael, she'd be shackled to a cot in the asylum." Seeing his face darken, she added, "She's as sane as you or I, and no mistake. I imagine once she's settled in, she'll tell us the truth of it."

"Settled in?" Daniel had been silent until now. He was just a lad himself when Felicity had come to stay with them in the summer of 1849. He barely remembered her now; it seemed a lifetime ago. "Has she come to stay?"

"Aye, for as long as she needs to, and certainly until we sort out how she ended up in the asylum," Martha told him. "Yer ma's got the tea on, so do come up and say hello."

By the time the three of them returned to the kitchen, Felicity had come back downstairs and was helping Ciara set the table. There was a bit of hesitation, as neither man knew exactly how to greet someone they had considered family when she was a small child, but didn't know as a grown woman. Felicity, however, felt no such uncertainty and hurled herself into their arms as she had often done as a child.

They listened carefully as Felicity told them of her experiences at the school for the deaf in New York City, and how she had left there to care for her uncle about a year ago. She signed as she spoke, as was the custom at the school. At Michael's request, she agreed to teach them sign language so that they might do the same.

"Now, Daniel, mind ye speak directly to her so she can read yer lips," Martha reminded him as he asked Felicity if she missed teaching.

Felicity seemed to just stare at Daniel, which startled him for a moment, but then he laughed as if they had just shared a joke. "Aye, I know fine how to speak to her." He grinned and picked up his cup to drain it. "I'd best get back to the loft. The beasts will be wantin' their hay." He got up and gave his mother and his auntie each a kiss on the cheek. "Thanks for the tea, ma." He looked at Felicity again and she gave him a knowing smile before he headed out the door.

Martha and Felicity went about clearing the table. Michael looked confused, unsure of what had just transpired, but Ciara remembered. "It still works between them after all these years," she said, smiling.

"What still works?"

"Do ye not recall the three of them when they were young, and seldom a word spoken between them?"

Michael smiled at the memory of Ian, Daniel and Felicity as children. "Oh, aye, they got up to their fair share of mischief, to be sure. I just thought it was the way of some children, to just know what the others are thinkin'."

"Well, I'm glad of it. It will do both of them good to remember when they were young." Getting up from the table, she asked Michael, "Do ye think she'll go back to the school?"

"I imagine so, if they'll have her. There's nothin' keepin' her away now that her uncle has passed."

"Aye, well, we best find out how she ended up in the asylum before she goes anywhere," Charlie added as he got up to make his exit.

"Aye, to be sure," Michael agreed. "Well, I'd best be off as well and see if I can salvage the day. Martha, shall I take ye back to yer trap?"

Martha wiped her hands on the apron she had borrowed from her sister and then removed it to the peg where she had found it. "Aye, I've a few patients to check on before the day is out."

They were silent for most of the ride back to the university but as they turned on to Main Street, Michael asked Martha if she knew anything of Mrs. Awalte before today.

"No, I can't say as I do."

"Well, now that I'm thinkin' of it, I do recall about a year ago Dr. Grant mention a woman claimin' to be a physician. She had an office on North Division. I'm wonderin' now if it was her he was talkin' about," he told her.

"Aye, I'd say so. She told me I could find her at 248 North Division Street if I should have need of her," Martha offered. "Did he speak well of her?" Martha had eventually won the respect of many of the local physicians, even if she hadn't won the confidence of their clients, so she wondered what they would make of Alva Awalte.

"No, he did not. She is not a trained physician, like ye are. She's a healer, and well ye know that's somethin' entirely different to most physicians." Michael knew more than anyone how hard Martha had fought for her place in the medical community and he did not want to see her lose any footing by virtue of her association with this woman.

"Were it not for Mrs. Awalte, Felicity would still be shackled to that bed, for ye know it would have been a day or more before ye would have been able to get out there," Martha reminded him.

Michael was quiet for a minute because he knew she was right. Martha would have asked for his help, but with an unknown patient, he would not have just up and left the university to come to her aid. "I didn't say we should not be grateful to the woman for her help. I'm just sayin' that she is a cause for concern among the other physicians."

"What ye mean is that they don't care for her treatin' patients who they feel require the services of a trained physician."

"Martha, she's not a physician."

Martha was not about to mention that Mrs. Awalte claimed to be a clairvoyant healer. If he hadn't already heard that part, it was just as well that he didn't know. "That doesn't mean she can't treat the common ailments. She must have treated one of Dr. Grant's regular patients to have angered him so."

"Dr. Grant is not a man ye want as an enemy." He knew as he spoke the words that they were futile. The Sloane women never turned their backs on anyone or anything they thought was important. If Martha wanted to befriend this woman, no words of caution from him would make a difference.

Chapter Nine

Daniel was forced out of sleep, disoriented and out of breath from the same old nightmare. As he calmed himself, he listened for the sounds around him that would confirm he was home in Buffalo, in his own bed, and not in the hospital tent at Fort Monroe. The dream brought the details fresh to his mind, conjuring up those dreadful days in Virginia during the war. Near death with typhoid, Daniel had seen his brother's death in a dream. When the fever finally broke, he woke in a panic, wanting news of Ian. The doctor assured him that it was just a dream brought on by his high fever, but later he would realize that the dream had been prophetic. It was meant to warn him of his brother's fate, but now it was a frequent reminder of Daniel's role in the events that had led to Ian's death.

The sound of footsteps carefully making their way down the stairs outside his chamber pulled him out of the downward spiral for which he was most certainly otherwise headed, for a deep depression always followed that particular dream. It was dark out, and by the look of it, much too early for his mother to be up yet. Daniel sat up, rubbed his hands vigorously over his face, and then reached for the trousers hanging on the

111

peg by his bed. Groping in the dark for his shirt, he quickly dressed and went barefoot down the stairs.

Felicity's back was to him as she lit the stove, but she could feel the change in the energy of the room when he entered the kitchen. "Did I wake you?" She spoke without the use of her hands, which were busy adjusting the flame and placing the kettle over it, but she turned so that she could read his reply.

"I'll need to be up soon anyway." Daniel moved further into the room so that she could see him clearly in the dim light given off by the single candle that had been lit. "Ye couldn't sleep again?" She nodded and then so did he. "It was like that when I first came home, too. For me it was sleeping on a bed that was hard to get used to. During the war we slept on the ground, and then after that I slept wherever I landed."

She smiled, but didn't comment. Daniel noticed that Felicity smiled a lot, not because she was happy, but rather as a sort of default appeasement gesture to people. A smile usually smoothed things over when she had trouble understanding someone, or when they had trouble understanding her. Some, like this one, said 'I understand but do not wish to comment further.' There was a sad edge to this smile that told him it was still difficult to talk about her recent experiences, but he got the sense she wanted to try.

"They were cruel to ye." Felicity nodded, although he hadn't asked a question. She rubbed her wrists, which were still red and raw from the shackles that had been used to restrain her. She was grateful to have use of Martha's old chamber and so would not tell Ciara or

Michael that it scared her to be in the small room alone at night.

Daniel saw the struggle on her face. He motioned for her to stay put while he left the room. Minutes later, he returned with a pen and paper. "I thought it might be difficult for ye to tell me the whole of it, but would ye maybe write it down?"

She hesitated for just a moment, and then reached for the paper and pen. Daniel waited patiently for more than half an hour while she wrote. He got up only to fix the tea and return to the study for more paper. She wrote in feverish spurts, all the anger and frustration flowing from the pen out onto the page, bringing to light all of the things too upsetting to speak or sign. Then she would stop, as if deciding whether or not to reveal a particular detail. Having made up her mind that Daniel could know everything, she continued. Finally, she handed the pages to him, watching intently as he read.

"Ye were evicted from yer uncle's house. Did they give ye any warning?"

She shook her head. The landlord had come and talked to her Uncle Taylor when Felicity first arrived, having heard rumors she had been in an asylum. He had tolerated their presence while her uncle was still alive, but he would take no chances that she would stay there by herself once he had died. She had been trying to work out transportation back to New York City but money was tight after the burial expenses were paid. Felicity had hoped to be able to stay in the house until she received word back from Mrs. Awalte, to whom she had appealed for help, but the constable had appeared at her door within days of her sending the letter. He brusquely demanded she leave and physically removed her from the house. When she struggled against such harsh treatment, he had her sent to the asylum.

"Dear God, he shackled ye?"

"I was scared and he was pushing me out the door. I just wanted a few minutes to gather some things." Her emotions were high as she relived the horror of those few days and her voice sounded choked off and difficult to make out. She had to force herself to slow down and try to speak clearly. "He was a brute!"

Daniel's eyes continued to scan the page, although he looked up occasionally to gauge her reaction as he read. "'Tis no surprise Mr. Kraus lost his temper with ye. He makes the constable in Laona look like a lamb."

"Mr. Kraus spoke too quickly for me to read his lips. He became angry with me when I couldn't answer his questions. Mr. Leonard was the same. He threw my tray onto the floor. They would not give me a meal until I answered their questions." Tears began to roll down her cheeks. "I tried to tell them I could not hear them. Mr. Leonard misunderstood and got up close to my face to yell at me. The force of his anger scared me, but I was shackled to the bed and I could not move away."

"Ah, well, 'tis over now and ye're safe." He took the pages and touched them to the flame, placing them in the sink where they both watched them burn. "We needn't speak of it ever again."

Felicity looked at Daniel. "I'm scared at night."

"I was, too…still am sometimes." Daniel got the feeling that being alone and afraid of the dark was something that had occurred often throughout Felicity's life. She had not known the stability of growing up in the same place with her family about her as he had. Suddenly he felt ashamed because she had been able to endure so much more than he had. Felicity had suffered a litany of losses during her life, yet she had managed to keep going. It might take some time to recover from this latest struggle, but she would. Of that, he had no doubt. He was not as confident he would ever fully recover from Ian's death.

Daniel was removed from his thoughts when she reached across the table and covered his hand with hers. "It wasn't your fault. Ian does not blame you. No one blames you." She knew what he had been thinking and was willing to put her own troubled feelings aside to comfort him. He felt a sense of profound gratitude and relief settle over him, displacing some of the overwhelming grief and guilt with which he had been living for so long. The candle between them began to sputter, but then, when Felicity gave his hand a gentle squeeze, it flickered back to life and the room became just a bit brighter.

The sounds of Daniel's parents beginning to stir made them both look up. It was just dawn and, within the next few minutes, they would make their way to the kitchen, Charlie not far behind them. It was just as well because he was not yet ready to discuss Ian. Felicity gave his hand another squeeze and rose to start breakfast preparations.

Daniel stood with her. "Aye, well, 'tis time I get out to the barn. I'll be back after a while."

Felicity smiled because she understood that to mean he would seek her out when he was ready to talk about his brother and that pleased her.

* * *

Martha was preoccupied on her way into the asylum and almost didn't notice the man sitting dejectedly on the bench under the big maple tree by the door. With his head down he didn't see her expression change when she recognized him. *Not again,* she thought as she altered her course toward the tree. Alanson Palmer had once been a wealthy man and was considered one of the most influential citizens of Buffalo until he lost his fortune during the panic of '37. He had spent the years between then and now trying to regain his wealth, first with the help of his many friends, and then, when they would no longer receive him, with his mother-in-law's estate. Try as he might, Mr. Palmer never did reclaim his prosperity or status in the community. His mental health began to deteriorate a decade ago. Forced to leave his offices on Main Street, Mr. Palmer gave up all hope of continuing on the glorious path he had once traveled with such confidence. His wife had long since left him, wanting to retain what connections she could to see their son and daughter married into respectable families. He had been picked up several times for vagrancy and had spent the last few years in and out of the asylum.

The man she saw before her was not insane, but he was broken and devoid of hope. She feared when he had been released the last time that, if he were to return, he would undoubtedly be considered by Mr.

Leonard to be incurable and thereby be transferred to the state asylum in Ovid. There would be nothing she could do to prevent that, so she put on her best smile and greeted him warmly. "Good mornin' to ye, Mr. Palmer."

"Good morning. It is a fine day, is it not?" The man spoke as he would to a passing stranger. In his younger days, everyone he came across on the street knew who he was. He had always treated strangers with respect and kindness, which was more than he received after his reversal of fortune. It wasn't unusual for Palmer not to seem to recognize any of the staff at the asylum, perhaps because he didn't want to believe that he was actually an inmate there. Whether he was putting on an act or genuinely confused she did not know, but Martha had given up a long time ago reminding him of who she was or where he was.

"'Tis a very fine day indeed, Mr. Palmer." He must have just arrived because she could see that he was still wearing his own clothes. His overcoat had once been of good quality, as had been his hat. They had both deteriorated over the years at pace with their owner and all three were now quite the worse for wear. These items, along with his other clothes, would be packed away, and he would be issued a pair of shoes, pants, a straw hat and blue denim over shirt that would mark his status as an inmate.

Martha looked quickly around the yard and did not see anyone else. If he had been ordered by the Justice of the Peace, he would have been escorted by the constable. Had Mr. Palmer made his own way to the asylum? "Are ye meant to be here today, Mr. Palmer?"

The man looked around, as if resigned to his fate. "Yes, Dr. Quinn, I am meant to be here. Justice Threadgoode saw fit to allow me to make my own way here." He paused to follow the flight of a red-tailed hawk across the sky, envying the bird its freedom. "There was a time when he regularly dined at my table." He sighed and stood up. "It seems there are still a few who recall the integrity of my character. May I escort you inside, doctor?"

Martha stood for a moment speechless. Her surprise at this moment of lucidity was overshadowed by profound sadness that Mr. Palmer did indeed understand his own situation, and seemed resigned to it. What recent events precipitated this, she didn't know. She also didn't know whether she should be sad for him, or relieved that he wasn't living on the street. It was helpful at times like this to call upon her training as a physician and put aside her emotions to do what she must for the person in need of her care. "'Tis most kind of ye, Mr. Palmer, and I thank ye." She took the arm graciously extended in her direction and walked toward the door.

Martha left Mr. Palmer in the reception room and went to inform Mrs. Boswell of the old man's arrival. "Thank you, Mrs. Quinn. I'll fetch an attendant to see him to the ward."

Martha knew that there were a few empty cells in the men's wing on the second floor and that Mr. Palmer would be comfortable there until the time of his transfer to Ovid. She began to climb the stairs to check on Miss Potter when she heard Mason Leonard call her name. It came as no surprise that he wasn't in the main hall when she turned to look behind her. He often summoned her to his office without leaving his chair. It was one of the ruder aspects of his character she knew she must overlook.

"Ye wanted to see me, Mr. Leonard?" Martha preceded her question with a polite knock on the open door.

Leonard kept his eyes on his work as he spoke. "Yes, Mrs. Quinn. The laundress is still in her cell claiming she is too ill to work. I thought I made it clear to you that we cannot afford to get behind with the weekly chores." He looked up from his desk to make his next point. "Need I remind you that there are 73 inmates in this asylum, and precious few able to do a day's work. I've had to remove one of the women from her duties in the kitchen in order to keep the laundry operational this week."

"I was just on my way up to see her now, Mr. Leonard, if ye'll excuse me." Martha turned to leave, feeling that no further excuse or explanation would be helpful.

"Just a minute, Mrs. Quinn. I'm not quite finished with you."

"How can I be of further assistance to ye, sir?" Her use of the word sir was deliberate. If the man needed reminding that she practiced medicine in the asylum at his discretion, so be it. It wouldn't kill her to feign a bit of respect if it would sooner end this discussion.

"You can get that woman down to the laundry by day's end, Mrs. Quinn, and when you are done with her, see to the two patients on the third floor. Kraus will be close by should they become dangerous."

The two women on the third floor in need of medical care were no more dangerous than Martha was, but she would not jeopardize her access to them by trying to convince the Keeper. "I'll do what I can, sir." Martha left the office before he could say another word.

The Keeper accepted few excuses for absence from work and she had no wish to continue a pointless discussion now. It was true that there were few able-bodied in the institution as a whole and that many chores fell to the inmates of the asylum as a result. She was certain it gave Mason Leonard an element of control over the Keeper of the Poorhouse to be able to supply labor when it was needed, which was often. It wouldn't do to have chores go undone in his own asylum when he was so quick to judge the conditions elsewhere.

Martha quickly made her way up to the second floor. She was pleased to see that, while Miss Potter was still in bed, the drapes were open and she appeared more alert than she had the previous few days. "Good mornin'. How are ye today, Miss Potter?"

"Good morning, Dr. Quinn. A bit better, I think."

Martha asked her to sit up and made note of the fact that the small task was easier accomplished today. "Do ye still have a bad headache?"

"No, I'm just tired."

Her color had improved and the look of anguish had left her face. "Have ye had anything to eat?"

"No, ma'am. Mrs. Sutton said she had orders that I was to come down to the dining room, but when I tried to rise this morning, my head began to throb. It's better now."

Martha hesitated for a moment and then asked if she felt able to return to work. While Miss Potter replied that she was, it was obvious that a bit more rest would be appreciated. "Well, get ye dressed and down to the kitchen for a wee bite. Best ye at least try to go back to work." As an afterthought, she added, "Tell cook that ye are to have a bit of bread and tea under my orders." The kitchen ran on a tight schedule and inmates were not to be fed in-between scheduled meals. Mrs. Boswell would not allow the kitchen staff to deviate from her strict policy. Only a doctor's request would permit special consideration, and even then, it could be difficult. "Never ye mind, I'll just run down there and tell them myself before I continue my rounds."

"Yes, ma'am."

"I've some other patients to see and I'll be back in a few hours. If ye're feelin' poorly, I'll tell Mr. Leonard ye must return to bed." Martha couldn't see why Miss Potter wouldn't be able to return to work. She seemed much better than she was a few days ago, and surely some food would go the rest of the way to see her feeling back to normal. Still, it was a case that required further thought in the service of reducing the number of lost workdays in the asylum. She recalled a paper on the topic of migraines by a fellow female physician in London about which Michael had told her. Making a mental note to ask her brother-in-law about it she walked quickly to the back staircase that provided a more direct route to the kitchen.

When she was assured that Miss Potter would receive the meal that had been ordered, Martha made her way up to the third floor to check on Mary McGuire. The poor woman had been transferred from Catholic hospital a few weeks earlier because the sisters there thought her insane. At just seventeen years old, Mary had complete ankylosis of both knees. With both knee joints effectively frozen, she had no use of her legs and so was forced, using only her arms, to crawl where she needed to go, but it was her howling and carrying on during the night that led ultimately to her transfer to the poorhouse asylum.

Martha had suspected rheumatic fever, specifically acute articular rheumatism. Mary was perhaps a bit older than the usual age of onset, but not by much. Sure enough, it was revealed that Mary had suffered severe tonsillitis just before she was let go from her position as a kitchen maid, which was further complicated by Rheumatic fever. The symptoms of articular rheumatism easily explained her outbursts at the hospital. Severe joint pain and swelling were often accompanied by convulsive type movements and outbursts of unusual behavior.

Mary McGuire wasn't insane. She was sick. Martha tried repeatedly to explain this to Mr. Leonard. He insisted that the girl stay on the third floor, shackled to her bed, but he did allow Martha to treat her because Kraus complained that her screaming was making the other inmates restless. At least on the third floor she would have a bed to herself where she could recover. Already, regular doses of salicin were reducing the stiffness and swelling in her joints. Remarkably, Mary was resting peacefully at night.

"Good mornin', Miss McGuire. How are ye feelin' today?" Martha noted that her color was good and her wrists showed no abrasions or other signs that she was struggling against the shackles.

"I'm better, thank ye, ma'am."

Martha pulled pack the blanket to examine her legs. "Would ye pull yer nightdress up just a wee bit so I can take a look at yer knees?" Mary complied and Martha placed a hand each underneath the leg and foot to flex gently the knee joint. "Does it hurt ye when I do this?"

"No, ma'am." Mary was able to achieve full flexion and extension of each leg with no pain.

"That's wonderful Mary." Martha moved to unfasten her restraints so she could sit at the edge of the bed with her legs dangling over the edge. "Try to lift your leg so that it's straight."

On her own, Mary could barely lift each leg, her muscles weakened from such a long period confined to her bed. "Don't ye fret over it," Martha told her as she eased Mary back into a position where she could refasten the shackles. "We'll work on it a bit each day."

Mary did not fuss when Martha restrained her once again. "How long until I can leave here?" she asked.

Martha fussed with the blanket and adjusted the position of her pillow so that Mary would be more comfortable. "Well, we need to get yer legs workin' proper again and then there's the matter of findin' ye a new position. I'd say a few more weeks."

"I'm no daft, ye know that, right?" Mary was concerned because when she asked the same question of the Keeper or of the ward attendant, she got a different answer.

"Aye, Mary, I do know that. In time, Mr. Leonard will see it too. Remember what I've told ye. Just ye stay quiet and don't resist the restraints." She placed a hand over Mary's wrist, gently placing it back in the leather cuff. Martha hoped Kraus would not notice that she had left the leather straps a bit loose. "Just ye leave Mr. Leonard to me. There's no arguin' with the man, to be sure, but when ye're walkin' again on your own, he'll see for himself." Indeed, he would see for himself, and take all of the credit for Mary's recovery. Mason Leonard knew well how it pleased the county Board of Supervisors when inmates of the asylum were discharged as cured.

The next patient Martha saw was a mystery that had her concerned and angry in equal measures. Anna Griffin was with child. She certainly wasn't the first unwed pregnant woman at the asylum. The mystery lay in the fact that Miss Anna Griffin had been admitted two years ago. She was feeble-minded, but not insane, although to Mr. Leonard they were one and the same. Up until her confinement, she had been assigned to the Keeper's kitchen. As long as the Keeper took his meals on time and she was present in her cell at the morning and evening bed checks, there would be no cause to keep track of her. Certainly there would have been opportunities to seek out the company of a man. However, Miss Griffin insisted no such liaisons took place. It was true that the woman was dimwitted, but Martha had very clearly explained to her how a man and a woman went about creating a baby, and still Miss Griffin could not recall such an event taking place.

Martha suspected that Anna was covering for the father of her child, who she believed was Mason Leonard. It would not surprise her to learn that a liaison with the kitchen maid was, in fact, responsible for his wife running off rather than anything the Spiritualists might have offered. Pamela Leonard had been consumed with grief over the death of her child. Martha did what she could to console her, but Leonard resented her involvement and insisted she leave his wife alone. After that, the poor dear had no one in whom she could confide. It stood to reason that if she had learned of his infidelity, she would have been devastated.

Another factor that supported Martha's suspicions was that Miss Griffin was confined to the third floor, where typically only the inmates presumed to be violent or dangerous resided. However, Mr. Leonard had made a point of telling the ward attendants that she did not need to be restrained. Martha found the woman pacing the floor when she opened the door to her cell.

"Is it time, Miss Griffin?"

"Oh, hello, Mrs. Quinn. I'm afraid I've a terrible case of colic."

"No, Miss Griffin. 'Tis just the babe ready to come."

Martha helped her back to bed and then went to inform the ward attendant that Miss Griffin would have to be moved to the hospital department. "No. Mr. Leonard's orders. She stays here," Kraus told her.

"Well, we'll just see about that!" Martha quickly descended the stairs in search of the Keeper, but was only able to find Mrs. Boswell.

"Mrs. Boswell, do ye know the whereabouts of Mr. Leonard? He's given instructions not to move Miss Griffin, but she must be transferred to the hospital to have her baby."

"I'm sorry, Mrs. Quinn, but the Keeper has left the premises. I do not know when he shall return."

"Mrs. Boswell, ye do know that women in this institution are always transferred to the hospital department to give birth, even the women here in the asylum." She spoke slowly, more in an attempt to reign in her frustration than to be sure the matron understood the situation. There would be no way of getting past Kraus if Leonard had left him specific orders. Martha knew that Mrs. Boswell had complete knowledge of her brother's schedule and could locate him if she had a mind to be cooperative.

"Mr. Leonard is not available just now. Miss Griffin can have her bastard right here in the asylum where they both belong."

Martha had delivered babies in worse places than the third floor of the insane department and decided this wasn't worth an argument. She made a quick trip to the hospital to gather what she needed and said a silent prayer on the way back that the birth would not be a complicated one.

Back on the third floor, Martha could tell by the unmistakable smell of his pipe tobacco that Kraus was hovering at the end of the hall outside Miss Griffin's room. "Did ye need somethin', Mr. Kraus?" She asked.

"I have orders." Kraus was a man of few words.

"Yes, I understand. I'll make do here."

"You will hand over the babe when it comes," he told her, his pipe clenched between stained teeth.

"I'll do no such thing, Mr. Kraus." Martha knew the best chance the child had for survival was to stay here with its mother. The women in the children's department did the best they could, but there the babe would be exposed to diseases the other children brought with them into the institution, in addition to all of the risks associated with feeding from poorly washed bottles.

"Mr. Leonard's orders."

"Aye, we'll see about that!" Martha closed the door to the cell, effectively ending the conversation.

Mason Leonard had seen to it that there would be no record of Miss Griffin's delivery because he had refused her access to the hospital. Kraus would then deliver the infant to the children's department of the poorhouse with some claim that its mother had come to the asylum with child and had given birth before she could be moved. There would be no way for anyone to know that this woman had become pregnant while under Leonard's care at the asylum, and no way for anyone to suspect that he was the child's father.

The feeling of being absolutely powerless to do anything about something to which she was so strongly opposed consumed Martha such that she had to keep her back turned to her patient until she was able to compose herself. There was no proof that the infant was Leonard's, and Miss Griffin denied having relations with any of the other inmates. If Martha spoke up, her only accusation would be that a woman under Leonard's care had fallen pregnant. It was doubtful that anyone on the county Board of Supervisors would take notice at all. If they did, Leonard would only receive a stern verbal warning to supervise his inmates better. She hated that she could do nothing to protect the patients under her care.

Martha took a deep breath and braced herself for both the delivery and the battle with Kraus that would follow. She had considered more than once during the four-hour travail simply to tell Kraus that the baby had been stillborn. Even if the babe should remain silent after birth, and be removed unseen from the asylum, Martha still didn't know what she would do with it. If she got into the habit of rescuing every child that was born into the misery of the poorhouse, she should have to build one of her own. As it turned out, there was no need to feign the infant's death. The poor thing did not survive the delivery and came into the world with its cord wrapped tightly around its tiny neck.

Later that night Martha wept in Johnny's arms. It had happened often in the beginning of her medical career, but over time, she learned to accept the realities of practicing medicine in an institution. As a veteran physician of the asylum, there were still cases like Anna Griffin's that broke her heart. There was nothing she could have done to save the babe, but instead of being frustrated and disappointed with herself, she was relieved. It was for Miss Griffin she feared, knowing this could, and likely would, happen again.

"Aye, well, the babe was spared a miserable life," Johnny told her. It was all he could ever think of to say.

He had been sent to the poorhouse as a young boy and had often shuddered at the thought of how things might have turned out if not for Ciara and her sisters.

"Yes, he was. It was a boy; did I tell ye that?" Johnny nodded and she continued. "It's just that I would have had to let Kraus take him, had he lived, and me powerless to save the child from his fate. Worse yet, I can't protect Miss Griffin from havin' to go through it all again, for well ye know he'll have her back in the kitchen, and on her back for that matter, as soon as she's recovered." She wiped her eyes and then turned to look at her husband. "Johnny, I've had to endure more than my fair share of ignorant Keepers, which I did gladly to be able to help the people in that asylum, but Leonard is different. The others only really had trouble with the fact that I was a woman, but once I proved myself, we got on fine. The more I try to prove myself to Mason Leonard, the more suspicious of me he becomes."

"He's a strange man, is Leonard," Johnny agreed. "He puts me in mind of a man I knew when I traveled. He had a son who was learnin' the way of the business, same as me. When I made a good deal, Grand Da Daniel was that proud of me, but when Jarvis did the same, his Da seemed cross. It was as if somehow he felt he'd been outdone by his own son. I think Leonard feels the same about you. Ye have the knack for knowin' when a patient needs to be treated with medicine or just needs a bit of kindness. Ye are able to cure the ones he's said are incurable. He thinks ye are out to undermine his authority."

"Perhaps, but in the end he takes credit for having cured all of my patients, and me never sayin' a word, so ye'd think he'd be glad to have me," Martha pointed out.

"Well, now that's ye thinkin' like the woman ye are and not like a man. Sure enough, Leonard will take the credit for all yer work, and ye are wise to let him to keep the peace. But deep down he knows that the good work done in that asylum is done by yerself and not by him. That sits about as well as a bee in his britches."

Part Two

Chapter Ten

It was still dark when Maude finally gave in and opened her eyes. The soft grunts of Don snoring beside her indicated that there were still a few hours before the night gave way to dawn. Back when she was a professor, there were many evenings when a particular student or the lack of progress toward a grant deadline kept Maude from a full night's rest. Her dreams, still so vivid in her mind, kept sleep at bay tonight. If she stayed in bed, Don would eventually wake up. He always did when she had a restless night. If she got up, one or both of the boys would likely hear her making her way downstairs. The living space above the shop was considerably less than the square footage of the home they had lived in, and to be shuffling around late at night would surely be noticed by those who were still in their beds.

Realizing she was up for the duration, Maude weighed the risk of waking the boys. If she could make it past them, there was the data collected from the poorhouse hospital ledger on her laptop that would help to pass the hours until morning.

"You won't make it past the bathroom." Don's voice was still heavy with sleep.

Maude smiled as she turned toward him. "How is it that you are able to read my mind?" She asked as he pulled her in.

"I'll never tell. Now that we're up, can I convince you to stay in bed for a while longer?" He kissed her slowly, and then with purpose, driving all thoughts of her unusual dreams away.

* * *

Maude unlocked the front door of The Antique Lamp Company and Gift Emporium just in time to see Mrs. Houston exiting the shop next door.

"Oh, I'm glad you are finally here, my dear," Mrs. Houston said to Maude as she entered. "While I was waiting for you to open I was drawn into a conversation with Mr. Northrup next door, which turned out to be rather uncomfortable."

"Come in, Mrs. Houston. I'm sorry; am I late?" Maude could not recall scheduling an appointment this morning.

"No, dear. I happened to be out running errands and I wanted to pop in and ask you for a reference. I was lost in my thoughts and wandered into his store by mistake; the window display looks very similar to yours. Of course, when I realized what I had done, I apologized and explained that I was waiting for you. He offered to show me around his new store while I waited. Well, I saw no harm in that. He seemed nice enough."

"What did he do to upset you, Alexandra?" Maude knew by now that Lester Northrup was annoying, but he hardly seemed dangerous.

"Oh, he didn't upset me, really, it was just how he engaged me in conversation. I got the distinct impression that he was trying to get me to do business with him instead of you. How many other people are likely to wander in there thinking it's your shop? Be careful with him, dear. It appears as though he's trying to go after your clients."

Maude smiled, having no intention of sharing what little she knew of Lester Northrup. Mrs. Houston was likely exaggerating, but she'd take a look just to be sure. "I appreciate the heads up. Now what can I do for you today?"

"I was hoping you could give me the name of a licensed appraiser. Mother Houston has decided to dispense with most of her estate while she is still with us so she can have the pleasure of giving things to her grandchildren. She has no granddaughters and her jewelry is neither to my taste nor my sister-in-law's. So we decided to sell a few pieces and she'll donate the money to charity."

"That's really a nice idea. Christine knows more about antique jewelry than I do. The pieces we carry are vintage, but you would really need an expert for the older pieces." Maude asked her a little bit about the jewelry she was interested in having appraised and left a note to discuss it with Christine. "I'll ask her to leave me a few names and I'll call you later today or tomorrow."

"That would be wonderful dear, thank you."

"Is there anything else I can help you with today?" Maude asked her.

"No, not today. I'm off to meet two of the ladies from my bridge club for coffee." She turned toward the door, but quickly turned back toward Maude as she walked out. "You mark my words about that Northrup man. He seems like trouble to me."

Maude laughed. "Okay, thanks Alexandra. Enjoy the rest of your day." It was kind of Mrs. Houston to be protective of their shop. Certainly, that kind of customer loyalty was rare in any business these days. Maude began reflecting on how lucky they were to have such wonderful clients when she heard footsteps on the stairs leading from their apartment. Don had been upstairs catching up on phone calls and e-mail. He descended the stairs with two steaming mugs in his hand.

"Hey, hon. What's up?" Maude asked as she accepted the cup of coffee he offered.

"I just got off the phone with the city inspector's office. Take a guess who called about our crumbling façade?"

"They actually told you?"

"More or less. They're not supposed to, but if you can catch the right guy in the right mood, he will make it easy for you to figure out who it was."

"Well, then, don't keep me in suspense. Who called?"

Don used air quotes. "'Your new neighbor.' That's exactly what the inspector told me. He also mentioned that he was pretty surprised to find minimal damage considering the nature of the complaint." Don took a sip of his coffee before he continued. "The guy told me that it's not the first time he's received an exaggerated complaint from someone who has a competing business. He also told me it would be fine to wait until next month to work on the repairs."

Maude just stood there for a moment, trying to reconcile what she had just learned with what Alexandra Houston had just told her. "Well, I guess I have something to add to that story." She proceeded to tell him about her conversation with Mrs. Houston. "I was just about to wander next door and take a look when you came down."

"Is he even officially open for business yet?" Don asked.

"Probably not, but it won't take long. That building is in great shape. It wouldn't take more than a day or two to set up inside. He'd be wise to keep the door opened while he worked, even if he weren't officially open for business yet. It would encourage curious people to take a peek as they are walking by. C'mon, let's go take a look."

The couple went over to find that the door was open, but the shop was apparently empty. They wandered in and took note of the fact that although the window display was clearly a work in progress, it resembled theirs in that the windows themselves were framed in lace valences and outlined in twinkle lights. There were also a few nineteenth-century lamps hanging from the ceiling, as well as other unique hand crafted items displayed on fabric-covered platforms.

Don went to examine the hanging lights more carefully. "These are reproductions. Look. There's no counterbalance. Even if it was removed, the ceiling mount isn't right." He turned to Maude to continue his scrutiny of the window display, but he noticed she had moved toward the counter, and was clearly eavesdropping on whatever conversation was going on in the back. Without warning, she bolted toward the door and motioned for Don to follow her.

"What was that about?" he asked when they were safely back in their own shop.

"I heard Lester talking on the phone. He was just hanging up and I wanted to be sure there was no way he could think we overheard what he was saying."

"What the hell was he saying?"

Maude cautiously looked out the front window, although for what she didn't really know. Reasonably sure that Lester was not aware that they had just been in his shop, she turned to answer Don. "While I didn't hear much, what I did hear didn't sound good." Don looked skeptical but she continued with her story. "It sounded like someone was laughing, you know, like a kind of sketchy laugh, so I figured Lester was just in the back of the shop. When I got closer, I realized that he was on the phone." She moved closer to Don and lowered her voice just a bit. "I couldn't make out much more, but I distinctly hear him say 'that's gotta be worth a fortune.' The person must have said something on the other end, then I heard Lester tell him 'just get it, do whatever it takes.' That's when I thought it was wise for us to leave." She looked at her husband, waiting for his reaction to what she obviously thought was suspicious behavior.

"Well, I agree it was wise to leave before he realized you were eavesdropping on his phone call. As for the rest of it, I think you are letting your imagination run a bit wild."

"I don't know, Don. That laugh sounded pretty sinister."

"You have upgraded it from sketchy to sinister?" Don did his best to hide a smirk, but ultimately failed.

"Okay, maybe it was somewhere in-between. My point is that it attracted my attention and motivated me to move closer to hear more," Maude argued.

"So, what do you propose we say to the man? You know as well as I do what goes on in the antique world. That's why I can count on one hand the number of people in this town I'd do business with."

"Point taken, but at the very least I think he is trying to go after our customers. The windows look enough alike and he doesn't have any signage, so a casual observer could mistake the two storefronts as belonging to the same business." He was considering that statement as she continued to argue her point. "Why else would he hang those reproductions in the window? Oh, and don't forget that he did try to lure Christine away, and Mrs. Houston got the impression he was trying to entice her into doing business with him instead of us."

"I'm not saying he is not a shady guy, Maude. He's no different than most of the people in this business."

Maude knew Don was right. The antique business was full of unscrupulous characters who would deliberately undervalue specific items to a seller only to turn around and make a substantial profit for themselves. It was just as easy to convince the next buyer that the item was worth more as it was to convince the original seller that the very same item was worth less. It happened all the time. There were also plenty of little shops in the city that wouldn't hesitate to steal clients from a competing shop. "Yeah, he'd just deny it if we suggested he was trying to make his storefront look like ours. So, how do we protect ourselves?"

"Well, assuming you're right about that, and I think you are, there isn't much we can do. Our existing clients know us by reputation and will see right through him. Hopefully any potential new people will see through him, too." It was a concern to Don, too, but he was much better about not worrying about things that were beyond his control than Maude.

"I'm more concerned about the walk-ins. They are not coming in for antique lamps. They are coming in for the other unique items we sell. I'm sure you noticed he had a few beaded purses in the window, too." She pointed to the far corner of the shop that sparkled brilliantly with hand-beaded purses, hair accessories and vintage jewelry. "I post those things on Facebook, so it will be very easy to see what we are selling without setting foot in our shop. All he has to do is like our page."

"Maude, although you are going to completely disregard my advice not to worry about this, I'm going to give it anyway." He took the empty cup from her hand. "Just steer clear of Lester."

* * *

Lester walked into the front of the store, sure he had just heard people talking, but there was nobody there. Grabbing the piece of paper off the front counter, he returned to his office mumbling, "Let's see if I can figure out who you are." He had been with Dawn long enough to know the value of that Michael Kors purse and the sapphire Levian ring on the hand that held it. The woman who had wandered into his shop by mistake had not given him her name, so he had quickly scribbled the license plate number on Alexandra Houston's BMW after she left. "Something tells me you're worth knowing."

* * *

Maude was preoccupied for the rest of the after-noon and was content when Don offered to watch the shop so she could have some time to organize her dream journals. She reread the sequence of the birth of Anna Griffin's unfortunate child, reconciling it with the case she had recorded in the hospital ledger. She was content, for now, to attribute this scene in her dreams to the recording of the actual case in the ledger days before. Still Martha's suspicions that Leonard was the baby's father occupied her thoughts. "Why do I get the feeling that Leonard blamed us for his wife's departure?" She was talking to both the notebook and to Martha, or perhaps the idea of Martha. It was hard not to think of her as a separate person. "There's nothing from this dream that would make me reach that conclusion. Did we know about the affair?" Maude felt foolish asking that question aloud, not because she was actually talking to Martha as if she were there, but because she remembered that Martha had only come to that conclusion during the delivery. She could not possibly have exposed Leonard's affair to his wife. "Why does he blame us? I mean you. This is so weird!"

Maude started a new heading in a fresh notebook entitled *Questions that need answering*. She wasn't quite sure how she would go about answering these sorts of questions, but still felt compelled to keep a list of them anyway. Why she felt Leonard blamed Martha for his problems with his wife was number one. Before she really knew what she was writing, she had a second question on her list. "What's the deal with Lester Northrup?" She was surprised when she read it out loud, as if she hadn't been aware of what she was writing when she was writing it. "Well, that's clearly a question for another list," she mumbled and crossed it out.

"What do you mean what's the deal with Lester Northrup?" Christine walked into the office and plunked down in the chair by the desk.

"Oh, hi. I didn't realize you were working today."

"I'm not. I stopped in because I was driving by on my way to the dry cleaners and I couldn't help but notice how similar Lester's shop looks to yours. I take it from your remark that you have already noticed."

"Yeah. Mrs. Houston came by today and actually wandered in there by mistake," Maude told her.

"I'll bet that's exactly what he was hoping for. What a snake."

Maude looked at Christine and a smile spread slowly across her face. "Don and I went over there a while ago to check out the place and I overheard Lester on the phone in the back of his shop." As Maude hoped she would, Christine leaned forward in her chair eager to hear more. When Maude was finished, Christine was hooked.

"He's up to something. He's gotta be. He doesn't have the brains to run a business like this. I wouldn't be surprised to find out that he set up right next door to deliberately drive you out of business."

Maude was immediately sorry she had filled Christine in on all of the details. "Boy, your imagination is worse than mine. I just figured he was trying to swindle some poor widow out of her Kittinger table."

"C'mon, think about it, Maude. He was furious after the deal for this shop fell through. Phil all but said so when he tried to convince the boys to sell next door."

"Christine, I know you love a good drama, but I think this is much simpler than you suspect. Lester is a sleazy guy and I wouldn't put it past him to cheat people out of their family heirlooms, but you said it yourself: he's not a very bright guy, so I doubt he's smart enough for revenge."

"I don't trust him." In those four words, Christine had told Maude that she would be keeping a close eye on Lester Northrup, which was really what Maude wanted, after all.

Chapter Eleven

It was an unusually breezy day in June and while the door was propped open, the bell remained silent at the arrival of Christine's favorite customer. The distinct perfume that had reached the front counter even before the woman crossed the threshold had alerted her to the identity of the woman approaching. "Hi, Mrs. Billingsley. What brings you in today?" Christine stepped out from behind the counter to greet the tiny round woman.

"Oh, hello, Dear. I'm in need of a gift for my niece. I thought perhaps something black and shiny."

Maude was in her office paying bills. Listening to the women chatting she couldn't help but smile. She so admired Lorna Billingsley for her progressiveness. Her seventeen-year-old niece Theresa had been in her Goth phase since freshman year of high school and Lorna had come into the shop just before each birthday and Christmas since then in the hopes of finding something unique. She had no problem parting with a considerable sum of money for some bejeweled insect or bat if she thought she might score some points with her sullen niece. Now both Maude and Christine kept their eyes out at estate sales for interesting insects and reptiles made of onyx, jet, agate or obsidian. Maude had found an onyx and diamond scorpion brooch a few months ago specifically with the younger Billingsley in mind. She smiled again at the appreciative *oos* and *ahs* when Christine took the brooch from behind the counter. At twelve hundred dollars, it would be the best sale of the month.

"That will do nicely, dear. Do you have a box?"

"Sure, I'll even wrap it for you. I think I have some black ribbon in the back."

Maude came out to say hello while Christine gathered the macabre wrapping supplies. "I always manage to find the perfect gift here," Lorna told her.

"We aim to please."

"Now tell me, Maude, what have you got going on next door? Are you expanding?"

"No. We have our hands full with the shop as it is."

"Well, you should have a word with your neighbor then. I believe he has taken your company's name."

"What?" Christine asked, approaching the counter with the black foil wrapped package.

"Well, I went in there thinking it was your place. It says Antique Lamp Company on the window."

Maude interjected before Christine could say a word. "Well, imitation is the sincerest form of flattery." She accompanied Mrs. Billingsley to the door, walking out to hold it open so she could casually glance at the windows. Her eyebrows shot up and as soon as Mrs. Billingsley pulled away Maude went back out for a better look.

"You're not going to believe this," she told Christine when she came back inside.

"Oh, God. What now?"

"That creep has the words *antique* and *lamps* stenciled on the window in the exact same font as ours. Between that and the general décor of the window, anyone could easily wander in there thinking it was our shop."

"What a jerk! You should go over there right now."

"What exactly should I say? Nothing short of legal action can make him stop doing this. Besides, I'll be damned if I'll let him think he's getting to me."

Christine went outside to check out the window for herself. "Maude, you know Don is going to flip when he sees that."

"Don't drag Don into this, Christine. He won't even see the windows. He uses the alley entrance to the shop." Maude held up her hand to prevent her employee from interrupting until she was finished. "Look, Lester is not the best of new neighbors, although I have no idea why, but in truth he has done no harm. He's been open a few weeks and even the people who have wandered in there by accident have eventually made their way over here."

"I know exactly why. He's still angry that he lost this building last year. Maude, you need to keep an eye on him. He's up to no good, I can feel it."

"Look, I'm not going to confront the guy, and neither are you." Seeing the look on Christine's face, Maude added, "and we are certainly not getting Don involved."

Understanding that there was no point in arguing, Christine changed her tack. "What if we just change the window display? You know, spruce it up a bit. We could change out the curtains, maybe paint the trim, and move a few things around."

Maude decided that keeping Christine occupied was the best way of keeping her out of this business with Lester Northrup and so agreed to a window overhaul. "I think that is a great idea. I have some big planters from the old house in the basement. We can do up a nice floral display on either side of the door, too."

Christine got to work immediately taking down the hanging lamps and lace valences in the window while Maude went down to the basement to haul up the planters and see what paint might be available. The part-time employee was distracted for the moment, but would not be deterred from what she knew was trouble brewing. In a day or so, Maude would forget about Lester Northrup in favor of her research project and that would give Christine an opportunity to do some snooping around next door.

Maude was busy packing away some of the items that would have to be stored until the window facelift was complete when a very pregnant Abby Stevens shuffled in.

"You didn't have to come all the way over here," Maude said, relieving her friend of the heavy canvas bag, which she could not imagine would ever be replaced with a pastel quilted diaper bag.

"Are you kidding? I was happy to get out of the house. In another week I won't be able to fit behind the wheel and I'll be stuck at home until his royal highness arrives." Abby laughed as she followed Maude back to the office.

After she settled herself in the chair and waved off Maude's offer of tea, Abby said, "I think I'll die if I have to choke down another cup of herbal tea! The thing I am looking forward to most after the baby is born is a good, strong cup of coffee."

"Well, you will certainly need many of those during the first few years!" Maude decided against tea as well and took a seat behind her desk. "So, what have you found out?"

"Well, I started with the Nolans because they were more public figures than the others by virtue of her association with the orphan asylum and his with the university." She reached into her bag, pulled out a flash drive and handed it to Maude. "I made a file for each person I've looked into."

"Interestingly, Alva Awalte appeared often in the period newspapers," Abby continued. "What a fascinating woman. Apparently, she had a very successful practice as a clairvoyant healer and was a wealthy woman in her own right. I can't imagine that went over well with the medical establishment at the time! A few of them had her arrested in the later decades of the nineteenth century for practicing medicine without a license."

"Well, that sounds about right." Although she could not mention her sources to Abby, Maude knew from her dreams that the male dominated medical community of Buffalo barely tolerated a traditionally educated female physician. From what little she knew of Alva Awalte, it stood to reason that she had triggered the same reaction.

"She appears to have had a friendly relationship with Dr. Nolan because he testified twice on her behalf," Abby told her. "Wait until you read her file! She had two daughters. One went to medical school and the other followed in her footsteps as a clairvoyant healer." Abby shifted a bit before she continued. "You've got the makings of a great story here, and a fascinating group of interconnected people to inspire your characters."

Maude nodded in agreement, while wishing she could understand why they were connected to *her*. She hesitated for just a minute, not sure if she was ready to learn more about Martha Quinn. Finally, she took a breath that she hoped Abby didn't notice and asked. "Were you able to find out anything about Martha Sloane Quinn or her husband, Johnny?"

"Well, there was not much about either of them with the exception of their admission to the almshouse in 1835. There is a record of Martha attending medical school, but virtually nothing about her career as a doctor."

"I can't say I'm surprised. It must have been difficult for a woman to practice medicine in the mid-nineteenth century," Maude suggested. "I looked at the Keeper's Reports for the Almshouse and she is mentioned as a physician there, and her name appears as the physician of record often in the actual hospital ledgers."

"There was not much to be found about her husband either. He owned the dry goods store that once occupied this building, so he was listed in the city directories," Abby told her. "Beyond the record of Johnny inheriting this building in 1855 and a brief mention of his death in a period newspaper, I couldn't find anything."

"Johnny Quinn died?" Maude was overcome with a profound sense of sadness, as if she had just been told about the death of a family member.

Abby chuckled, "Well, of course he did. You didn't expect him to still be alive now, did you?"

Maude smiled, embarrassed to realize what she had blurted out. Abby had no idea of the true nature of her connection to these people or the dreams she had been having about them. "No, I didn't. I guess writing fiction has destroyed my objectivity. I'm becoming attached to these people." She cleared her throat and glanced in the direction of the flash drive that likely contained the answers to questions she was reluctant to ask. "Was there any record of Martha's death?" She didn't really want to know, but couldn't stop herself from asking, so she hastily added, "Don't tell me when she died. I just want to know if there was any record."

"I get it," Abby said. "I would think it might be difficult to write the story you have in your head if you know too many of the real details. I will only tell you that there is a record of Martha's death."

"Thanks." Maude was hoping the uncertainty she felt didn't show on her face. It would take her a while to wrap her head around the fact that she now was in possession of information surrounding her own death, all the weirder that it was her death in another life.

"I'll continue with the other names on your list, but I think what I have found so far should keep you busy for a while." Abby struggled for a minute to get up from the chair, but waved away Maude's offer of help. "Thanks, but it is a point of pride that I can still get out of a sitting position on my own steam."

Maude laughed, sharing a similar experience late in her own pregnancy when she was still able to get her own shoes on without help. "At least let me take your bag out to the car for you."

Abby hoisted the bag over her shoulder and proceeded toward the door. "Honestly, I'm fine. I know you are dying to get into those files. I'll let you know when I have more for you."

"Okay. Thanks, Abby. I'll come to you next time." Maude watched long enough to see Abby drive away before returning to her office. For a few minutes, she just stood and stared at the flash drive sitting on her desk. The news of Johnny's death left her feeling empty, and for the first time in her life she wondered what life would be like if Don passed away before she did. She could pick up the phone and call him, reassure herself that he was still here. "Oh, get a grip Maude!" she spoke aloud to break the deafening silence that had snuck in after Abby left.

Maude sat down at her desk and continued to stare at the flash drive, hoping it contained some kind of warning like "open at your own risk" or "use with discretion," but it just sat there keeping its own secrets. "Okay, clearly I need to talk to Charlotte before I take a look at this," she told herself. A quick glance at the clock revealed that there were only a few more hours before Christine left for the day. Maude had wanted to use that time to review the transcription of her latest dream. After a few moment's consideration, she decided to send an e-mail rather than call. An e-mail would allow her to organize her thoughts, state them without interruption and allow Charlotte to do the same in her reply.

After she hit the send button, Maude turned off the computer and opened the spiral notebook. There were new details she needed to ponder while she had a few hours to herself.

Chapter Twelve

Charlie and old Beau both hobbled out of the barn, age having caught up to both man and beast. Daniel watched carefully as the horse came toward him, still favoring his right hind leg. "He looks a bit better today," he remarked.

"Aye, a few more days and he'll be sound again," Charlie agreed, leading the horse up to a large pail. By now the old gelding tolerated soaking his hind leg in a warm solution of bitter purgative salts, but earlier in the week, when they discovered the heel abscess, he hadn't been so willing.

Both men were focused on the horse and hadn't noticed Felicity approaching until she was standing before them. Clearing her throat loud enough to get their attention without startling the horse, she rotated her fingers to sign the letters T, E, and A.

Daniel nodded and turned to Charlie. "Go on up. I'll be along when old Beau's done."

"Are ye daft, lad? Ye can't hold him and put his leg in the bucket."

Felicity reached for the lead rope and after a moment's consideration Charlie handed it over.

Confident that Beau would behave like a gentleman, the old man made his way up to the house for tea.

Daniel could hear Felicity murmuring to the horse as he settled its leg comfortably in the pail. "I can take him now," he told her, extending his hand.

Swirling her fingers around the white star on Beau's head, Felicity just smiled, content to stay while the horse completed his treatment. She continued her attention, alternating murmured words of endearment with gentle kisses on the muzzle.

"He's a fine beast, is Beau." Daniel was close enough for Felicity to feel his breath wash across her as he spoke, but her attention was on the horse. Their ability to communicate without the use of words or gestures was strongest when they focused on each other, but that connection was easily broken with other distractions. Felicity faced him, pointing first at her eyes and then his lips. "I have to see you," she said.

Her voice was constrained and nasal, but he understood enough to remember that he needed to be facing her so that she could read his lips. "Oh, right, sorry." He spoke louder, exaggerating each syllable, which made Felicity laugh.

"You must learn sign language." Both hands moved rapidly as she spoke, her index fingers, then thumbs extended and swirling around her chest as if she was tying a bow, indicating the gestures for the words *sign language.*

Daniel laughed too, this time responding in a normal tone, "Aye, 'tis not enough, I think, for us just to know the alphabet ye taught us." They managed simple communication by using it in combination with the gestures and pantomime they had used when she was a child. Longer discussions were becoming problematic for everyone. Often, Felicity would simply sign what she wanted to say, forgetting that they hadn't learned yet. Daniel and the others had a tendency to forget that she needed to be facing them when they spoke to her. It was very frustrating for all.

Felicity kept a steady hand on old Beau's head as Daniel removed the leg from the bucket and applied an onion poultice. "Go ahead," he said, waving her forward. Beau kicked out his right hind leg, annoyed by the gooey glob attached to the base of his heel, but the wrapping was secure so his efforts were in vain.

Daniel caught up to Felicity as she put the horse in his stall. He extended his left elbow in her direction while at the same time using his right hand to sign the letters T, E and A.

With a smile and a nod, she took his arm, signing back Y, E and S.

* * *

Alva Awalte waited on the bench outside the asylum for Martha to arrive. She made eye contact just for a moment with a young man pulling weeds along the side of the building. Muttering to himself, the man interrupted his task every so often to check over his shoulder, but Alva deliberately looked away, sensing her presence made him uncomfortable. She was just contemplating whether or not to wait elsewhere when Martha arrived.

"Good day to ye, Mrs. Awalte. Have ye business at the asylum today?"

"Good day to you, Doctor Quinn. May I have a moment, or is there an urgency to your visit this afternoon?"

"I've many patients to see today, but I can spare a few minutes."

"Perhaps you might walk with me for a bit," Alva suggested, and with a furtive glance at the gardener, steered Martha in the opposite direction.

"How can I be of assistance to ye, Mrs. Awalte?"

"Well, I'd like it if you called me Alva, Dr. Quinn."

"Then ye must call me Martha, Alva. Now that we have accomplished that, what else brings ye to the asylum today?"

"Martha, you will find as you get to know me that I get straight to my purpose, so I'll do no different now. There is an odd sensibility here and I seek to understand it better."

"I'm sorry, but I don't take yer meaning."

"My dear, people such as we are able to understand more about our patients than just the outward manifestation of their symptoms. Surely you know what I mean." Alva stopped and turned fully toward Martha, wanting an answer to this question before she continued.

After a moment's consideration, Martha shook her head. "I can't say that I do." It wasn't entirely the truth.

Alva blew out a sigh of frustration, then quickly gathered her composure. She hoped Martha would learn to trust her in time. "Put plainly, Martha, I can sense things about people, and I think you can as well." She saw the hesitant look on Martha's face and decided to try a different approach. "That young man over there, he talks to his guides often because he has suffered great loss since he has come to this country. To him they are guardian angels."

"Aye, 'tis true what ye say of Mr. Rubino," Martha agreed. "He came here from Italy last year with his family, and he the only one who survived the journey."

"Take a moment, Martha, and look at him, then close your eyes and tell me what you are feeling."

Martha watched as the man stood, steadying himself with the shovel as he reached down to grab the bucket full of weeds. She stood quiet for a moment with her eyes closed, breathing steadily. "He is very sad," she said without opening her eyes. "There is confusion, too. He wants to go home, but he can't figure out how."

Alva smiled, relieved and pleased in equal measures that Martha had been able to feel Mr. Rubino's grief for herself. "Martha, part of the sadness you are feeling is the collective grief of the people here. They grieve lost loved ones, as Mr. Rubino does, or their loss of freedom. Many have given up hope. It is like a wall of pain surrounding the place. If you quiet your mind, you will feel it too."

"What would ye have me do?"

"Let me work with you. I can help Mr. Rubino. I know a man fluent in Italian. Perhaps we can help him get home." She had Martha's full attention now. "We have gifts beyond our abilities to heal the body. Would you deny these desperate souls the full power of your ability to help them?"

"Alva, 'tis kind of ye to offer your services. To be sure this asylum could use another set of eyes to watch over these people and another pair of hands to help them heal, but I think ye know it will not be easy to gain the approval of Mr. Leonard. We ruffled his feathers but good by taking Felicity Taylor and he'll not soon forget that."

"Dr. Nolan is held in high regard here, I think," Alva argued. "Surely Mr. Leonard would allow me here as your assistant at his suggestion."

Martha started to say something, thought better of it, deciding that if Alva Awalte could speak without pretense, so could she. "Dr. Grant has expressed concern about ye treating patients. If Dr. Nolan were to intervene on yer behalf, it could cause trouble among the other members of the Medical Association."

It was easy for Alva to see where this argument was heading. "Dr. Grant felt foolish when I diagnosed and successfully treated a case of Bright's disease in a patient whom he had examined previously. He could not determine the true source of the illness. Many trained physicians overlook the patient in favor of studying only the symptoms." She waved her hand dismissively, not at all concerned about Dr. Grant's bruised ego. "You are concerned that if Dr. Nolan intervenes on my behalf it will cause trouble with the Association for you."

"Yes, I am, and rightly so. Alva, I have worked for two decades in this asylum because it is the only place I can practice medicine. Mr. Leonard is not the first difficult Keeper for whom I have worked. Dr. Grant has been an ally as much as Dr. Nolan has when I have needed him."

"You do not hesitate to call on your protectors when it is in the best interest of a patient," Alva argued. "This is such a time, Martha. You and I are able to help these people in a way that Drs. Grant and Nolan cannot. Do not deny them that."

Her brutal honesty fell like a blow to the chest. Martha had worked hard to become a member in good standing of the Buffalo Medical Association. For the past twenty years she had considered many of its members her allies, but they had merely taken her under their wing, one of their own, to be sure, but one who could not function as they did without them. It was a bitter reality.

Martha glanced over to where Mr. Rubino had been working, but he was long gone. She stared at the spot where he had stood as she considered what Alva was asking of her. "I must get in to see my patients. May we continue this another time? I can call on ye next week, perhaps."

"Yes, I think that would be a good idea. You have much to consider."

At the end of the day, there was Johnny, waiting at the livery. "I've a mind to see the house on Linwood Avenue, if ye don't mind walkin' for a bit," she suggested as he helped her down from the trap.

"Aye, 'tis a fine time for a wee stroll." He offered his arm and with a nod to the stableboy, they were off.

They made their way down Main Street, absorbed in the cacophony of hoofbeats, creaking wagons, and boisterous shouts coming from all directions, but the noises of the city receded as they turned onto North Street, and then onto Linwood Avenue. Johnny waited for Martha to offer up the real reason she wasn't quite ready to return home.

They approached the large wrought iron fence surrounding the home of Dr. J.J. Hackstein. One of her senior colleagues, Dr. Hackstein had recently built the house for his third wife. Tragically, the woman died in childbed and her husband was devastated. He put the elegant brick and sandstone house up for sale and left the city. It was indeed a fine home, and spoke of how far she and Johnny had come since they had left the poorhouse as children. "Is it not too big for just the three of us?" she asked.

"'Tis grand, to be sure," Johnny agreed, "but one day Robert will have a wife and a family of his own. Picture the wee ones and all their cousins comin' over for supper on a Sunday." He pointed to the side entrance of the house. "There's room for an office just there, one large enough to see patients, if ye had a mind to."

The thought of having the whole family over made her smile. As for trying to establish a practice of her own, Martha was not sure she wanted to and she told him so. Ultimately, they agreed that they could be happy in this house. They stood outside the fence for a while discussing when they would tell Gertrude of their plans and how soon they could take possession of the house and move. It wasn't until they were walking home that Martha told him of her conversation with Alva Awalte.

Johnny listened, hearing all of what she said as well as what she didn't. "Ye've a special gift, of that I've been sure since the day I first met ye. I'll admit, I don't understand it, but I'm that sure the good Lord put ye here to help those people, for even if ye had been able to establish a practice of yer own early on, ye'd have been there as well."

"Are ye sayin' I should go to Michael and ask for his help?"

"Aye, and what's so wrong with that? Do ye think he'll refuse ye?"

"'Tis not that simple. I've told ye the other physicians don't care for this woman. It could cause trouble for me down the road if I help her now."

"Sounds to me as if she is offerin' to help ye."

"Ye said yerself that Mason Leonard sees me as a threat. Do ye not think he would be even more threatened by Mrs. Awalte? He despises the Spiritualists, and should he find that he has two such gifted women under his roof, we'll likely end up in shackles on the third floor."

"Do ye fear the man?"

Martha did not hesitate to answer. "For myself, no; but for the patients, I do fear him. If he should forbid me to practice there, they would suffer for it, surely. The few other physicians who would even come to the asylum would do so at their leisure. They would neglect the chronic patients in favor of the other patients who can pay."

"Ye truly believe he would do that?"

"I do."

Johnny was surprised by her certainty. "I think he'd be a fool to do such a thing. When the fiscal year ends, the number of people who leave there cured reflects favorably on him. The county is pleased for every penny he saves them when a patient is discharged. Leonard may resent ye, but he needs ye, and well he knows it."

His words infuriated her, although he hadn't meant them to, and she made no effort to hide the anger in her voice. "We live in a world where the opinions of women mean nothing. Were we to work as a team, think of all Mason Leonard and I could do. So many people suffer because he thinks only of himself."

There were no words of comfort to counter those statements because Johnny knew that she was right, and to suggest otherwise would just prove her point. "It seems to me that ye must work with this woman if she has a mind to help ye, for she may be yer only true ally in that place."

They walked along in silence for a while as she considered Johnny's advice. "She's like no other woman I have met," Martha commented, more to herself than to him. "She speaks of her gifts so boldly, even as she sees what can happen to people like us."

"God gives ye what ye need to do his bidding. He has given ye powerful gifts, Martha, and now he has given ye someone who can teach ye how to use them. Consider that before ye make yer decision."

Chapter Thirteen

On the first Sunday of each month the entire Nolan clan gathered after church for their midday meal, and so there was a steady train of wagons and carriages as the Thomases, the Quinns, the Friedlanders and the Behringers made their way down North Street to the farm where they'd all grown up. The summer heat beckoned the men to the porch and the children to find what trouble they could outside.

"We cannot all fit in the kitchen," Gertrude remarked after Patricia and Ellie had arrived. "Ciara, take your sisters into the parlor and leave us to our work." She directed Felicity toward the bushel of potatoes and Ellie toward the bushel of string beans before shooing the older three women out of the kitchen.

Felicity fell comfortably into the rhythm of meal preparation, as few words were required for each woman to apply themselves to the tasks before them. Trading off a cauldron of potatoes for several heads of chard that needed chopping, she sat at the table across from Ellie. With her eyes focused on the cutting board, she was not aware that Ellie had asked her a question until she saw a hand enter her field of vision.

"Did you enjoy teaching?" Ellie asked again.

Felicity smiled and nodded enthusiastically. Making a fist with her thumb curled around her first finger and shaking it twice, she signed *yes*.

"Would they have you back, do you think?"

Felicity had returned to focus on her work and had missed the second question, so once again Ellie waved to regain her attention. Felicity shrugged to indicate that she was unsure. The question was one that required a lengthy answer, and no clear way to relay it to Ellie, so it was just easier to express uncertainty.

She smiled again, and picked up the knife. Nodding briefly down at the chard, Felicity attempted to get Ellie to understand that she could not chop vegetables and watch her at the same time. This was one of the many frustrations of living with hearing people. They often needed reminding that communication required her full attention.

It was much easier around Ciara. They worked companionably throughout the day in the kitchen, the garden and the laundry exchanging few words. It was even easier with Daniel because when it was just the two of them, they did not need words or gestures to know what the other was thinking. It wasn't as if they held entire conversations in their minds. Much of their communication as children involved doing things that did not require many words. Felicity smiled, remembering their games of hide and seek when they were children. They had become experts at reading each other's body language and facial expressions back then, although they knew each other's thoughts as well. The ease she felt around Daniel was a special gift and she cherished it.

A hand placed gently on her shoulder brought Felicity out of her thoughts. "Bitte, die mangold," Gertrude told her, extending her arms out as if she intended to receive something. "That is enough, I think." She pointed to the pan, full to the brim with the leafy greens.

Felicity looked confused, unable to understand the first sentence. "Bitte, die mangold," Gertrude repeated.

"She doesn't speak German," Ellie reminded her and when Gertrude's attention turned toward Ellie, so did Felicity's. "Give her the chard," Ellie directed Felicity and nudged the cast iron pan in Gertrude's direction.

"Oh, sorry." Felicity offered a conciliatory smile to Gertrude, who was embarrassed that her broken English made her hard to understand. It was the easiest way to stay in the good graces of people who found it difficult to communicate with her. In Felicity's experience, if a person became frustrated they would often just give up trying and either ignore her completely or rely on a third party to interpret the message. For the first time since she had arrived at the Nolans, Felicity longed to be back at her school where the use of a standard set of hand gestures and motions united everyone, regardless of age, social status or native language.

The meal was served in shifts, with all the young children seated first. At this point Ciara exercised her right to hold dominion over the kitchen. Shooing the younger women out to the porch, she and Patricia managed the seven little ones.

"Now, Frederick, mind ye wait until everyone is served before ye start," Patricia reminded Gertrude's middle son.

"Just ye keep yer eyes on yer own plate, Robyn," Ciara scolded Ellie's oldest girl. "The lads have the same as ye do. If ye want more, ye must clean yer plate first."

Ellie, Martha and Gertrude chuckled, their heads leaning toward the open window so as not to lose a word of the conversations going on inside the kitchen. "If I close my eyes, it was us sitting at that table," Martha reminded Ellie.

"Aye, and we were not so easy to wrangle around the supper table, were we?" Ellie replied and the three women laughed out loud this time.

The joke was lost on Felicity, and with the other women so focused on the goings on inside the house it was easy for her to sneak away.

It had become something of a habit, as the children got older and louder, for the men to find a reason to remove themselves to the barn, the porch being too close to the chaos at the table. After a brief discussion of whatever drew them there, a carriage in need of repair or the loan of a particular tool, they made themselves comfortable on bales of hay until they were called for supper. Charlie always managed to find a bottle of whiskey to share while they discussed the news of the day. It was something of a rite of passage for the lads to be sent down to the barn and Daniel remembered with fondness the first wee dram of which he'd partaken with these men. With his mug in hand, Daniel stared out the barn door thinking of that day, which he had shared with his older brother. Ian had been quite put out that Daniel was also sent down to the barn along with him, and he a full year and a half younger than Ian.

Someone walking down from the house pulled Daniel from his thoughts. It was Felicity. The other men were absorbed in a discussion over the latest news on the acquittal of Peter Rimmer, a young man accused of murder in Schenectady, but who had been apprehended in Buffalo. Daniel slipped out of the barn unnoticed.

She seemed to be wandering without purpose, her loneliness evident in the stoop of her shoulders and the slowness of her pace. Daniel was aware that she still rose each morning well before dawn, but made efforts to be quieter, either not wanting to disturb him or needing the time to herself. He thought it might be a combination of the two and had left her to her privacy. She saw him approaching and smiled. Daniel had become an expert at reading her smiles. Her lips flattened more when she was frustrated, but it showed more in her eyes when she felt foolish over having misunderstood something. This smile indicated relief as he caught up with her.

For a few minutes, they walked companionably toward the far end of the pasture, old Beau trotting alongside them from inside of it. "He is well?" she asked, and Daniel nodded, watching the horse stride with confidence.

They stopped close to where the path met the road and leaned on the fence rails, feeling no particular need to say anything. Daniel was reluctant to break the easy silence between them with talk of Ian. He had thought often about their conversation that morning in the kitchen, but still couldn't find a way to forgive himself for letting his brother and his parents down. His eyes followed the horse as the beast grazed his way around the field, content to keep his own counsel on the matter. Finally, Felicity took his hand and turned him toward her. "Tell me," she said.

"About Ian?" Of course, she was aware of what was going through his mind as they stood there. "I should have been there to protect him." He couldn't bring himself to say that their mother had told them to look out for each other, or that Ian had always had Daniel's back, but his feelings showed plain on his face.

Felicity looked at him and then just behind him. She made an effort to speak clearly, feeling speech was the most effective means to convey Ian's message. "He is still here looking out for you. Your grief keeps you from seeing that he does not hold you responsible for what happened." She gave his hand a gentle squeeze. "If you will stop blaming yourself for his death, you will see for yourself."

Daniel looked behind him, trying to understand what she saw. "Can ye see him?" He had heard there were such gifted people in the world that could see the dead, but he wasn't sure he really believed it.

Felicity nodded and smiled. "Forgive yourself, Daniel, and you will feel him beside you."

Daniel closed his eyes and felt the gentle breeze on his face. Could it be that simple? In his heart, he knew his brother did not blame him anymore than his parents did. Perhaps the only way for Ian to be a part of his life again was for Daniel to forgive himself. "I'll try," he said.

Beau was doing his best to get her attention, so Felicity approached the old horse. The smile she wore when the horse nuzzled the hair at her shoulder was lighthearted and cheeky. Daniel seldom saw her smile simply because she was happy and it comforted him to see that she was healing. "Old Beau's got a way of puttin' a bit of joy in yer eyes." He had been speaking to her from behind, but she turned and he repeated the statement. Irritated that her attention had shifted, Beau nudged at her back, pushing her forward. Daniel reached out and steadied her, both of them laughing. He went to scold the horse for his bad manners and then turned back toward Felicity to see her silly grin now directed at him.

"I'm happy you're here," she told him, briskly waving her extended hand above her chest to sign the word happy. There was no need to tell him why, the softness in her eyes gave away her reasons.

For the first time Daniel was confused by what he saw, and more so by what he felt. There was both gratitude and relief in her words, but there was something else underneath. It was more than just affection and it took him by surprise. Felicity saw him working through this revelation and waited calmly for a response.

"For the first time in a long time I'm happy to be here, too." Although he meant what he said, it would take him some time to accept truly the weight of his own words.

Felicity took both of his hands in hers and looked at him, the warmth in her eyes telling him that it was okay to be confused. She had revealed more than she had been aware of herself until just that moment and they would both need time to think about it. "C'mon," she motioned with her hand as she turned to walk toward the house. "Let's go eat."

Martha made her way down to the barn to fetch the men who were engaged in a lively debate over the fate of Mr. Rimmer. Her presence was enough to effectively end the debate and send the men eagerly toward the dining table. "Michael, may I have a word?" She asked, placing a hand on his arm to keep him back.

"Aye, of course, what's on yer mind, then?"

"I had a visit the other day from Alva Awalte." He looked interested but not concerned, so she got right to the point. "She'd like to serve as my assistant in the asylum." Martha was surprised to see that Michael was not opposed to the idea.

"She'd be a help to ye, to be sure," he told her. "What's yer concern?"

"Ye did tell me that the other members of the medical association didn't care for her."

"Aye, 'tis true enough, but she's less a threat to them workin' in the asylum, isn't she? I'd think they'd be pleased to see her distracted and out of their way."

Michael's reply startled her. Had they intended to keep her distracted and out of their way, too? It was a question she decided she hadn't time to ponder. "There's still Mr. Leonard. He'll not take kindly to another woman seeing patients, particularly one who speaks her mind."

"Just so," he agreed. "Ye're askin' me to have a word with the man?"

"Aye. He'll not refuse ye, I think."

Michael considered her request. "Have ye thought about what might happen should the woman stir up trouble?"

Martha recalled her discussion with Mrs. Awalte and knew well they'd be stirring up trouble. "She can help them in ways that I can't." When he looked confused, she amended her statement. "She can teach me to help in ways I don't yet know. Michael, she has gifts similar to mine that help her to see what is inside a person's mind." She waited for him to interrupt with more words of caution, but when he seemed willing to listen, she continued. "You and I are in agreement that many of the patients in the asylum do not suffer from sickness or injuries of the brain, as others in our profession now think, are we not?" He nodded and she went on. "Many of these patients have just given up hope. More's the tragedy, they can't always say why. Alva Awalte understands what weighs on their minds, even when they don't know themselves. I think we owe it to them to let her do what she can to help them if she's willin' to try."

Before he and Ciara were married, she and her sisters had come to stay with Michael's parents. His mother, Katherine, had told him about the gifted children. Every so often, a babe was born with a wisdom and empathy far beyond that even of the average adult. These children possessed a charm that drew people in and an ability to speak without using words. They also had great capacity for love and forgiveness. As adults, they often became healers or pursued other professions that allowed them to help people. The gifted ones were supposed to be rare, but he felt he had been blessed to know a few of them: Martha, certainly, and Felicity. They had realized she was special early on. He also suspected Daniel was among them, although Michael had never said so aloud, even to Ciara. It couldn't be a coincidence that all of these people had found their way into his life, and now Alva Awalte had joined them. Perhaps God had sent them all to him so that he could help them use their gifts. "Aye, just so. I'll have a word with Leonard tomorrow. In the end, he'll think it was his idea."

The kitchen being too small to accommodate eleven adults, they ate in the dining room. Martha and Michael came in to find the rest of the family already seated and serving themselves. The rotation of bowls, platters and chatter didn't miss a beat as they took their seats.

Daniel sat at the end of the table by the door, his attention diverted by Felicity and Rolland. Their hands were gesticulating as they carried on a discussion amid the loud chatter. Daniel had no idea what they were discussing and was impressed with how quickly Rolland had picked up the language of signs. Daniel had realized that Felicity was unaware of what she was really telling him earlier until the moment that she spoke. She was glad he was here, but was she glad that *she* was here? Would she stay long enough for them to explore what was happening between them, for something was happening. He'd felt it at the same moment that she had. Daniel had found relationships with women to be difficult because so often what they said and what they really felt were very different. There was a time when he was just out of common school that he thought he was in love, but his feelings were not returned. When he was an attorney, the ability to read people was a gift, but when it came to personal relationships, it seemed a curse. There would be none of that with Felicity. Her feelings were genuine and she would be patient while he sorted things out in his head.

As soon as Martha took her seat across from him, Johnny exchanged a brief glance with his wife that told him that she had spoken with Michael and it had gone as she had hoped it would. The two physicians spoke easily now of the upcoming months when medical students would tour the poorhouse and asylum, but Johnny got the sense that their brief discussion in the barn was the beginning of a very different relationship between them. Michael had been both a mentor and a father figure to Martha and he was very much to credit for the fine physician she had become. But Michael could not provide the kind of guidance that Alva Awalte would, and Johnny dearly hoped he would not stand in the way.

It did not escape Ciara that her son's attention was focused on their houseguest. He was not obvious about it, stealing glances while he filled his plate, but she had noticed. There had been no appreciable change in Daniel's behavior since Felicity arrived. He had gone about his business and their paths only crossed at meal times, so what was in his thoughts now she could not say, for nothing in his expression betrayed his mind.

Chapter Fourteen

Maude was exhausted by the time the day was over, but one of the advantages of living above the antique shop was that there was no great rush to get home to get dinner started. There was time to check her e-mail. Sure enough, among a few items of spam that seemed to have slipped through the filters there was a response from Charlotte.

Hello Maude. It was lovely to hear from you. It looks as though your spirit guide is keeping you busy! Regarding your dreams, be patient and let them play out. Your guide has used this method before to provide you with the information you need to understand what she is trying to tell you. Record them as you did before, and feel free to call me if you need to discuss anything in particular.

I think it is wise of you to continue to do research on this side. That seems to be your role in all of this. Remember that the people you are looking into have lived their lives and have passed into spirit. Of course, you would be saddened to learn of their deaths. You were connected to them during that life, particularly to Johnny. It would also serve you well to keep in mind that nothing you learn will change their fate. It might, however, change yours. Remember, we are often surrounded by the same cast of characters, so to speak, in each life. They behave in much the same way as well. Often negative karma will continue into subsequent lives until someone does something to break the cycle. My feeling is that all of this may be leading up to something like that. (It is only a feeling. I'm not keeping anything from you.) Be mindful of the people in your life now and of any situations that seem familiar, for better or for worse.

Whether or not you look specifically at Martha Quinn's life is entirely a personal choice. Reincarnation seldom offers that kind of opportunity. Personally, I would not be able to resist, were I in your shoes. Just be aware that you may not be happy about what you learn. The same would be true should you have chosen past life regression, where hypnosis would take you back into Martha's consciousness. Looking into the historic record gives you only the perspective of the person who recorded the information, and so is quite different from past life regression. You might meditate and ask for guidance on this issue.

My dear, I am pleased that you have chosen to embrace this journey. Know that I am here for you. Charlotte

"As usual, more questions than answers," Maude said aloud as she read the e-mail over a third time.

"Questions about what?" Don had come in through the back door, but Maude had been too engrossed in her e-mail to notice.

"Well, I took your advice and I consulted Charlotte Lambert."

"And you now have more questions than answers?"

"Yes."

Don came around the desk and pulled Maude to her feet. "Let's go upstairs and grab a couple of drinks and you can elaborate."

"Corner of Lincoln Parkway and Forest Avenue...why does that address sound familiar?" Don had followed Maude into the kitchen and pulled the most recent edition of the weekly newspaper from their old neighborhood out of his back pocket. It had been his habit since they moved out of that area to keep up on the latest news.

"That's Mrs. Billingsley's house. Well, one of the houses on that corner is hers. Why?"

"That location is listed in the Blotter. There was a break-in last week."

"You're kidding me! That place is a fortress; I can't believe it. Did they say what was missing?"

"Jewelry and some cash."

"Do you think I should call her?"

"I wouldn't; it might not be her house, but if she happens to pop in the shop, you could ask."

"Yeah, you're right. I wouldn't want to bother her."

"Boy, that would be an odd coincidence if it was her."

176

"Why?" Maude got the feeling that she really didn't want to know the answer to that question.

"Well, I went over to pick up the chandelier from the DeMonteforte's on Nottingham yesterday and Mrs. DeMonteforte told me they had a break-in last week, too."

Maude felt her stomach tighten as she spoke. "Mrs. Billingsley and Mrs. DeMonteforte were both in the shop this week."

"Well, I doubt that had anything to do with it. That's a pretty fancy neighborhood, but it's pretty close to the park. I'm surprised there aren't more break-ins."

"I guess." Maude didn't sound convinced.

The conversation shifted back to the e-mail from Charlotte Lambert, but did little to ease Maude's mind. There was so much to consider for an over-thinker. She doubted she would even fall asleep, let alone dream up the answers to her questions. Two things in particular were keeping her from slumber: first, the idea that what she might learn in the process of doing her research might change her fate. *What fate?* That thought played over and over again in her mind. Fate implies the inevitable, and Maude wasn't really sure she believed in that. Charlotte seemed to indicate that Maude's fate might be changed by what she learned which would imply NOT inevitable. Can something be considered one's fate if it were possible to change it? If so, how did that work? Maude thought it might be wise just to accept the possibility of Charlotte's suggestion rather than to dissect the meaning of the word fate. Now all that was left was to figure out what cycle needed breaking and how she might do that. That thought led directly into the second thing keeping her up: *Be mindful of the people in your life now, and of any situations that seem familiar, for better or for worse.* Just what the hell did that mean?

Charlotte could not possibly understand the power of those words to an over-thinker. Maude knew she would be scrutinizing everyone who crossed her path. She would drive herself crazy wondering what might be about to happen, with whom it might happen, and how she might stop or change it. How was she supposed to carry on with her life if she was constantly stopping to take stock of every interaction? Were there enough notebooks for such an endeavor? Still, it might be worth making a list of any new people who had entered her life when her dreams started up again. Maude began to tally in her head those who had crossed her path just that day. It was a bit like counting sheep and she was asleep before she got to the person who had handed over her afternoon coffee in the drive-thru at Tim Hortons.

Chapter Fifteen

Martha walked down Division Street, absently smoothing the wrinkles from her skirt and straightening her hat as she approached number 248. She opened the wrought iron gate and walked up the path with the feeling that something exciting was about to begin. After a quick rap on the door and a few words to the maid who answered it, she was seated in the parlor waiting for Alva Awalte to receive her.

"Martha, how wonderful to see you. I'm delighted you came to call. Have you time for tea?"

"I thank ye, Alva, but I must be off shortly."

"Well, then, let us not waste a moment!" Alva said as she took a seat across from her guest. "What brings you here today?"

"I've come to take ye up on yer offer to help me at the asylum...but there are a few things we must have clear between us before we are in agreement."

"I'm listening."

Martha looked at her directly and spoke in a tone that would brook no argument. "Ye must understand and accept that ye'd be practicing as my assistant. Ye are not a physician and if we are to keep Mr. Leonard out of our business, ye must remember that he will not tolerate yer presence there in any other capacity." Alva nodded, not yet in agreement, but in understanding, so Martha continued. "Ye speak boldly of yer gifts, but Mr. Leonard must never know of them, for should he find out, he'll have the both of us removed."

Alva considered these conditions before she responded. "Martha, I know your position in that asylum is dear to you and I would do nothing to place it or you in peril. You have the formal education that I lack, but there is still much I can teach you. I am sure that our meeting was no accident."

Martha nodded in agreement. "We can do much together, but Mr. Leonard will claim every success as his own. We will not be recognized for our accomplishments; ye must understand that as well."

"I have suffered the ignorance and indifference of men longer than you have by a decade or more, I think. What you are telling me comes as no surprise."

With a brief nod of acknowledgement, Martha looked around the well-appointed parlor before issuing her final condition. "There's very little pay involved. I am considered a consulting physician and were I not a married woman, I could not live off the wages I am paid as such. As my assistant, ye will receive far less."

Alva smiled, waving off the discussion of money as if it were an annoying insect buzzing between them. "Martha, my dear husband left me comfortable when he passed. Beyond that, I have a very lucrative business as a healer, which I intend to continue. I can offer my help to you three afternoons each week at the asylum, but I must continue to see my existing clients as well."

It was difficult for Martha to suppress a smile, but she managed it anyway. Alva Awalte would hardly be distracted and out of the way, and that pleased her beyond measure. "Well, then, if we are in agreement, we should settle on a schedule before I depart."

"As it happens, I am available for the remainder of the afternoon. I can accompany you now, and meet you there on Thursday and Saturday as well, if it suits." Not waiting for Martha to agree, she added, "I will ride with you and leave word for my driver to fetch me at day's end."

* * *

Mason Leonard watched out his office window as Martha and that dreadful German woman approached the building, heads bent in conspiratorial discourse, he was sure. The last thing he needed was another woman who thought she knew better than he did about the place, but Michael Nolan was held in high regard by the Board of Supervisors and he would not risk losing their favor by refusing Nolan's request.

A knock on the office door drew his attention from the window. "Come in," Leonard commanded, not taking his eyes off the women as they climbed the stairs to the entrance. A barrel of a man appeared in the open doorway with a clean shorn head and a full beard.

"Ah, Kraus, perfect timing, man, perfect timing. Do come in."

The man stood silent before Leonard's desk with his hands folded behind his back, waiting for the Keeper to speak. "Mrs. Quinn will be working with a new assistant. The woman is new to the care of the insane and will need close supervision over the upcoming weeks as she learns the way of things. See to it and report to me if she should undertake any methods inconsistent with our own."

Kraus nodded and returned to the hall, standing like a sentry outside the office as the doctor and her assistant arrived. Martha acknowledged him with a nervous jerk of her head as she approached Mrs. Boswell. "Mr. Leonard is expecting us," she said, and waited in the hall as the matron announced them. Martha could feel Kraus' eyes on her back as she entered the office with him directly behind her. Once inside, he took up the same post, but just inside the door instead of just outside of it.

Leonard looked up from his desk, scowling as if he had been rudely interrupted. "Is there something I can do for you, Mrs. Quinn?"

Martha used the smile she typically adopted when Mr. Leonard was insistent about something and then annoyed with her when she complied. She spoke calmly and reminded him that he had wanted to meet Mrs. Awalte. It seemed a gift from heaven that he did not remember her from the day Felicity had been discharged and neither woman saw the need to remind him of that.

"Ah, yes, Mrs. Awalte, it is no easy task we have set out for ourselves, caring for this most unfortunate class. One must be sharp at all times. Many of our inmates are not above using trickery as a means to their devious ends." With a pointed glance at Martha, he continued. "I daresay others in this institution are too easily led astray when certain inmates feign illness to shirk their duties. Do not fall prey to their ruses, Mrs. Awalte, for if you do, it will become a regular habit for them to try and deceive you." Alva had become a master at hiding what she really thought behind an impassive mask and simply nodded as Leonard continued speaking.

"All difficult medical cases must be transferred to the hospital department unless specifically indicated by me." Again there was another pointed look at Martha, which Alva pretended not to notice. "Make no mistake, Mrs. Awalte, I have achieved a high standard of care unmatched by my predecessors." Pointing to the large, bald man by the door, he added, "Mr. Kraus sees all and reports directly to me. Do we understand each other, Mrs. Awalte?"

"We do, thank you, sir." She and Martha turned and left without another word. Alva resisted the urge to make eye contact with Kraus on the way out because she knew her attempt to see what was in his thoughts would be interpreted as defiance. She did not want to give him a reason to pay closer attention to her. Besides, she had plenty of time to read Mr. Leonard as he delivered his instructions. What she saw was a desperate man who hung his own self-worth on the opinions of others. He appeared harmless enough on the surface, but desperate men were dangerous and she was sure that Martha did not see Mason Leonard as a dangerous man. Alva kept pace with Martha as they climbed the stairs to the patient wards, relieved that she had gotten here just in time.

* * *

A gust of wind caused a ripple across the bed-clothes hanging on the line, revealing a pair of legs in well-worn boots just behind them. Felicity hadn't noticed them as she wrestled the heavy, wet sheet onto the clothesline. Daniel was content to watch her go about her work. There was still a wee bit of the girl he knew in her eyes and in the way the stray hairs came loose from her bun and danced around her face, but she had grown into a fine young woman.

She was still for just a second before she reached back into the basket, realizing he was there. They had played this game as children, and Daniel could no more sneak up on her now than he could then. He reached over and flung the sheet aside, laughing as he wiggled his fingers as if to tickle her. It was what he had done when they were children. He had tickled her mercilessly until she laughed so hard, she couldn't catch her breath. Not to be left out of the fun, Ian would tickle Daniel and they would all end up rolling around the ground in a squealing ball of arms and legs.

"Don't even think about it," she giggled, snapping a wet pillowslip in his direction.

Daniel raised his hands in surrender then reached to secure the sheet back onto the line. He raised his eyebrows and looked toward the basket to see how much was left.

She took the last pillowslip out, clipped it to the line and smiled. "Done!"

His hands moved rapidly as he spoke. "I must turn the horses out. Will ye come along?"

She nodded and fell into step alongside him. They emerged from the maze of hanging bed linen and followed the path that wound around the barn, each content to enjoy the sunshine and cool morning breeze. The easy silence between them was a comfort as Daniel gathered his thoughts. He stopped at the large maple tree just outside the back entrance to the barn. There were things he wanted to say, but when he looked into her eyes, he understood that she already knew what was in his heart.

Felicity had been attracted to other men before, but she did not feel that giddy nervousness around Daniel she had felt around them. Perhaps it was because she had known him as a child, and so knew the real person behind the façade of this grown man standing before her, or perhaps it was because they were just right together. She felt at ease as she never had before. It settled comfortably around her, drawing Daniel in as well.

They both stood under the tree, an arms width apart, and without a single spoken word realized that each had been waiting for the other to come home. Taking her hands, he drew her in. She was close enough to kiss, but he was content just to watch her for a moment. Her smile was one he hadn't seen before and he watched as it traveled from her heart all the way up to her beautiful eyes as her lips met his.

Kissing Felicity was the homecoming he was long overdue. He pulled her closer and the world around him righted itself. There would always be a small place where Ian lived, but he could let the light in now. Felicity had brought the light with her and allowed him to see the joy that had once been in his life, and more importantly made him realize the joy that was still there.

The kiss seemed to go on forever, at first filled with gratitude for the gift she had given him, and then longing for the woman that she was.

Daniel tried to ignore the sound of hooves against the stall door, but she could feel the subtle tensing of his shoulders and drew away. He looked with regret toward the barn, not wanting to let her go to sign that he must see to the horses.

Felicity smiled and gently pushed him in the direction of the barn. "Go and finish your chores," she signed. "Come and fetch me when you are done." She leaned in and kissed him one last time before she turned to go and retrieve her basket.

* * *

Ciara came into the barn to remind Charlie that she would need a ride into the city later that afternoon. The sound of hooves striking wood drew her to the last stall. Nora, the bay mare, was growing impatient waiting for Daniel. Ciara walked toward the back door and was about to call out when she saw Felicity lean in and kiss her son. It was just a quick brush of the lips, but the look on Daniel's face as he watched her walk away told Ciara that things had changed between them. Not quite sure at that moment how she felt about this new development, Ciara quickly made her way to the front of the barn and out the door.

Later that afternoon, when Charlie dropped Ciara off at Patricia's house on Franklin Street, she still had Daniel and Felicity on her mind. Patricia may not have had Martha's gift of second sight, but she knew when her older sister was distracted. "Out with it," she demanded after Ciara's attention had drifted for a second time during their conversation.

Ciara let out a long sigh, rearranged her cup on the saucer, and finally looked up at Patricia. "Daniel's in love with Felicity," she blurted out. "I saw them behind the barn, by the big maple tree. She kissed him."

"Oh, that's wonderful news!" With a conspiratorial smile, she added, "If she kissed him, I guess there's no need to ask if his affection is returned." Noting that Ciara was not smiling, she asked why. "Do ye not think it's a good match?"

"Oh Patricia, I don't know what to think. Recall it was only a few weeks ago that Martha and Michael pulled her out of the asylum. We still don't know how she ended up there."

"Surely ye don't think her insane?"

"No, of course not, but Martha told me that the woman who helped them suspected that the Constable in Laona took a dislike to her because of her special gifts. He aims to rid the town of folk like her."

"Well, I don't know why she'd return there with her uncle gone," Patricia told her. "Do ye think she might go back to the school in New York?"

"I don't know. She hasn't mentioned any plans to leave, yet." Ciara's disquiet at the mention of New York told Patricia that this had more to do with the possibility of Daniel leaving than any danger Felicity might be in.

Patricia laughed, and seeing her sister's expression struggling between anxiety, confusion and annoyance only made her laugh harder. "Ye saw an innocent wee kiss behind the barn and ye've got them married and off to New York, never to be seen or heard from again."

Ciara smiled, if only to give the impression that she was in on the joke. "Laugh if ye must. The kiss might have been innocent, but, sure enough, the look on my son's face was not. 'Twas not that long ago that yer own daughter married and left for Albany and ye were not laughin' then, were ye?" Ciara raised her brows, daring her sister to deny it.

"No, I cried for a week and well ye know it, for it was mostly on yer shoulder."

Ciara remembered shedding her share of tears as well because not only had she lost her niece, but she was losing her sister as well. She had been heartbroken when Martha had left the farm to begin her new life with Johnny, but Patricia had been there and together they had raised their children. She dearly missed her middle sister, but Daniel was still there and he needed her so. She could not bear to think of him leaving.

"'Tis something all mothers must face," Patricia told her. "Sooner or later, our children grow up and leave us. Still, ye must wait and see what happens between them before ye continue to fret over it."

"Aye, maybe ye're right." Ciara put the discussion aside for now, but thoughts of Daniel leaving had taken root in the back of her mind and would not be so easily discarded.

Chapter Sixteen

Maude rotated the flash drive through her fingers as she reviewed the notes from her dream journal. Much like last time, nothing in the journal seemed to reveal the purpose for these vivid portrayals of the past. There was definitely another novel there but the scope of it had not taken shape in her mind yet. Her eyes traveled from the page to the flash drive still twirling in her left hand. She still hadn't looked at any of the files, although she was not sure why. It sort of felt like cheating, and Maude suspected that there was value, or maybe power, in letting things be revealed in their own time. Still, if the new novel would be based on these people, it would be useful to have more details about their lives. "You're being stupid," she told herself. "Just plug the damn thing in and get on with it." Her hand was hovering over the USB port when the shop phone rang.

She looked at the caller ID and recognized the number. "Good afternoon, Alexandra. What can I do for you today?"

"Oh, Maude, something terrible has happened. I was on my way to the appraiser and my car was broadsided in the middle of the intersection. It caused a dreadful mess."

"Oh my gosh! Are you okay? Was anyone hurt?"

"Thankfully, nobody was hurt. I'm fine for the time being, but I don't think that will be the case when Mr. Houston finds out."

"Well, it wasn't your fault, right? You didn't run the light or anything, did you?"

"No, someone went speeding through the intersection, slammed into me and kept right on going. It all happened so fast that nobody even got a license plate number."

"Well, I'm sure Mr. Houston will be relieved to know that you were not harmed. Insurance will take care of the rest."

"I'm afraid that the insurance may only take care of the car, dear. I was on my way to the jewelry appraiser you had recommended. I had several valuable pieces of Mother Houston's jewelry in my car when it was hit. In all the chaos of police reports and the exchange of insurance information with the other vehicle that was also hit, someone stole the jewelry out of my car."

"Oh no, that's horrible." Maude considered not asking, but then couldn't help herself. "When you say 'several valuable pieces', exactly what do you mean?"

"There were two necklaces, a tennis bracelet and four rings. All together they were worth about 200K, I expect, maybe more."

"Two hundred thousand dollars?" Maude stopped herself from asking why she had left the house with jewelry that valuable instead of making an appointment for the appraiser to come to the house. She knew Mrs.

Houston did not like strangers in her home. "Did you tell the police who were on the scene?"

"Yes. Just before the tow truck left, I remembered the jewelry was in the car, and I opened the glove box and the small case was gone. The poor tow truck driver insisted we search his entire truck and his person so there would be no doubt that he didn't take them."

"What did the police say? Do they think they can recover your property?"

The anger rose in Mrs. Houston as she continued to tell her story. "They told me it was foolish to transport items that valuable by myself and that I should have locked the car when I got out after the accident." She tried to get control of her frustration as she went on. "I suppose I can't be angry with them. They are right, after all."

"Well, that may be, but I'm sure you were more concerned with the people at the scene of the accident than you were about locking your car."

"Truthfully, I had forgotten they were even in the car. The woman I hit when my car spun around had children with her. Thank God they were unharmed." Alexandra paused, again feeling her emotions getting the better of her. Maude could hear her take in and expel a deep breath before she spoke again. "Maude, I'm calling because I am hoping that you can answer some questions for me."

"I can certainly try. What do you need to know?"

"The police think this was a random crime. Someone saw an expensive car and rummaged through it for whatever they could find."

"That makes sense to me."

"I'm wondering if you are aware of any disreputable dealers. Where would a petty thief try to sell such jewelry?"

Maude thought for a few moments before answering the question. "It would depend on whether they knew what they had. It would be pretty foolish to try and sell valuable pieces without some kind of proof of ownership. Even most of the shady dealers might not want something they knew the police are looking for. Having said that, there are always buyers who don't ask questions, but I don't know who they are."

"The police are faxing pictures of each piece to every jeweler and pawn shop in every major city. I'm sure the insurance company will leave no stone unturned as well, but I know my husband and he will have a private investigator on this the minute he finds out. I was just hoping to offer up a lead."

"I'm sorry, Alexandra, but I really don't know. Don and I have never dealt with anything that valuable before."

"The woman who works for you, is it possible that she would know anything that would be helpful?"

Maude was glad they were speaking on the phone and that Mrs. Houston hadn't seen her choke back the smile on her face and in her voice. This was just the kind of intrigue Christine loved, but Maude was sure all of her contacts were reputable...pretty sure, anyway. "I'll certainly ask Christine, but I don't think she can help you either."

"Thank you, dear. If you hear anything, anything at all, please call me right away."

"I will, Alexandra. Same goes for you. Give me a call if there's anything else I can do. Better yet, stop in soon and we'll have a cup of that tea you like so much."

No sooner did Maude hang up the phone than she heard a voice from the front of the shop and footsteps heading toward her office. "Ask me what?"

There would be no way of keeping such big news from Christine, so she motioned for her to sit down. "Mrs. Houston had some jewelry stolen out of her car today."

"I heard you say two hundred thousand dollars. That's more than some, I think."

"I don't suppose you know any fences in the area?" Maude was only half kidding and so was only mildly surprised by Christine's answer.

"I might. What was stolen?"

"What do you mean, you might? Do you have a secret life in the underworld of the jewelry business?"

Christine laughed. "No, but I dated a guy a few years back who did."

"Get outta town! You did not."

"I most certainly did. I met him at an auction in New York about 10 years ago. He was ridiculously good looking, and so debonair, you know, like a jewel thief in the movies." She looked wistfully up to the heavens as she recalled his charming British accent.

"Only he was a jewel thief in real life."

Christine let out a sigh of lament. "Sadly, yes. Of course, I had to end it. He was heartbroken; so was I." Her voice dripped with sarcasm and regret as she painted a picture of her brief but sultry romance with a noble cat burglar.

"I don't suppose you and your thief in the night still keep in touch?"

Her eyes lit up like a lioness who had just spotted her prey. "It could be fun to have a reason to call him."

The eagerness with which Christine was willing to jump into this mess had Maude second-guessing whether she should have said anything in the first place. "Wait a minute, how well do you know this guy? Keep in mind that the objective here is to get the jewelry back. The original plan was to sell the pieces and donate the money to several local charities. The last thing we need is for you to tip the guy off on a big score."

"Not to worry, he is definitely the Robin Hood type. He only steals from the wives of greedy corporate pigs."

Maude laughed out loud. "He sounds divine. I don't know why you let him go."

"I ask myself that often," Christine commented absently as she scrolled through the contacts in her phone. The bell above the front door announced a customer and she slid the phone back in her back pocket.

"I guess tall, dark and felon will have to wait!" Maude chuckled as Christine exited the office.

* * *

Between the regular customers and Christine's schedule, the window facelift took over two weeks to finish completely. Jobs thought to take just a few hours like painting the trim and arranging the container landscaping took a few days because the trim and the planters needed a bit of TLC before they could be transformed. On the day when Maude was putting the window back together, no thoughts were spared for the nineteenth century or how those thus far revealed details might change her fate or be worked into a book. To Maude's surprise she wasn't able to remember much of her dreams the night before, which was attributed to the fact that she had gone to bed thoroughly exhausted. There were persistent but vague whispers of Mason Leonard that left her feeling odd when she woke, but the reason she rose from sleep unsettled eluded her.

Maude was hanging the last lamp with her back turned to the open door. She turned to reach for the switch that would turn on all of the lights in the front window and was surprised to find Lester Northrup standing in the door. His lips curled into a defiant smirk, like he had been watching her unawares and wasn't the least bit abashed at having been caught. It was an effort, but Maude showed no reaction to his rude behavior. Instead, she did her best to smile and greet him like she would a valued client for whom she didn't particularly care.

"Oh, I'm sorry, Lester, I didn't notice you standing there. Is there something I can do for you?"

He made no secret of inspecting the new window display, as if he'd come to give his approval. Finally, in a tone that indicated that he was pleased with himself, he said, "You've been hard at work these last few weeks."

"Well, we were due for a facelift." Maude was careful to keep her own words neutral. It certainly appeared as if he had come to gloat, but over what she had no idea. It was a relief to see the mail carrier approaching and she nodded toward the street to draw

Lester's attention to the woman as she entered the doorway behind him.

He laughed in a way that made Maude feel that he was in on a joke that she wasn't and backed out, allowing the woman to enter. "You just keep up the good work, honey."

Maude took the time to close the door behind him, although it was warm enough to leave it open.

"Hey Diane, what have you got for me today?" Maude asked the mail carrier as she offered over a fist full of envelopes.

"Oh, the usual, bills, bills and more bills."

"Just once I'd like you to bring a letter from a long lost relative telling me I've inherited millions." Maude had told her that at least once a month over the last ten years and her reply was always the same.

"Maybe tomorrow!" With a wink and a smile, Diane left the shop, the bell on the door jingling behind her.

With the flick of a single switch the front window came to life. Blown glass chandeliers and Victorian hanging lamps reflected off the smaller lamps and antiques, creating a twinkle effect that would be even more dazzling as the sun went down. Most of the jewelry and accessories had been moved out of the actual display, but could easily be seen through the window. Beautiful peach colored begonias and pale pink New Guinea impatiens cascaded out of the planters, catching the eyes of both pedestrians and commuters as they came by. Putting the mail on the counter, Maude went outside to assess the full effect. The display looked beautiful from both sides of the glass, and she was so busy admiring the results of her efforts that she didn't hear the man who approached from across the street, although he had called out to her.

"Excuse me, but are you the business owner?"

"I am. Is there something I can help you with?"

"My name is Trent Doyle." He handed her a business card that indicated he was from the building inspector's office. "We've had a report that you are doing renovations to your building without a proper permit."

"I don't understand. Do we need a permit to re-point a few loose bricks?"

Mr. Doyle looked at the window display and frowned. "This is not about re-pointing loose bricks." He looked at the clipboard he was holding for a moment before he continued. "The complaint had to do with renovations to the entryway and new signage. Do you intend to mount some sort of sign?"

"No. We scraped and painted the windows, added some flowerpots and put in new curtains. The most complicated thing we did was to rearrange the lighting fixtures that hung in the window."

Doyle went inside for a closer look and Maude followed him. "Well, it looks as though everything is in order here. I'm sorry for the interruption." As he headed out the open door he added, "It looks very nice, by the way."

Maude stood at the front of the shop looking dumbfounded when Christine came in through the back. "What was that all about?"

"I think our new neighbor is at it again. That was the building inspector. He got a complaint that we were doing renovations to the front entrance without a permit." Maude told her.

"Are you kidding me?"

"Nope."

"Maude, you've got to go over there and find out what the hell is wrong with that guy."

"No, Christine, that's the last thing I should do." There was no point in telling her that Lester had been by not five minutes ago. He had likely seen the building inspector parking his car as he left. "I think you're right that he's still mad about not getting the building from his brother. If I confront him, it will just make things worse - that's assuming he's the one who called the inspector." Maude argued.

"Of course it was him. He knows we're on to him about the windows, so he's called the building inspector just to screw with us. He's a bully."

"All the more reason to ignore him."

"Are you going to tell Don about this?" Christine asked.

"Of course, and I'm sure I'll have the same discussion with him that I'm having with you right now. There is nothing to be gained by antagonizing Lester Northrup. By the way, what are you doing here? It's your day off."

"Basil returned my call." Christine said, her lips curving into a mischievous smirk.

"Dare I ask who Basil is?"

"Basil Hewitt is my friend in the jewelry business from New York."

"Oh, the jewel thief - you actually called him?" Maude laughed out loud. "Dear God! Basil Hewitt is the perfect name for a cat burglar! It can't be his real name."

"He's really more of a broker these days."

Maude rolled her eyes. "Well, does he know anything about Mother Houston's jewelry?"

"He can't say with just the information I gave him. He'd really need to see the pieces for himself."

"I can't believe we are having this conversation. No, wait - it's you. I can totally believe we are having this conversation! Only you would know a big time jewel thief in New York. Do you really think this guy can or would be of any help in recovering Mother Houston's jewelry?"

"If there is a finder's fee, then, yes, I do. He knows the underside of the business and he can provide contacts in just about every major U.S. and European city."

This had to be one of the most unusual discussions Maude had ever had. "Seriously?"

"Seriously."

"Exactly how am I supposed to suggest this to Mrs. Houston?"

"Are you kidding? She'd offer you a kidney for a contact like Basil." Christine handed her a small piece of paper with a name and phone number printed neatly in her own hand. "Just give her this; he's expecting her call."

Maude was a little concerned with the idea of Alexandra Houston speaking directly with a jewel thief. "I'm guessing she'll just pass the number on to her private investigator." Maude was hoping she would.

"No. Basil won't deal with anyone but her." Seeing the look on Maude's face, she continued, "It's not like they are meeting in a dark alley. It's just a phone call, and really, Basil is a great guy. There's no need to worry."

"That can't be his real name."

Christine smiled, "If you saw him, you would not care what his name was, and neither would Mrs. Houston."

Shaking her head, Maude laughed as she reached for her phone. "I can't believe I'm doing this, but I'll call and let her know there is a cat burglar who is willing to help."

"He's a broker."

"Sure he is."

* * *

Lester chuckled at the confused look on Maude's face as she spoke to the building inspector. "You go ahead, sweetie, and try to outsmart me." He walked away from the window still talking to himself. "I've still got a few tricks up my sleeves." It really didn't matter if the inspector issued a summons or not. With a few well-chosen lamps and curtains, he had inadvertently manipulated her into spending considerable time and money in order to distinguish her storefront from his. He smiled, wondering what else he might do to send her jumping into action. After a while, she would realize that he was in control, and that's when he would deliver the final blow. She had it coming after all the trouble she had caused him.

Lester had never seen Maude in person until the morning he walked into her shop to announce that he was starting a new business next door, but something about her was so familiar. It wasn't just that he thought he knew her; he also realized that he detested her. The feeling stayed with him for a few days until he recalled the warning of his ex-wife. "You are connected to that woman in your past life," she had insisted, although he was certain he had never met Maude. Dawn had felt the connection that day she had come to the shop to confront Maude for stealing the building out from underneath them. She could be such a drama queen when she slipped into what he often referred to as 'psychic mode' and rambled on about the spirit world, but he hadn't paid much attention to her at the time.

After meeting Maude and feeling a palpable sense of familiarity mixed with contempt, he began to remember Dawn's ominous warning. The reason he relentlessly pursued the opening of his own shop was evident to her the moment she laid eyes on Maude. "You have business yet to finish with that woman and it will not end well." She could not get him to understand the gravity of her words and, ultimately, Dawn left him. Lester had never really believed his wife had any special abilities. After all, if she were truly psychic, wouldn't she have made her fortune in Vegas or at the track? What's more, she thought if Lester continued to pursue the idea of owning an antique shop, he would meet the same fate he had before. "You paid a steep price for whatever transpired between the two of you in the past," Dawn told him, making it clear that she would not stick around if he ended up in trouble again. There was no point in arguing with her. Lester thought she had finally lost her mind. She'd get over it in a day or two. Instead, Dawn left without another word and never came back. He considered calling her to see if there was anything else about this supposed past life connection, but decided not to give her the satisfaction of knowing he now suspected what she had said was true.

Lester's anger and resentment toward a person he had never met before were explained as past life experience according to the few sources he had Googled on the subject. The feeling that there was a shared past between them became stronger the more he watched and interacted with Maude. He came to realize that there was also a definite sense that their previous connection had not ended well for him, although details of their past remained elusive.

He became so angry over Maude's role in his downfall that he never even stopped to think about the significance of these revelations or why he was so certain that what Dawn had told him was true. Resentment blinded him and didn't allow him to consider any behavior on his part that might change the outcome of their interactions in this life. All he could see was that Maude had caused him great suffering and that she would continue to do so in this life unless he stopped her. Dawn had been right: Maude and Lester had unfinished business, and he was in the perfect position to finish it.

A year ago, Lester was interested in the Antique Lamp Company and Gift Emporium as a front for his illicit business interests. If he could sweet-talk a few packed widows out of their family heirlooms at a reasonable price, he'd turn around and sell them to the highest bidder. If not, he knew a few people who could get around even the most expensive security system for a cut of the take. The original plan included Dawn, who would have run the retail end of the business and identified the marks. When that fell through, he realized he could easily do the same thing from his own shop next door, even without Dawn. Putting Maude out of business was an added bonus, but the more he watched her, the stronger his connection to the past became. She had ruined him and she needed to pay with more than just her livelihood.

* * *

"I would have loved to see the look on Alexandra Houston's face during that conversation," Don told his wife as he helped empty the truck of a week's worth of groceries.

"Oddly enough, she didn't sound that surprised." Maude laughed, handing him another bag. "Be careful, that one has the eggs in it." She continued talking as they hauled the bags into the back of the shop and upstairs to their apartment. "I'm just hoping she shares whatever details come of this connection."

"I still can't believe you hooked up one of our best clients with a jewel thief."

"Christine says he's a broker."

"Sure he is."

Maude laughed again. "That's just what I told her."

"Did you ask how this man would be able to recover two hundred thousand dollars in jewelry?"

"No. I was afraid to ask, although I'm hoping to get a full debriefing from Mrs. Houston if he manages to pull it off."

"Something tells me she won't want to know the details...you know, plausible deniability and all that."

The laughter faded as Maude realized that Mrs. Houston had been the third customer of theirs who had been burglarized in the last few weeks. "Don't you find that odd? I mean we have been in business a long time and I don't think I have ever heard that any of our clients had been robbed."

"Well, as you said, you have not heard. Most people aren't eager to broadcast that kind of news. It makes them appear vulnerable, plus we don't actually know it was Mrs. Billingsley who was robbed." He looked briefly around the kitchen. "Hey, did you bring the mail up?"

"Yeah, it's on the counter. I didn't get a chance to look at it yet. Are you expecting anything?"

"Just an invoice."

Maude wasn't yet ready to give up the discussion of the robberies. "You don't seriously think there's any link between those women being robbed within days of visiting our shop..."

"No, I don't. What are you thinking? I doubt someone was parked on the street watching our shop. I mean, something like that wouldn't get past Christine."

Realizing Don was right, Maude laughed and gave up the topic.

Don opened the refrigerator and surveyed the possibilities for dinner. "Were you busy today?"

"No, but we had a visit from the building inspector." Maude gave him the details of her brief conversations earlier with the building inspector and their troublesome new neighbor, adding an appeal just to let it go. Much to her relief, Don agreed to steer clear of Lester Northrup.

"There's only so much the guy can do, because he actually needs us...well, you, really." Don told her.

"How do you figure that?" She took the half-frozen package of ground beef from him, placed it back in the fridge and handed him a takeout menu instead.

"Well, you're the one who has turned this shop into a destination for downtown shoppers. It's all the unique gifts and vintage jewelry that brings most of the people in the door. Don placed the menu on the counter in favor of a quick perusal of the mail. "He certainly isn't smart enough to build a business like this from the ground up like you did."

"Like we did, Don. We built this business together."

"Maudie, you are the one who created the 'Gift Emporium' part of the Antique Lamp Company and Gift Emporium. I couldn't have done what you did either. I think all these bullshit games he's playing are less about some revenge trip and more his way of dealing with the fact that he needs you to stay in business. He doesn't like you, but he needs you, and, somewhere deep down inside, he knows it."

"I don't know about that, and I can't run the business worrying about what ideas or clients he might steal." Maude blew out a sigh of frustration. "Why can't Lester make his living poaching off of someone else?

"We're just lucky, I guess. By the way, a couple of these envelopes are addressed to him. Want me to bring them over there tomorrow?"

"No, don't go over there!" Maude was surprised at the urgency in her own voice. Regaining composure, she added, "You won't be able to resist confronting him. Besides, you said you'd drop the boys at camp early tomorrow on your way to Ellicottville. Just leave them on the counter and I'll take them over."

"You think I'm gonna get into it with Lester. Don't worry, Maude. As long as he doesn't cause any real trouble, I'll stay out of it." Don's stomach rumbled and he took up the menu again.

Later that night, Maude had what she considered a brilliant idea. Instead of trying to piece her dream journals together to try and make sense of them, she thought she would build a story around the dreams as she recorded them and let her creative mind fill in the gaps. Perhaps she would be able to determine her new fate and have another novel in the bargain. Feverish with ambition, she wrote well into the night.

Chapter Seventeen

Martha pulled her trap into the long drive of the asylum with Alva Awalte's carriage just behind her. It was their usual habit to arrive at the same time and use the few minutes as they walked toward the building to discuss any important cases, procedures or treatments that might prove problematic that day. Both women were thus far pleased with the arrangement they had worked out and were especially delighted to see much improvement in several of the patients who had been labeled incurable.

Alva approached Martha's trap, a pint sized bottle in her hand. "What's that?" Martha asked.

"It is my remedy for pain relief. I thought Miss Potter might benefit from it."

Martha read the ingredients printed neatly on the bottle: oil of cajeput, sassafras, origanum, hemlock, cedar and powdered capsicum mixed in alcohol. It was likely an effective combination, although Martha suspected that the oppressive heat and humidity in the laundry were the likely culprits for Miss Potter's headaches. "Aye, well, I should think so, but we will have to see her in the hospital this morning. Mr.

Leonard insisted she be transferred yesterday," Martha told her.

Miss Potter had experienced severe headaches several times since her initial examination. A few days of rest seemed to put her at ease, only to have the problem recur when she returned to her duties. Martha argued that perhaps a reassignment to the kitchen, or better yet, the garden might end the problem, but Mr. Leonard wouldn't hear of it. "Clearly she is feigning illness in order to shirk her duties," he had told her. He was certain Miss Potter's deception would be exposed by the hospital staff. Martha wisely had kept that to herself, knowing it would only irritate Alva.

"The man is a fool." Alva thought it absurd to burden the hospital department with another patient who would be better treated in her own bed. It spoke of the lack of confidence the Keeper of the Insane Asylum had in their abilities as healers, something Martha was used to, but Alva was not.

"Aye, ye'll get no argument from me on that point. In a day or two, when the pain has passed, he'll have her down there in the cellar again until it starts all over again. Eventually he'll see the way of it."

"So we must wait for him to see for himself?"

"Aye." There was nothing Martha could add to her reply that would make any sense and she did not have the heart to tell Alva that it was possible Mr. Leonard might just persist in his opinion that a reassignment of duties was not the answer.

Martha's attention was diverted to the prisoner carriage approaching the asylum from the back. Alva picked up on her distraction and followed her gaze.

"Dear God, she is but a child!" The two women watched as the attendants led a girl of perhaps fifteen or sixteen from inside what could best be described as a cage on wheels. She was tall, but had not yet developed the curves of a woman. The poor thing was dressed in rags and her hands were bound in front of her in a leather restraining muff. She looked terrified and tried in vain to resist as they pushed her toward the door.

Alva stared at the child, hoping to catch her eye, wanting to connect. Finally, the girl looked in her direction and held her gaze. Martha could see her begin to relax and walk willingly. Alva turned to her. "Go and fetch Dr. Nolan immediately. We will need all the help we can get to release this poor child. She is one of us."

Martha just stood and stared at the girl, wondering what could have gone so wrong in her young life that she ended up here. "No, we must speak to the attendants before they get up to the third floor. We'll never get past Kraus once the lass gets up there. Mr. Morrissey!" Martha ran toward the attendant with Alva right behind her.

"Best you keep away, Dr. Quinn. She's a dangerous one. Mr. Leonard gave us strict instructions. She's to go straight to the shed." Morrissey was referring to a small wood frame building that had been hastily built more than a decade earlier when the old insane department had become overcrowded. Even with construction of a new building for the insane, the shed was still pressed into service when the cells on the third floor were full. It was now in a terrible state of disrepair, unfit for human habitation and entirely inappropriate to house a young girl.

As Martha got closer, she noticed the girl had a rather deep bruise around her left eye. "She's hurt. Surely, there is no harm in examining her injuries. She is restrained, after all." Martha was already coming forward, opening her medical bag as she moved toward the girl.

Alva moved to take the bag and helped the girl over to the bench by the big elm tree. "See what you can find out," she mumbled to Martha as she helped the girl sit down.

Martha was glad it had been Morrissey and Felber transporting the patient. They would at least talk to her. Motioning for the attendants to follow her out of earshot, she still spoke in hushed tones. "She's just a lass. Surely she doesn't belong here."

Mr. Morrissey shook his head, no happier about the girl's arrival than the women were. "I'm afraid she does, Ma'am. The Justice of the Peace in Chautauqua County sent her here. They've no room for the violent ones."

"What has she done?"

"She come from the orphan home to Roach's tannery in Laona," Felber told her. "Mr. Roach himself said she attacked him and darn near killed him."

Martha could hardly credit what she was hearing. "Why?"

"Don't know, but she's a strong one, so she is. Took Morrissey and me both to get her in the cage." He leaned down and rubbed his thigh. "She kicked me right hard, so she did."

Martha glanced at the door hoping Mr. Leonard had not seen them talking. If they didn't hurry, he'd be out here wondering what was taking so long, and furious that she and Alva had interfered with his direct orders. "May we have a word with her?"

Now it was Felber's turn to look toward the door. "Aye, but make it quick. We'll all get the shove for sure if Mr. Leonard sees the two of ye out here."

"There's swelling, but nothing is broken," Alva told her as Martha came toward them. Luckily, they were obscured by the branches of the tree and the prisoner carriage stood in front of them, so they could not be seen by anyone looking from the door or the ground floor windows. The two attendants were standing by the carriage with their backs to the women, more concerned with being caught than with what was actually going on behind them.

There was no time to gain the girl's trust. If they were going to help, she needed to tell them what had transpired between her and the owner of the tannery. Martha told her that and after a moment's consideration she spoke. "He barely fed us, us who came from the orphan home, only bread and coffee at midday. My brother and I decided to try it out on our own, but he found us." The girl shuddered as she recalled what happened next. "He laid poor Julius out with one punch. He's dead. I saw his fetch." Her voice broke and tears welled in his eyes. "It scared me and I screamed."

"Did ye harm the man?" The girl looked suspicious and Martha tried to put her mind at ease. "Ye were frightened, I know, but Mr. Roach said ye attacked him."

"I hit him before he could get at me. He wasn't expecting it and stumbled, so I ran, but the constable caught me. He gave me a wallop when I tried to get away." The girl gingerly touched the bruise around her eye, as if to see if it still hurt.

"Young lady, what is your name?" Alva asked.

"Patrice...Patrice Gulligan."

"Come with me, Patrice." Without another word, Alva quickly ushered the girl toward her carriage parked a few yards away on the other side of the tree. She helped her inside and then spoke quickly to the driver. "Wait until the men have gone inside and then take her home. Mrs. Metzker will see to it that she is freed from these restraints, cleaned and fed. I shall be along in a few hours." She closed the door to the carriage and turned to find Martha just behind her, eyes wide with shock.

Martha looked quickly in the direction of the attendants, who were still deep in conversation. "What are ye doing?" she asked in a panicked whisper.

"You heard her, did you not? I am certainly not leaving a child in the hands of Mason Leonard, and worse yet, Mr. Kraus." She pointed to the wooded structure. "That shed is not fit for man nor beast and you would have a child in there? My housekeeper can see to her until I get home."

"And then what? Will ye take the lass in?"

"If I must, Martha. She saw the tannery owner kill her brother. I sense there is more to this story than she is willing to tell us right now. She is not safe here."

Although she could not condone Alva's actions, neither could she argue with the intentions behind them. "Just how will ye go about explainin' that she's gone?"

"Just leave that to me, dear." She turned and walked calmly toward the two attendants and told them matter-of-factly that the girl had run off. She held her hand up to stop them when they made to give chase after her. "Now, gentleman, it is not unusual for patients to abscond from here, and you are unlikely to lose your positions over it. However, should you mention that she ran off from us, Mr. Leonard will be furious that you defied his orders and allowed two women near a dangerous patient. Surely we will all lose our positions." She paused for a moment, looking like the schoolmarm nobody would dare cross. "So, tell me, how will you explain this to Mr. Leonard?"

Martha stood behind Alva, waiting for the two men to make up their minds. Mr. Felber rubbed his sore leg again recalling the struggle to contain the child the first time and not looking forward to it again. "She chewed off the muff, so she did. When we stopped to take a piss, she jumped out of the wagon and ran off."

"Gave Felber here a right good hoof to the leg, so she did," Morrissey chimed in. "I chased her through the woods for near a quarter hour." He thought their explanation would be sufficient to keep them out of trouble with the Keeper. Mrs. Awalte was right. It wouldn't be the first time a patient had gotten away from them. "Still, Mr. Leonard will be a bit huffed to hear the girl's run off. Mr. Roach insisted she be sent to Ovid at the first opportunity. He'll check sooner or later to see it was done."

"He'll be mad as a March hare to find she's run off," Felber added. "Given the choice, the wee wretch may well have chosen the shed to wanderin' the streets with the likes o' Morris Roach after her."

Martha gave a quick nod, understanding what they were trying to tell her. "Best ye get in there and tell Mr. Leonard. He'll not be any kinder to ye if ye wait." The men didn't notice the carriage heading down the long drive as they went inside.

"The girl has come from Laona?" Alva asked and Martha nodded. "We must keep her well-hidden. I know of Morris Roach. He is a fierce man and has friends on the Board of Supervisors in Chautauqua County. Mr. Leonard will be huffed indeed if they get wind that a violent patient transferred to our insane department has run off."

"Do ye think they'd find out?" Martha asked.

"If Morris Roach is determined to see Patrice transferred to the Willard Asylum in Ovid, he may well use what connections he has to do so," Alva told her. "It will surely reflect poorly on Mr. Leonard if there is an issue between the two counties over the escape of a dangerous patient."

"Let us hope he does not intend to follow up on the matter."

"Indeed." Alva turned in the direction of the poorhouse hospital. "Now, shall we see to Miss Potter?"

After a brief trip to the hospital department, the two women set out to do a general tour of the asylum wards. It was a regular part of Martha's routine, but had become far more productive since Alva had joined her. She was teaching Martha to read the energy given off by each patient, which helped her to understand the things they often had difficulty telling her. Sometimes it was because they couldn't bear to speak of it, and other times because they did not know themselves. In the weeks since Alva had joined Martha, five patients had been discharged as cured, of which three had been thought to be incurable.

Usually the women were more receptive than the men, but there was a young war veteran with whom Alva was making some progress. There was another young male entity constantly hovering around Andrew Faulkner, a man named Thomas Mooney, who had died during the war. That much she had learned. Still, whatever had passed between them that was causing Andrew's nightmares - dreams so frightening that he woke each night screaming - Alva could not determine. It seemed that neither Andrew nor his comrade in spirit were able to reveal what had brought them together again.

At first, Andrew did not credit the idea that the spirit of Thomas Mooney was with him, but the more Alva described his young friend, the more he could not deny it. Mooney had been able to tell her about the girl Andrew had kissed under a large magnolia tree in Virginia, and how her father nearly chased him all the way back to their encampment. Sadly, there was no person alive but Andrew Faulkner who knew that tale, and so he began to listen.

"Hello, Mr. Faulkner. How are you feeling today?" Alva asked. She could see from the dark smudges under his eyes that he had not slept well again last night.

"I'm tired, Mrs. Awalte." Andrew spoke to Alva, while Martha looked on. Although Martha was a gifted

215

seer and was beginning to focus her ability to pick up on people's emotions and motivations, she was not a medium and could not see the dead.

"Your friend Thomas is still with you."

"Can't ye tell him to leave me be?"

"Andrew, you can tell him to leave yourself, but you know why he is still here."

"I can't, Mrs. Awalte; I just can't talk about it. Please don't make me."

"I would not force you to speak of something that troubles you so, but I have told you before: Thomas wants you to move on from this. He does not blame you."

"I see it over and over again in my head. Every time I shut my eyes, the same horrible thing every time. Tell him to stop."

"Do you think Thomas is making you see what you don't want to see?"

Andrew was sitting in the chair. He began to rock slowly back and forth as he became more agitated. "Yes. How can he forgive me if he keeps showing me what I did?"

"Maybe he wants you to see something you continue to overlook. Maybe he is trying to show you that it wasn't your fault." She placed a hand on his arm both to gain his full attention and to calm him. "Maybe we can discuss it and I can help you to see what he is trying to show you. Will you think about that for next time?"

He nodded.

* * *

While Mason Leonard should have been pleased, particularly at having spared the county the burden of paying indefinitely for the care of those patients whom he had determined to be incurable, instead he was more irritable and condescending than ever toward Martha. As soon as the women descended the stairs, Martha was called into his office. "He wants her, too," Mrs. Boswell told her, pointing at Alva, who usually had no direct contact with the Keeper.

"Ye wanted to see us, Mr. Leonard?" Martha stood in front of his desk, with Alva just behind her.

"An inmate was to be brought here from Chautauqua County this morning. The accompanying note from Justice Pennyworth told me that this woman is very dangerous." He paused and gave each woman a penetrating stare. "The attendants responsible for her transfer tell me that she has absconded just outside the city. Are you aware of this?"

"No, sir," Martha answered and Alva shook her head in agreement, understanding that it would not be appropriate to speak. Leonard gave her no status other than that of an assistant and expected Martha to answer for the both of them.

"Mr. Kraus reported having seen the both of you speaking to the two attendants when they arrived." Leonard nodded to the attendant, who had followed them in and was standing by the door.

Martha wondered if Kraus had seen them from the third floor window, if so, what else had he seen? "We did speak, but nothing more than a cordial greeting," she informed the Keeper.

"I see. That is all." Leonard went back to his work and left the women to see themselves out.

They headed back up towards the women's ward and waited until they were out of earshot of Mrs. Boswell, who had been outside the office in the hopes that she might overhear something interesting. "Will he search for her?" Alva whispered.

"I don't know." Martha stopped at the top of the stairs, hesitated for a moment, and then asked Alva a question she wasn't entirely sure she wanted answered. "Do ye think Kraus saw us?"

"You were in the same room with the man as I was. What do you think?" It was Alva's usual answer to a question like that. She was trying to get Martha to pay more attention to her feelings and impressions when she interacted with people.

Martha's expression indicated that this was not the time for a teaching moment. "All I felt was their dislike of me."

"That should tell you what you need to know. The Keeper does not like you and he does not trust you. That does not mean he will act on any information Mr. Kraus might have given him." She continued to explain in response to Martha's confusion. "To openly accuse you would be an admission he has lost control of his staff. He would also have to acknowledge that the two attendants defied his direct orders. I do not think he would do that."

"Aye, ye're right, not publicly, anyway," Martha told her as they made their way down the hall.

Part Three

Chapter Eighteen

At the end of the day, Alva came home to find Patrice Gulligan scrubbed, in clean clothes and sound asleep. "Did she speak to you?" she asked Mrs. Metzker.

"A bit," the housekeeper answered, "but she listened, too."

"And what did you tell her?"

"That she was safe here, and that you would see that no harm came to her." Miss Gulligan was not the first person nor even the first child in need that had been entrusted into Bethany Metzker's care. She had worked in the household of Alva Awalte for more than twenty years, during which time she had fed the empty bellies and dressed the wounds, both physical and emotional, of a dozen or more men, women and children who had needed rescuing. They had all been gifted with the second sight or the ability to see the dead. Alva hid them until they were able to recover from whatever cruelty had been inflicted upon them and then saw them safely into the hands of someone who would nurture their gifts and help them to find a way in this world filled with fear and hatred of that which lay beyond the boundaries of tolerance.

"Her story, so far as I know, is troublesome," Alva told her. The fact that the girl had been the second person to have been transferred to the Buffalo asylum confirmed her suspicions that many of the Spiritualists were no longer safe in Laona. She had managed to find many a safe haven among the Free Thinkers of Chautauqua County over the years for the troubled souls that found their way to her door. The majority of the Spiritualists there had the resources and connections that placed them above what trouble Constable Schaeffer could cause, but the poor souls like Felicity Taylor and Patrice Gulligan, with neither of those things, were not so fortunate.

"Where will she go?" Mrs. Metzker asked. "Surely she is not safe in Buffalo after what she has told me."

"First I must hear the rest of the girl's story; only then can we decide where she will go. Tell me what you have learned." Alva spoke with more confidence than she felt. If Laona or the surrounding area of Cassadaga Lake was no longer safe, she would have to reach out to other Spiritualist communities. There were friends in Ohio, Pennsylvania and Massachusetts, but was there time to send word and arrange for travel so far away? She suspected not.

* * *

"I spoke to the broker about the Hackstein house," Johnny told Martha as they walked home from the livery. "We can have it straightaway if ye're still sure."

"That's wonderful news."

"Aye, 'tis, but ye've somethin' else on yer mind and there's no sense in denyin' it."

Martha stopped for a minute to make up her mind and then asked her husband if he had a mind to take a wee stroll. "I've somethin' I must tell ye, but we dare not speak of it on the street."

Johnny raised his brows but allowed himself to be steered toward North Division Street. They spoke of inconsequential things during the fifteen-minute walk to Alva Awalte's house. Mrs. Metzker answered the door. "Mrs. Awalte thought you might come to call," she informed Martha as she moved aside to let them in.

"I do apologize for the hour," Martha said as she made her way into the hall.

"Not at all, Dr. Quinn, your business is urgent, I think. You will stay for dinner, yes?" Without waiting for an answer, Mrs. Metzker showed them into the sitting room where Alva was waiting for them.

"Martha, I was hoping you'd come." Alva stood to greet them. "We have much to discuss." She gave a quick nod of her head in Johnny's direction. "Mr. Quinn, how good of you to join her. Your thoughts on the matter at hand will be welcome." Turning to the housekeeper, she added, "Mrs. Metzker, please set two additional places at the table."

Johnny listened while Mrs. Awalte filled him in on what she knew of Patrice Gulligan. "It is worse than we expected," Alva told him. "Mr. Roach, it seems, has an eye for the older boys from the orphan home. They do not need to be paid and he receives compensation from the county for their keep. They do the work of grown men and are fed scraps." Alva grew angry as she continued telling Patrice's story. "He is heavy-handed with the boys if they fail to do their tasks. Our Miss

223

Gulligan had seen the darkness in that man's soul. Worse yet, she and her brother came upon Mr. Roach beating one of the other boys nearly to death. That is why they ran off, and likely why her brother Julian lost his life. Mr. Roach has the blood of that young boy on his hands, and likely the other boy as well. Patrice was fairly certain he could not have survived his punishment."

Johnny weighed his words carefully. He, too, was outraged over the circumstances that had brought Patrice Gulligan to them, but he also knew that things like this happened all the time. "'Tis an outrage, to be sure, but I doubt much would come of it were the lass to accuse Roach of murder," Johnny told her.

Alva nodded, understanding all too well what little interest there would be in the death of two orphans. "That was his hope, I'm sure, when he claimed Patrice was insane, but there would be an investigation just the same when the boys turned up missing. In all likelihood, the orphanage would stop sending him children, if only for a while."

"Aye, he would have to hire men for wages. That would surely take a bite out of his profits," Martha added.

"So the question is, how safe is the lass here in Buffalo?" Johnny asked.

"I think Mr. Roach will make sure she is sent to the Willard asylum," Alva told him. "Better to have her locked far away in a cell for the chronic insane."

Johnny turned to his wife. "Ye know Mason Leonard better than I. Will he go lookin' for her?"

"Aye, if he has an idea that the board would get wind of it, he would. He may have Kraus out lookin' already." Martha went on to tell him that she feared Kraus had seen Alva's driver take Patrice away.

The conversation continued over dinner. "We must get the girl out of Buffalo as soon as can be arranged," Alva said. "I have friends in Cape Cod who would take her in at least until other arrangements can be made.

"To be sure, if Leonard suspects ye've had a hand in her disappearance, he'll have someone watchin' yer house," Johnny said. "It will not be easy to leave here."

"Mr. Quinn, we have outsmarted a constable or two in our time," Alva told him. "I'm sure we can outwit Mr. Kraus. We will allow the poor child her sleep and be ready to leave at first light."

It was just getting dark when Alva saw her guests to the door. She stood by her front window, having moved the drapes just enough to see Martha as she and her husband made their way down the street. After they had passed a good distance from the elm tree across from her house, she saw a large person descend from it and follow them toward Main Street. Although it was difficult to be certain in the dark, Alva was reasonably sure the man was Kraus. "Mrs. Metzker, wake the girl! There is no time to waste!"

Mrs. Metzker hurried into the sitting room where her employer still stood, watching as the man continued to follow the couple at a distance. "Mr. Quinn was right; the house was being watched. Mr. Leonard will surely come once he realizes I live here. I will tell Mr.

Metzker to bring the carriage to the back door. They must leave within the hour."

Bethany Metzker nodded in agreement as she exited the room. Forty minutes later she helped her husband settle a groggy Patrice Gulligan into the carriage. "Be safe," she told him, passing up a basket of provisions for the trip.

"The girl will come to no harm, and neither will I," Brian Metzker assured his wife. He patted the breast pocket of his coat, double checking that the letter of explanation Alva had hastily written to her friends in Massachusetts was secure and slowly guided the carriage out the back drive onto Eagle Street. It would not do to arouse the neighbors with a dramatic exit. He would quietly make his way to Genesee Street and exit the city, thereby avoiding the Keeper, who would undoubtedly be traveling toward the house on Main Street.

"Come, Mrs. Metzker." Alva's words were both calm and quiet. "I suspect we will have visitors soon enough."

* * *

Kraus stood in the main hall of the Keeper's quarters. Mr. Leonard had insisted on a full report regardless of the hour. It was quite late. Mrs. Quinn and her husband had stayed in the house on Division Street long after the dinner hour. He followed them home per Mr. Leonard's orders and then made his way back to the asylum. Exhausted from his efforts, Kraus was eager for his bed and not pleased to be waiting still. Why Leonard had not accused the women outright was beyond him. From his perspective of the third floor window, Kraus had seen them lead the girl under the tree. He had been going down to report this observation to the Keeper and found the two attendants in his office reporting that the girl had run off. If Leonard hadn't insisted on making him wait, Kraus would have made his report in the presence of the attendants and demanded they explain themselves. He could not understand why Leonard had insisted he not confront the men. All of this sneaking around in the middle of the night was foolishness. Leonard should have dismissed the lot of them and been done with it.

"Mr. Leonard will see you now." The housekeeper was similarly displeased at the lateness of the hour as she showed Kraus to the Keeper's study.

"That will be all for tonight, Mrs. Hurley," Leonard told the woman as she closed the study door. Redirecting his attention to Kraus, he asked, "What did you learn?"

"I followed her to the livery on Main Street. From there she and her husband walked to North Division Street. They spent four hours at number 248 and then walked home."

Leonard opened the drawer to his desk and took out the city directory. He spent a few moments thumbing through the pages. "It is as I expected. Number 248 belongs to Alva Awalte. If they have taken the girl, she is surely there. We must go back there immediately. Prepare my carriage."

* * *

227

An hour had passed before the clattering of hooves on cobblestone announced the arrival of the Keeper, time enough for Alva and her housekeeper to change into their nightclothes and put out the lamps in their chambers. When Mason Leonard pounded on the front door, the house was dark. "Take a look around the back," he instructed Kraus.

Not wishing for Mrs. Metzker to handle the man alone, Alva followed her to the door. "Mr. Leonard, whatever can I do for you at this late hour?" she asked, stepping aside to allow the man to enter.

"Mrs. Awalte, I've reason to believe that you are harboring the patient that escaped this afternoon." Leonard saw no need for a formal greeting or apology for the intrusion in the middle of the night. "I demand that you turn her over immediately."

"Mr. Leonard, I can assure you I am not in the habit of taking dangerous patients into my home."

"Do not try to deceive me, Mrs. Awalte. Mr. Kraus saw you and Mrs. Quinn usher the patient away from the prisoner carriage."

"Mr. Kraus is mistaken." Alva locked eyes with the Keeper and held his attention for the few seconds that were needed to learn what she needed to know. He was certain the girl was here. That was a good thing. If she could just keep him busy long enough for Mr. Metzker and the girl to be well on their way. "Search the house if it will put your mind at ease."

"I will do just that, madam."

Alva and Mrs. Metzker sat calmly in the parlor for a full hour while Mr. Leonard searched every room, closet and cupboard large enough to hide a person.

Kraus had gone to check around the back of the house and barn and found the carriage was missing along with the two horses that pulled it.

"My daughter left this afternoon to visit her aunt in Erie," she told Leonard when he questioned her about it.

"Madam, you have made a grave mistake associating with Mrs. Quinn and you have placed the good citizens of this city in peril by putting a violent woman back into civilized society."

It had been no problem to keep her temper in check until now, but it took considerable effort not to remind Leonard that the violent woman he was so concerned about was really a terrified young girl. "I have done no such thing, Mr. Leonard. Should you care to take the trip to Pennsylvania, Barbara is staying in the home of Hans Awalte on Sixth Street." Alva did not raise her voice. It would serve no purpose to agitate the man further. "Now, sir, I must allow my housekeeper back to her bed." She walked toward the door and opened it.

Leonard motioned for Kraus to take up his position at the reins. "Hurry! They could not have gone far!"

"In which direction? They are ahead of us by an hour or more," Kraus pointed out. He wasn't foolish enough to suggest that the girl may never have been here in the first place or that if she was here, she was likely long gone. Still, Kraus was tired of this business and felt compelled to argue the futility of giving chase in the middle of the night.

Leonard considered the point and heaved a frustrated sigh. "Back to the asylum, then." Kraus was right, the patient was likely long gone, and Leonard needed some time to think about the possible consequences of that. Were it not for the letter from Justice Pennyworth that accompanied her, he wouldn't have given it a second thought. A patient who absconded was a patient they no longer had to clothe or feed, violent or not. Morris Roach had told the constable that she had been odd from the beginning, the bastard of a feeble-minded woman who fancied herself a Free Thinker. There was no hope for her from the minute she drew a breath, for when she took her first, her mother took her last. Roach only sought to provide her with domestic skills so that she might one day make her own way in the world, but the girl was violent. Had Roach been a slighter man, he may very well have met his end when she brutally attacked him.

Justice Pennyworth thought Leonard the only man who could safely house such a dangerous patient, but Morris Roach insisted that Patrice Gulligan had a long history of violence and could not be cured. Pennyworth could not in good conscience send a young girl to Willard, an asylum for the incurably insane, and sentenced her instead to six months at the Buffalo asylum in the hopes that, under Leonard's expert care, a cure might be managed. It was very likely, the Justice of the Peace wrote in his letter to Leonard, that Morris Roach would use what influence he could to see the patient locked away for good.

What an accomplishment it would have been to have seen the girl cured upon discharge. Leonard was very pleased with the discharge rate recently and had no doubt that under his management she could be turned around. Now instead of receiving accolades from the Board of Supervisors for his tireless efforts, he would likely receive a formal reprimand for allowing the patient to escape. That insufferable Martha Quinn and her accomplice had no idea what they had done. Such an act of defiance could not go unpunished.

Chapter Nineteen

Michael walked down to the barn to find the wagon hitched up and Daniel at the reins. "Where are ye off to, then?"

"Ma has a long list of places," Daniel told him, "...again."

"To be sure she's kept ye busy this week," Michael commented. Ciara had Daniel running errands on behalf of the orphan asylum all week, leaving him no time to himself when his chores about the farm were finished. It had also not escaped Michael's notice that Felicity seemed unusually busy as well. The two young people hadn't spent a moment alone together since their first kiss behind the barn, which Michael had heard about from his very distressed wife. There was no point in telling her there was nothing to worry about, although he did try. Ciara would need time to adjust to the idea that her son was in love.

"Aye, she's been a bit cross with me as well. Have I done somethin' to anger her?"

Michael sighed and leaned against the carriage. "Yer ma's not angry with ye. She's just scared ye might leave." Daniel looked confused and so his father explained. "She saw ye the other day, with Felicity behind the barn. Things have changed between the two of ye, it seems."

Daniel smiled. "Aye, so they have. I'd have told the both of ye, but I haven't had a minute alone with her since that day. I'd wanted to have a few things settled between us before I spoke to ye." He paused, looking confused. "Ma doesn't approve?"

"I don't think it's that. As I told ye, I think she is afraid the two of ye will leave Buffalo."

"I don't even know if she'll marry me, so 'tis a bit early to consider the matter, I think."

"So ye intend to marry her?"

"I do, if she'll have me."

Michael reached up gave his son an affectionate clap on the shoulder. "I'm that happy for ye!"

"I'm glad of it, Da, but what about Ma?"

Something had settled in Daniel. Michael could see it in his eyes and in his smile as he spoke of Felicity and marriage. When Ciara decided to look, she would see it too, he was sure. "Give her some time. She'll come 'round." He looked in the direction of the house and saw Ciara coming toward them. "A long list of places, ye say? There should be time enough for a bit of conversation along the way, I think."

* * *

Mrs. Boswell gave a quick rap on the door, waited for permission and when it wasn't forthcoming, knocked again and entered. "Mr. Leonard, I'm sorry to disturb you, but..."

"As well you should be, Mrs. Boswell. Didn't I just give you strict orders not thirty minutes ago that I was not to be disturbed under any circumstances?" The Keeper interrupted her, barely looking up from his desk to chastise her.

"You did sir, but Mr. Prowett is here." As Keeper of the Insane Asylum, Mason Leonard served under Nicholas Prowett, the Superintendent of the Poor. Leonard's contact with Prowett was limited to quarterly meetings unless there was a problem. Mrs. Boswell now had the Keeper's full attention.

"Did he state his business?" Leonard asked.

"No, sir, he did not."

The Keeper rose from his desk and walked toward the door. "Show him in, Mrs. Boswell."

Mr. Prowett came in and Leonard gave a short bow. "You look well, Nicholas. What brings you to the asylum today?" he asked, gesturing toward the seat in front of his desk.

Prowett dispensed with a formal greeting and got right to his business. "I have received a letter from a Morris Roach of Laona. He seems very concerned about a young woman who was sent here a few days ago." Prowett took the letter from his jacket pocket and scanned it briefly. "Patrice Gulligan is her name. Are you familiar with this case?"

Leonard appraised Prowett's demeanor carefully and nodded. "Yes, the patient arrived earlier this week, along with a letter from the Justice of the Peace. He mentioned Mr. Roach's concerns."

"He feels strongly that the patient should be transferred immediately to the asylum in Ovid. What is your assessment?"

Leonard appeared to consider the question, but was trying to recall the letter from Justice Pennyworth. After a moment, he said, "The patient is only sixteen, Nicholas. I agree with the Justice of the Peace that we should wait and see what we can do for her here before we send a young girl to the Willard Asylum."

"Very well, I shall expect a report at our next meeting." Prowett rose from the chair. "If she is not showing progress, you will transfer her to Ovid. There is no sense in supporting a patient at this institution who in all likelihood should have gone there in the first place. Mr. Roach made it clear that he is not without influence, and I do not want the Board involved in this. Are we clear, sir?"

Leonard stood and met the eyes of the Superintendent. "Yes, we are."

Prowett left and Leonard immediately consulted his journal to confirm that the next quarterly meeting was in two weeks. That meant that he had fourteen days to either produce Patrice Gulligan or a record showing the girl had been transferred to Ovid. Producing a false report would do no good. If Morris Roach was concerned enough to contact the Superintendent, he was likely to follow up on any transfer. "Damn those women!" he said aloud. He was certain that Martha Quinn and her assistant had a hand in the girl's disappearance. There was no telling where she was now.

Leonard briefly considered simply telling Prowett the girl had died, but there hadn't been a death in the asylum for nearly two years and he would not tarnish his record to cover up the defiance of two women who hadn't the sense to obey their superior. "There must be someone else." He spoke the words as he scanned the open ledger on his desk in search of a woman he could transfer in Patrice Gulligan's name. Leonard was desperate and had looked over half of the oversized page before he would allow himself to consider the consequences of such an ill-advised plan. With a heavy sigh he was just about to abandon the idea as foolish and dangerous when his eyes fell upon the record of Felicity Taylor.

A smile spread slowly across his face. "You'll do nicely, my dear," he said as he rose from the desk. Felicity Taylor was deaf and unlikely even to know she was being passed off as someone else. He glanced at the record of her age and decided she looked young enough to pass for a girl of sixteen. Leonard also had to admit that there was a certain justice in knowing that at the Willard Asylum she would be safely locked away where she belonged. He opened his office door, startling the matron, who was speaking to one of the kitchen girls. "Mrs. Boswell, get Kraus down here right away!"

* * *

The carriage turned on to North Street and Daniel cursed himself for a coward. They were just a few minutes from home and he'd not found a way to bring up certain matters of importance with his mother. He glanced over at Ciara enjoying the sunshine on her face, satisfied with her day's efforts on behalf of those less fortunate. Perhaps now was a good time, while she was in a good mood.

Ciara glanced over at her son, who had been preoccupied all day. "Out with it, Daniel," his mother told him. "Ye've been frettin' since we left the church. Tell me what's on yer mind."

Daniel took a deep breath and turned toward his mother, who looked as if she were holding hers. "Well, I've got somethin' I must tell ye, but I fear ye'll not be pleased."

Ciara felt a flash of remorse for the way she had been treating her son all week. "Ye want to tell me about Felicity, don't ye?" He nodded warily and she made an effort to put his mind at ease. "Ach, Daniel, I can see how it is between ye."

"But ye don't approve?"

"'Tis not that I don't approve. Felicity is a fine woman and I can see she makes ye happy." Ciara looked away, reluctant to say more but Daniel stayed silent, willing to wait her out. She took another few moments to gather her thoughts and continued. "I just don't think ye've thought it through is all." She placed her hand on his arm to be sure she had his full attention. "Daniel, she had a life in New York before her aunt passed. Now that her uncle's gone too, will she not want to return to it?"

Daniel did not say what was on his mind because he knew it would upset her to hear that he would follow Felicity wherever she wanted to go. "Ma, ye've not given me five minutes to myself all week, let alone time to speak with her. I can't promise ye that we'll stay, but we've no plans to leave either." Ciara looked ready to argue the point and Daniel was relieved the house was in sight. He twitched his hand and the horses turned into the drive. The conversation was over for now, but it left him feeling unsettled.

Felicity was at work in the garden when the carriage pulled into the drive. Out of the corner of her eye, she saw old Beau take off at a trot across the paddock to meet Nora as she entered the drive and follow her to the barn. Felicity watched as Daniel helped his mother down, sensing that there was still some tension between them. It did not require any special gifts to see that Ciara was not pleased at the change in her relationship with Daniel and it grieved her to be at the heart of this disquiet after all the kindness the Nolans had shown her. She stood to greet them as Ciara and Daniel approached the house.

"Good," Ciara said pointing to the basket of freshly harvested vegetables by Felicity's feet. "We'll need those for supper." She picked up the basket, continued toward the house and motioned for Felicity to follow. Turning her head, she called out to her son, "Away and help Charlie with the horses."

Felicity smiled wistfully, catching Daniel's eye. He had intended to turn in the direction of the barn but then thought better of it. "Charlie's got the horses well in hand, Ma. If ye please, I did promise Felicity some of my time a few days back." He reached out and took her hand. "She'll be back in time to help ye with the supper." Without waiting for his mother's comment, Daniel steered Felicity away.

Ciara struggled with the urge to call them back, but ultimately admitted to herself that she could not begrudge them a bit of time to themselves. With a sigh, she walked to the house, determined not to fret over it.

238

As soon as they were out of sight, Daniel tried to pull her in but Felicity moved away, her hands gesturing rapidly. "Your mother does not approve."

There was no sense in arguing the point. "Aye, I know and we'll talk about that, but a few days have passed since last we were alone together and I've missed ye." Daniel smiled and this time she did not resist his attempt to draw her in. Their kiss was filled with reassurance and longing after days apart and he held her for a long while after, enjoying the feel of her in his arms.

Finally, they separated but only so Felicity could see Daniel's face. Neither of them wanted to let go and so they would have to rely on the spoken word rather than signs. "I have missed you, too," she told him.

"Well, I shall have to marry ye straightaway then if we're to have any privacy 'round here."

It was just the proposal she was expecting, without pretense, understanding that they both wanted to be married as soon as it could be arranged. Still there were some things needing to be discussed. "What about your mother?"

"Ma will come to her senses soon enough."

There was a sadness in Felicity's smile and Daniel knew she was trying to understand why his mother was concerned with the change in their relationship. "Ye know she loves ye as if ye were her own daughter, don't ye?"

Felicity nodded and then held his gaze. "It is you she is worried about. She does not want you to leave."

Daniel couldn't help feeling frustrated. This was all still so new to both of them and he didn't want to be rushed into any decisions to gain his mother's approval. "I'm a grown man, Felicity, and I've earned the right to make my own decisions."

He immediately regretted the tone of his remarks, but Felicity seemed to understand his irritation was not directed at her. "Your mother has opened her heart and her home to me twice when I had no place else to turn. I have no wish to repay that kindness by being the cause of discord between the two of you."

Daniel took another step back. He wanted to be sure she understood what he was about to tell her and his hands formed the gestures that accompanied his words. "There is much we have to work out between us, and I, for one, am in no rush to do so. Whether we stay or go, I'd like to do it as man and wife, if ye'll have me. Will ye marry me, Felicity, and we'll take our time to figure out the rest of it?"

She moved closer, held his gaze once more and smiled. There was no need to nod or to sign. He knew her answer was yes. This time their kiss was long and lingering, filled with the promise of what would happen in private as man and wife.

* * *

Every so often Maude became aware that she was dreaming because she felt as if she were a bystander in her own life, or rather in Martha's life. Still deep in sleep, she could actually feel a dark shadow hovering over the blissful scene of Daniel and Felicity kissing. It was such an odd feeling because she wasn't present in their moment, but she could feel the danger approaching, whereas, apparently, they could not.

Chapter Twenty

Maude was startled out of sleep and sat bolt upright in bed. The early morning light permeated the sheer curtains and it took only seconds for her to realize that she was in her bedroom in the twenty-first century. There was confusion in the fact that she couldn't remember actually going to bed. So wrapped up in writing, it had to be well after midnight when she called it quits. Don's side of the bed was empty. Her eyes traveled to the clock on his bedside table. It was just before seven and she remembered he was headed to an estate sale in Ellicottville.

A few deep breaths helped to regain some focus on the present. Maude heard the shower shut off and Don moving around in the bathroom. She closed her eyes and took another deep breath, hoping for a bit more composure before he came back in the bedroom. She must have failed because when he opened the door his smile turned to a concerned grimace.

"Are you feeling okay? You're as white as a sheet."

"Yeah, just gimme a minute. I had a weird dream."

Still wrapped in a towel, Don came and sat on the bed beside her. "What, like a nightmare?"

"No, it wasn't like that at all." Maude moved back just a bit so she could lean against the headboard. She took a deep breath and attempted to explain. "Normally, when I dream about the past, I don't have any feelings about the people in the dream one way or the other. This time it was different. I could tell something bad was going to happen."

She gave him the details about Mason Leonard's plan to abduct Felicity and send her off to the Willard Asylum as Patrice Gulligan. "Well, that doesn't sound so strange."

"No, you don't understand. I couldn't tell who was in danger. I don't think it was Felicity. Someone dies, Don, as a result of her abduction. I'm sure of it, but I don't know who."

Don could see that she was starting to panic, so he moved closer and took her hands. "Just take a minute and breathe. Whatever happened, it was a long time ago and there is nothing you could have done to prevent it."

"I don't know. This feels important, like a crucial piece of the puzzle just fell into place."

Don saw the spiral notebook by the bed was open to an empty page. "Why don't you write all of this down and I'll put on some coffee. Maybe in a few hours you can give Charlotte a call and get her opinion on this."

"Yeah, that's a good idea."

Maude sat in bed and wrote in her journal until her fingers could no longer hold the pen. Massaging her hand, she reread the pages hoping something would jump out and answer the nagging questions she still had. The feeling that something was wrong became even more intense as she reviewed the pages, so much so that she had to stop reading. *Shake it off, Maude*, she told herself as she placed the journal on the bedside table. *Whoever died is long gone and there is nothing you can do to save them.*

It was too early to call Charlotte, so Maude did the best she could to push the dream out of her head. But her thoughts wandered to Felicity and her impending abduction until Christine came into work later that morning.

The energy in the room changed when Christine walked in the door. She had the wide-eyed sparkle of someone who couldn't wait to reveal a juicy secret and her words came tumbling out as though she would burst if she held them back any longer. "Oh my God, I thought I'd never get here. You aren't going to believe this!"

"What?"

"The thief has contacted Basil! In a million years, I wouldn't have thought it would happen!"

"Mrs. Houston's thief? Are you serious? Who? Who contacted Basil?"

"Well, I should say that Basil was contacted, but not directly by the thief," Christine told her as she stowed her purse underneath the counter. "It's one of those 'a guy who knows a guy' kind of things, but Basil was informed last night that someone in Buffalo is looking for a buyer for some high-end bling."

Maude couldn't help but laugh. "He didn't really say 'high-end bling' did he?"

"Of course not. Basil is classier than that, but you're missing the point, Maude. We may be able to find out who this guy is."

"What exactly would *we* do if we did? Forget it. I don't want to know." The mischievous look on Christine's face confirmed Maude's suspicions that there was more to this story, and it likely meant trouble in one way or another. "What haven't you told me?"

"Basil is coming to Buffalo to meet with the guy and appraise the pieces himself before he brings in a buyer." Christine was positively giddy over the idea of somehow being involved with catching the jewel thief.

Maude suddenly felt like she was in the middle of a bad movie. "Christine, don't get involved in this. It could actually be dangerous."

"Relax. I only told Basil I'd meet him for a drink when he got to town. He's not even staying with me." She sounded disappointed, but laughed it off.

Not fooled for a minute, Maude gave it one more try. "I'm assuming Mrs. Houston is aware of all this, so no doubt her people will handle the situation." Maude chased away visions of Christine lurking behind a door during a clandestine meeting between Basil Hewitt and the thief by changing the subject. "All of the globes and lampshades need dusting, but before you get into that, would you mind taking these envelopes over to our new neighbor?"

"Sure, no problem." Christine took the envelopes and walked out the front door.

Lester Northrup was sitting at his front counter playing with his phone when Christine walked in the door. He greeted her with his usual creepy smile as she approached. "Did you change your mind about working for me?" he asked her.

"No."

"How about dinner, then?"

"No, Lester, I just came to bring you these." She handed him the letters. "They were delivered to us by mistake."

Lester's phone rang and he glanced casually at the caller ID. He looked again more closely and decided he had to take the call. "Hold on for a minute, sweetie, and we'll talk about that dinner." He turned and went into the back room.

Christine turned to make a hasty escape, but turned around when she heard the words 'some Brit' coming from the back room.

"I don't know, tonight, I think." Lester said. "I'll let you know. Just sit tight."

His voice sounded like it was coming toward the front of the shop and Christine pretended to be admiring one of the purses in the window. She had seconds to decide if she should stay or go. Had she heard him right? Was some British man on his way to see Lester tonight? She took a deep breath and turned around as Lester appeared at the counter. "So, about that dinner, does tonight work for you?"

Lester was pleasantly surprised and it showed on his face, but his expression quickly transitioned to disappointment. "Sorry, sweetie, can't make it tonight." With a lecherous smirk, he added, "I'll give you a call in a few days and we can celebrate, just the two of us."

Christine did her very best to sound casual. "Yeah, sure." She didn't care to ask what they would be celebrating and exited the shop before he could ask for her phone number. It all came together in the few footsteps it took to return to the shop. Christine took a deep breath before she entered the Antique Lamp Company and Gift Emporium, but it didn't help. She still blurted out her suspicions the minute she crossed the threshold. "It's Lester! Lester Northrup is the thief! I can't believe I didn't realize that before now."

"Slow down. What are you talking about?" Maude asked her.

"I overheard him on the phone talking about some British guy who was on the way to see him." She came forward and leaned both hands on the counter, looking Maude directly in the eye. "He also tried to ask me out again. He said he wants to get together in a few days to celebrate, just the two of us. Don't you find that strange? I mean what does he want to celebrate? His newly acquired fortune, perhaps?"

"I'll admit he is totally lacking in social skills, but that doesn't mean he's the jewel thief, Christine. There are at least four British men who live here in the neighborhood, probably thousands more in the city. He could be talking about anyone."

"Think about it: three of the robberies occurred to clients of ours within days of them having been in the shop."

"We don't actually know if it was Mrs. Billingsley's house that was broken into," Maude interrupted, correcting her.

"Well, there's one way to find out." Christine picked up the phone and handed it to her.

"I'm not calling her to ask if she was robbed."

"Look at this objectively, Maude. Both Mrs. Houston and Mrs. Billingsley actually went into Lester's shop by accident. Mrs. DeMonteforte's driver always parks that fire engine red Lincoln of hers right outside the door, so I doubt it escaped Lester's attention. He saw enough of each of them to know they had a lot of money."

Maude thought about that for a minute. She did find it odd that three of her clients had all experienced burglaries after visiting her shop. "I agree it's an unusual coincidence, but c'mon. Lester would have to have known when Mrs. Houston was on her way to the appraiser and furthermore would have had to have orchestrated a car accident. I don't think he's that ambitious."

"Mrs. Houston's jewelry was worth two hundred thousand dollars. I think that would motivate most thieves."

There was no sense in arguing with Christine, not with a drama like this unfolding in her head. "Well, we'll find out one way or the other soon enough, I expect. Assuming your friend has informed Mrs. Houston that he was contacted, the police will undoubtedly come up with a plan to catch the guy, whoever he is." She still wasn't convinced that Basil Hewitt would be able to pass up a hefty broker's fee in favor of cooperating with the authorities.

"I should call and tell her what I overheard," Christine stated, reaching again for the phone.

"No, you should not. Stay out of this and stay away from Lester. He may not be a jewel thief, but he is a creep." Maude was determined to keep Christine out of it, but couldn't help thinking that she might be right. Maybe it wouldn't be a bad idea to give Mrs. Billingsley a call after all. If it wasn't her home that was robbed, it would put Christine's suspicions to rest, at least for Maude.

As soon as Christine took her break, Maude picked up the phone. She eased her way into the conversation by asking how Theresa had liked the brooch and complimenting Mrs. Billingsley on the lovely pearl necklace she had worn the last time she had come to the shop. The pearls, it turned out, had been stolen along with matching earrings and two diamond rings. The police hadn't made any progress in finding the thief.

There was a lull in the conversation, giving Maude a chance to respond, but she couldn't think of what to say. Shock was quickly giving way to anger and Maude was trying to think of a way to get off the phone so she could process what she had just learned. "I'm so sorry, Lorna, but the UPS man has just pulled up outside and I'm going to have to sign for a delivery. I'll call you back later."

Maude hung up the phone and turned in the direction of the shop next door as if that somehow might reveal what Lester was up to. Was it really possible that he had been targeting her clients? She looked at her watch. It was just after one. Don probably hadn't left Ellicottville yet, so there was just enough time to call him before Christine came back from her break. She quickly picked up her phone and dialed his cell.

"Is everything okay?" Don asked.

"Yeah, I just wanted to run a few things by you." She quickly told him about her conversations with Christine and Mrs. Billingsley.

"So you think Lester might be involved in all of this?"

"Don, I don't know what to think. There's enough of a coincidence that I feel like I should at least call Mrs. Houston and let her make up her own mind." There was a sense of urgency taking root and it could be heard in her voice. "I don't have a good feeling about this."

"Yeah, I am picking up on that. Are you sure you're not still rattled about your dream this morning?"

"I don't think so. I haven't given that any thought since Christine came in." Maude hesitated a moment and then added, "I don't know, maybe. It's hard to know where one bad feeling leaves off and the other begins."

"Think about this for a minute, Maude. You are accusing our neighbor of being a thief and at the same time suggesting to one of our best clients that she was targeted because she came to our shop." There was silence on the other end of the phone and he knew she was considering his words. He waited a few seconds more before he spoke again. "Have you had a chance to talk to Charlotte? Tell her exactly what you just told me and ask her to help you sort it out."

"Yeah, that's a good idea, but it will have to wait until after work. The less Christine knows about this the better."

"Agreed. Hey, listen, the boys are at camp so we're on our own tonight. Let's go out to eat. You need to get your mind off all of this."

"Great idea. Text me when you're on your way home."

"Will do. Love you, Maudie."

Maude could see Christine walking down the street toward the shop as she pondered what to do between now and dinner. By the time the door opened, she made up her mind. "Hey, do you mind holding down the fort. I have some research I've been meaning to finish up and it's pretty slow today, so if I get going now, I can be back by the time Don gets back."

Christine was intrigued. "Yeah, sure. What kind of research?"

"It's book-related." Maude ducked into her office and grabbed the flash drive that had been sitting on the desk waiting for her to find the courage to examine its contents. "Lock up when you leave." She headed out the back door before Christine could ask any more questions.

Chapter Twenty-One

Maude pressed the digits on her cell phone as she started up the car. "Hi, Charlotte. It's Maude. Are you up for a visit? Good, I'll be there in about an hour."

Exactly an hour later Maude passed through the gates of The Lily Dale Assembly and parked on Cottage Row in front of the gingerbread Victorian belonging to Charlotte Lambert. There was a moment of hesitation at the door. She had driven an hour in the middle of the day for Charlotte's serene wisdom and the overall tranquility of Lily Dale that would calm her mind and help her put the pieces of this strange puzzle together. Still, Maude couldn't help but think that maybe this had been a knee-jerk reaction. Sixty miles away, the idea that Lester Northrup had been targeting her clients seemed a bit of a stretch.

The door opened, leaving her no more time to consider the fleeting thought that she should just get back in her car and drive home. "You made good time." Charlotte had lost a few pounds since Maude had last seen her. Her thin dark skin hugged the bones of her bare arms, revealing the superficial tendons and blood vessels on the back of her hand as she held the screen door open and stepped outside.

"Thanks for seeing me on such short notice."

Charlotte smiled, the wisdom of a lifetime spent counseling people like Maude reflected in her dark eyes. "It's not a bother. I'm happy to help. Besides, the season hasn't started yet, so I've got all the time in the world for now." In another few weeks, Lily Dale would be inundated with visitors, many looking to connect with lost loved ones, some seeking the unique energy found only in the Leolyn Woods, and others just curious to see what all the fuss is about. Maude felt guilty for intruding on Charlotte's much coveted tranquility.

"I just didn't think I could express everything I need to tell you in an e-mail or a phone call."

"Maude, I have told you before, Spirit has brought us together for a reason. I'm on this journey with you." She gestured toward the porch, where a pitcher of lemonade and two tall glasses sat on a small wicker table. "It's a lovely day. How 'bout we sit outside?"

The intensity of Charlotte's attention was unsettling as Maude relayed the information she had learned earlier in the day, and she periodically took long sips from her glass to break eye contact. Charlotte took the time to refill both glasses and then sipped from her own before she responded. "You are connected with this man Lester in a past life, I think."

"Lester? Really? How so?" Maude was hoping for a bit more detail than that.

"I don't know, dear." The frustration was evident on Maude's face and so the old woman did her best to elaborate. "I can tell you that he resented you then as he resents you now." Charlotte closed her eyes to focus on the image she was getting. "I'm seeing a road block and I take that to mean he thinks you stood in his way." Her expression grew wary as she continued to process the images being presented to her. "He is dangerous, Maude. He means to do you harm."

Maude considered what she knew of her past life, Martha's life, searching for a connection with Lester Northrup. "The Keeper!" Maude stood up and began pacing the porch. "Mason Leonard was the Keeper of the Insane Asylum, where Martha worked. She was always locking horns with him." She stopped pacing and stood before Charlotte as the woman's words penetrated her thoughts. "Are you saying that Lester Northrup was Mason Leonard?"

"No, dear; that's what you are saying."

Maude could not help but feel relieved, but she was still confused. "So Lester has been stealing from my clients out of some sort of revenge over what happened in a past life?" Just like that, she labeled Lester a thief guilty of stealing from her patrons.

"I can't say for sure, but it is possible that he, too, recognizes the connection between the two of you. It is unusual, but it happens sometimes."

The frustrating thing when discussing anything with a psychic medium was most definitely the lack of clarity over important details. Maude understood that Charlotte could only relay her interpretations of feelings and images she received with the help of Spirit, but at times like this, she couldn't help feeling frustrated. "Okay, so let's just say out loud that Lester is aware of the relationship between Martha and Mason Leonard, and he is stealing from my clients to get back at me for whatever Martha did to him. Now what? How do I find out what transpired between them? How much danger am I really in?"

Charlotte considered the questions for a moment. "I remember you mentioned in your last e-mail that you had the opportunity to research some of the more public figures from your dreams, including Martha. Did you?"

Maude looked away briefly and cleared her throat. "Not exactly, I asked a colleague to do some digging for me but I haven't yet looked at the files she gave me." She paused, weighing the pros and cons of looking at the files for what might have been the hundredth time. "All I have are public documents, so if something personal transpired between them, I doubt there would be any record of it."

"You are afraid of finding information about Martha's death."

It wasn't a question, but Maude nodded reluctantly. How could Charlotte zero in on something that specific, but not fully understand Lester Northrup's connection to her past life drama? She had a lot to learn about Modern Spiritualism. "I know it's silly; she's been dead for over a century."

Charlotte got that look in her eye which Maude had learned meant she was about to say something vague but important. "Don't dismiss your feelings, Maude. There is a reason you are reluctant to look at those records."

It was hard not to show her exasperation knowing Charlotte was trying to help, so Maude took a deep breath. "I don't understand what you are trying to tell me. Should I look at the files or not?" She asked the question and then braced herself for what she knew would be the answer.

"I can't answer that for you. You have to decide for yourself how important it is for you to have the answers to your questions."

Maude rolled her eyes, not at Charlotte, but at herself for being afraid of what she might learn. If Lester was a threat to her or her clients, she would have to suck it up and look at the files. After all, whatever she might find had already happened. There was no way to change any of it now. "May I use your computer?"

The spare bedroom on the second floor doubled as an office. The door opened, bringing with it a gentle breeze from the open window that sent the papers on the table fluttering to the floor. "Do you want me to stay with you?" Charlotte asked as she bent to retrieve the sheets and restore them to their respective piles.

Maude watched her setting the desk to rights and couldn't help but wonder who had come in the room with them. After all, it was not unusual for potential allies from the spirit world to join them when Maude needed Charlotte's help. "Only if I'm not keeping you from something," Maude told her. She was relieved when the old woman proclaimed that the rest of her day was free of commitments.

Maude inserted the flash drive into the desktop computer and waited while the files came up. Each was labeled with an individual's name and it struck Maude that she was about to dig into a part of her past. She had spent most of her adult life researching people, places and events from the past, but this was different.

Would she recognize the people, places and events chronicled in these files? Would it cause her distress?

Charlotte picked up on the change in energy as Maude scanned the names of each of the files. "This is a great gift. I hope you know that. How many people get the opportunity to look themselves up in the historical records?"

Those words gave Maude the courage to click open the file on Mason Leonard. This was a great gift and she'd be a fool to turn her back on it. Maude recognized the notation of the first row of PDFs as the Keeper's reports from the Erie County Poorhouse insane asylum. It was unlikely that municipal reports would contain the information she was looking for. Next was a newspaper article that appeared to be a death notice. "Aha!" Maude said as she clicked open the file.

Charlotte adjusted her glasses and peered over Maude's shoulder. "It appears Mr. Leonard died in the Willard Asylum."

Maude hardly heard the woman speak. She was scrolling to the top of the page in search of a date. Finally, she turned to Charlotte. "Wow, I didn't see that coming!"

"Neither did I." Charlotte admitted. Maude hadn't meant the remark literally, but realized who she was sitting with after the words left her mouth and tried unsuccessfully to hide a smirk.

"This happened in 1873, so sometime between the summer of 1870 and December 3, 1873, Mason Leonard was committed to the Willard Asylum." She leaned back from the screen. "Willard was for the chronically insane. I wonder what happened..." The brief death notice did acknowledge the Mason Leonard had served as the Keeper of the county insane asylum in Buffalo and made vague reference to a scandal that had evidently cost him his position and his sanity, but there were no details.

Maude clicked open the folder labeled 'Martha Sloane Quinn' in the hopes that there might be some more information. There was her record from the day she entered the Erie County Poorhouse, which Maude had already seen, and the record of her admission into the Medical Department of the University of Buffalo in 1849. The only file left in the folder was a newspaper article from the *Sunflower* in Lily Dale. It was dated 1912. "I'm not ready to open that one yet." It was most certainly the notice of Martha's death, which Abby had told her was included among the files, and judging by the date it occurred long after the scandal with Mason Leonard.

"Now what?" she asked Charlotte. "How does any of this information help me figure out what is going on with Lester Northrup?" Charlotte gave Maude one of those long and thoughtful stares that sent Maude reaching for the glass of lemonade again. After a long sip she placed the glass back on the table and waited for a reply.

"You need to undergo a past life regression," Charlotte told her. "The answers to your questions are wrapped up in your memories of Martha's life. Once we unlock them, you will have the information you need."

Past life regression, the idea of being hypnotized to bring back the conscious memories of one's former life, had been suggested to Maude by Charlotte a few times since she learned of the connection to Martha Quinn in a past life. Maude was vaguely familiar with the process and was surprised to realize she was considerably less intimidated by it than she had been earlier. "Is that something we can do now?" she asked.

"Yes, if you're sure." Charlotte said.

Maude nodded confidently before she lost her nerve. There was no point in overthinking it. She needed answers and this seemed the only way she could get them, if it worked.

"I think you might be more comfortable over there." Charlotte pointed to the overstuffed chair in the corner of the room. Maude moved to the chair and looked at Charlotte to receive more direction. When none was forthcoming, she asked, "Is there anything else we need to do? Close the blinds, maybe?"

"That is not necessary, dear, unless you would feel more comfortable in a darker space. Your willingness to undergo this process is the most important part."

After a moment's consideration, Maude decided she did not need the room to be dark. She did, however, turn off her laptop and cell phone. "Okay, I'm ready."

"Okay, take a deep breath and close your eyes. Relax and empty your mind. Remember to keep breathing." Charlotte watched as Maude began to relax. When she felt the time was right, she spoke again. "Concentrate on the images conjured by my words. Enter the picture in your mind. I'll be there with you."

Maude opened her eyes in surprise. "You can do that?"

"Not everyone can, but, yes, I can. I won't be present in your journey, but you will know I am there. I'll see what you see."

"That makes me feel better already." Maude took another deep breath and closed her eyes. She was no stranger to meditation and within a few minutes her mind was clear and receptive.

"Okay, continue your breathing. Relax and concentrate on my voice." She waited again while Maude completed five deep breaths. "Picture the big building on Main Street, the one that once served as the insane asylum." Maude nodded and Charlotte continued. "Just in front of the modern day building is a subway station. Do you see it?"

"Yes."

"Okay, go inside." Charlotte closed her eyes and was silent as she connected with Maude's energy. "I'm here too. Come with me down the escalator."

Maude was still for a moment. She could clearly see the escalator in her mind and although she could not see Charlotte, she was aware of her presence. When Maude put her foot on the first step, she could feel Charlotte coming right behind her.

As they descended each level, it was like passing through a different phase of the subway's history. Each level looked older than the previous one until they reached what looked like the train platform from the nineteenth century. Maude could hear the steam engine hiss and whistle as they approached the tracks.

"The train will take us where we need to go," Charlotte told her.

Chapter Twenty-Two

Maude sat on the cool leather seat as the steam powered locomotive moved slowly along the tracks. Looking out the window, it felt like she was watching a movie. The train would stop, she knew, at the most important part. The scenery was different as the train passed along Main Street. The modern landscape of bars and fast food chains was replaced with clusters of two story brick or timber buildings separated by farm land and clumps of old forest.

At some point, Maude couldn't say when, the sun rose higher in the sky. By the time the train came to a stop behind the brick two-story building on the corner of Main and Chippewa it was early evening. Maude didn't recognize it as the building she currently worked and lived in. There was a porch and a large oak door overlooking a small yard, as opposed to the steel door that opened out to a small alleyway where she usually parked her SUV. "What is this place?" She asked.

"It's your home," Charlotte told her and Maude understood that to mean both her home and Martha's.

"Something's wrong," Maude told Charlotte, pointing to the carriage parked along Chippewa.

"Yes, Daniel and Michael just arrived. You need to hear what they have to say."

"They seem very upset," Maude observed. She exited the train and walked up to the porch, knowing she was watching what had already happened and that she was not a part of what was transpiring before her. Moving closer, a cold stone settled in her stomach as she saw the smile fade on Martha's face when she met her brother-in-law and nephew at the door.

"What brings the two of ye here at this hour?" Martha could clearly see the tension on both of their faces and knew immediately this was not a social call.

"Felicity is missing," Michael told her.

"She was taken, Da. Ye know she was taken from us!" Daniel corrected his father.

Turning to his son, Michael made an effort to speak calmly. "We don't know that for sure." Redirecting his attention to Martha he added, "'Tis why we've come, Martha. She's not here with ye, is she?"

Martha shook her head, but Daniel didn't give her a chance to respond. "See, I told ye! She'd not have gone away without leavin' word."

"Just ye both come in here and tell me what's happened." Martha stood aside and the two men entered just as Johnny was coming down the stairs.

"What's amiss then?" Johnny asked.

"'Tis Felicity," Martha told him. "She's gone."

Daniel looked panic-stricken and his uncle placed a reassuring hand on his shoulder in an effort to calm him down. "Take a deep breath, man, and tell us what ye know."

"Earlier this afternoon Ma got word that she was needed at the poor farm. One of the families she had helped before had returned. Charlie was feelin' poorly, so I drove her." It was evident that Daniel was making a supreme effort to speak calmly as he continued. "When we got there, the Keeper seemed confused, said he hadn't sent for Ma and that the woman and her daughter had been discharged weeks ago and hadn't returned. We got back and Felicity was nowhere to be found. We found a basket of wet washin' out by the line. Surely she'd not just have left it there, had she been called away for some reason."

"What about Charlie?" Johnny asked. "He'd have noticed if someone had come on to the property.

"Poor Charlie is beside himself with worry," Michael told them. "He was in his bed most of the mornin', says he didn't hear anyone come on to the property, nor see any sign of foul play. If someone was there, they were canny to be sure. Not even the horses were disturbed and Old Beau does love to greet a stranger on the road."

"Was she needin' to go into town for anythin'?" Martha asked.

"No. I even asked her to come along for the ride, but she still had chores to finish." Daniel told her.

The four of them sat around the kitchen table in silence for a few moments and Martha was glad that Gertrude had taken the boys to visit their aunt Ellie. It would do no good to worry them. Finally, Martha asked, "Ye say she'd left the washin' still wet in the basket, but was there anything else amiss about the farm?"

"Aye, there was. I found this right next to the basket." Daniel held out a corncob pipe, which Johnny took and examined with care.

"I've never seen its like," Johnny commented.

Martha looked closer and even went so far as to take the pipe from her husband. "Oh, dear God, I have! 'Tis Kraus' pipe! I'd know it anywhere." The unusual pipe had been a gift from his brother in Missouri, where they were just becoming popular.

Suddenly Martha began to tremble as she stared at the pipe. "What is it?" Michael asked her. "What do ye see?" He had been witness to her visions before and immediately understood that her physical connection with Kraus' pipe had allowed her to see something. It was a few more minutes before she was able to speak. "Take yer time," he told her.

"He snuck up on Felicity while she was hanging out the washin'. He forced something down her throat, laudanum, I think, and carried her off. She struggled a bit; that's when he lost his pipe. It fell out of his shirt pocket."

Daniel felt as if he had been punched in the stomach. He'd snuck up on Felicity a few times while she hung the wash, only his intention was playful, not malicious. Perhaps she hadn't struggled in earnest because she thought it was him again. He would never forgive himself if she came to harm at the hands of that brute. "Did ye see anythin' else, Auntie?"

"Aye, he carried her off to a carriage parked down the road."

"In which direction were they headed?" Michael asked her.

"Toward Main Street, they were headed toward the water, I think." She closed her eyes to concentrate on the images the pipe had given her. "Yes, there is a boat on the shores of the lake, but they are not in it yet."

Johnny considered all that his wife had told them. "Well, if Kraus took her, ye can bet it was at Leonard's behest…but why? More to the point, where the devil is he takin' her?"

"I'm afraid I've given him plenty of reasons to be angry with me of late," Martha admitted. "First, I used Michael's influence to have Felicity discharged, then again to have Alva as my assistant in the asylum. I'm afraid I may have pushed him beyond reason by helping poor Patrice escape."

At first, Johnny thought the young orphan girl's disappearance had nothing to do with Felicity's abduction, but as he was pushing the thought out of his mind, a dangerous idea took root there. Placing his hand on Martha's shoulder to steady himself as much as to comfort her, Johnny realized with terror the truth of Leonard's intentions. "He's headed to Ovid, to the Willard Asylum!"

"The Willard Asylum, why would he…" A look of confusion quickly transitioned to panic as Martha understood what her husband meant. "Oh, God, ye don't think he intends to pass off Felicity as young Patrice?"

Johnny's face was grim. "Aye, I do. 'Twould be faster to travel through the canals than over land."

"Are ye sayin' Leonard took Felicity so he could send her off to the Willard Asylum?" Michael asked.

"Why would he do that? I assured him I'd take full responsibility for her care."

"It wouldn't be Felicity's name on the intake form." Martha said. She told them about Patrice Gulligan and how she and Mrs. Awalte had helped the young girl flee the state. "We did fear that Kraus was watching the house on Division Street, and sure enough he was. Alva told me today that Kraus and Mr. Leonard returned there not long after we left, but they managed to get the lass away safely."

Daniel listened carefully as Martha described the cruelty of the owner of the tannery in Laona, and how he had insisted young Patrice was dangerous in an effort to keep her from revealing his crimes. "Do ye mean to tell me that they are tryin' to pass Felicity off as the other lass?" Daniel asked.

"We knew there was the possibility that Roach would follow up when she was brought to Buffalo," Martha told them. "Leonard would never admit she had been allowed to escape under his watch and he'd stop at nothing to stay in the favor of the Board of Supervisors."

"Aye, and it would be easy to pass a deaf woman off as another patient to be sure," Michael added.

Daniel made for the door. "Not if I can help it!"

Michael reached out to stop his son. "Just ye hold on a minute. Kraus can't just walk down to Canal Street with an unconscious woman over his shoulder. He'll have to wait for nightfall when the folks are well into their cups and more concerned with their next pint than with what's goin' on about them."

"We've got some time yet, I think," Johnny agreed as he turned to address his wife. "Ye saw a boat on the lake shore? I'll bet she's on it, just outside the city. Kraus will wait until it's safe to make his way to the canal."

"I expect he'll be with her, wherever they're hidin'," Michael speculated, "and he's not a man I care to fight. 'Tis best to wait until he is on the move again and take him by surprise."

"Aye, just so," Johnny agreed. "He'll have to pass through the slip, to be sure." The Commercial Slip was a narrow channel that led directly into the Erie Canal which would carry Kraus and his prisoner eastward toward the Finger Lakes and ultimately to the Willard Asylum. It would be easy to float through the slip and into the canal unnoticed by passersby, and with all of the raucous late night activity on Canal Street, nobody would even bother should Kraus actually have Felicity's unconscious body heaved over his shoulder.

"We can wait for him on the bridge," Michael suggested. A foot-bridge passed over the slip, connecting Canal Street on either side. Any boat heading into the canal would pass under it. Timed correctly, it would be an easy jump from the bridge to any vessel passing through.

"I can't just sit here knowin' she's with that brute," Daniel protested. "God knows what he'll do to her while we're here waitin' for the scoopers and the boatmen to drink their pay."

"If ye have a mind to be movin' on, ye can come with me to the asylum," Martha told him.

"Aye, 'tis a good idea to make sure they've not stashed her there," Michael agreed.

"They're expectin' me back this evenin' anyway to check on Miss Bauman. She's got a touch of the grippe. I'll insist that I be allowed to examine the third floor patients for symptoms." Flu-like symptoms always made the staff of the poorhouse and asylum uneasy and Martha knew she could bully her way onto the third floor, particularly since Kraus was unlikely to be there. "I'll get the keys from Mr. Morrissey and send him on his way. It will go faster if two of us search." Daniel reluctantly agreed and arranged to meet the other men on the bridge over Canal Street at ten o'clock.

* * *

"What do we do now?" Maude asked Charlotte as she watched Daniel and Martha depart.

"Just focus. You are connected to Martha's energy as I am connected to yours. We go where she goes," Charlotte told her.

Maude wasn't sure how or when it happened but in the blink of an eye she was standing outside the asylum, the presence of Charlotte Lambert felt if not seen. She saw Martha glance up toward the windows when she arrived, and then turned in that direction herself to see Mason Leonard staring down from his office window. It was almost as if he was waiting for Martha to arrive. Her intuition had grown strong enough to realize that Leonard was watching for her so she made eye contact and smiled making him immediately look away. Maude noticed that she could recall exactly how that felt, the satisfaction of making him turn away.

"Good evenin' to ye, Mrs. Quinn." Martha smiled as she saw Michael Kinney approaching from the barn. A kind old man, Michael was one of two longtime residents of the institution. He first came to the poorhouse at the age of 47, when most men already had a foot in the grave. Now fifteen years later, he still could dance a jig, and often would with anyone willing to be his partner. He arrived without a penny to his name after a lifetime of adventure, so he told people, and hadn't expected to live this long.

"Good evenin' to ye, Mr. Kinney." There was a joyful energy around Michael Kinney that always made Martha feel happy. Unlike so many others who came and went, Big Mike seemed content to live out his life here. "Ye recall Daniel, I'm sure."

Kinney nodded and turned toward Daniel, offering a short bow. "I do. What brings ye here this evenin'?"

"Miss Margaret is feelin' poorly," Martha told him. "Daniel's brought me to look in on her one last time this evenin'."

"I'm that grateful to ye," Kinney replied. Margaret Bauman was the other longtime resident of the institution. She had been in the asylum for nearly a year when Big Mike arrived and the two became fast friends. There was quite a big difference in their ages and Kinney took it upon himself to look after her as a father would. Where he was outgoing, Margaret tended to be distant, almost melancholy at times. Kinney filled his days wandering about the place offering help where it was needed, but Margaret did not venture out much.

She kept to the women's dormitory, or the adjoining sitting room.

"I'll check in on her straightaway," Martha assured him.

Daniel waited outside the women's dormitory while Martha looked in on Miss Bauman. She found the old woman sound asleep. Sinus congestion resulted in an audible snore produced by mouth breathing, but there appeared to be no sign of chest congestion to the naked ear. Martha placed a hand gently on Margaret's forehead and found she only had a slight fever. A few words with the woman in the cot next to Margaret's revealed she had been resting, without the discomfort of a cough most of the afternoon and evening. A brief tour of the ward produced two more women who had similarly mild symptoms whom she would check on again in the morning.

It was not a surprise to find Mason Leonard waiting on the landing of the second floor after Martha had left Margaret Bauman resting comfortably in the women's dorm. Martha met his eyes and again took pleasure in his discomfort. "Good evening, Mr. Leonard, what has kept ye here so late?" Martha asked.

"Good evening, Mrs. Quinn, Mr. Nolan. I wanted a full report on the condition of Miss Bauman. Influenza mustn't be considered lightly," he told her.

He shifted his weight just a little and looked off to the side as he spoke to her. Martha knew he was lying but used the opportunity to her advantage, reporting that symptoms were spreading in the dorm. "They're to stay in bed for the next few days. Give them beef tea, if they'll take it, and plenty to drink." Martha noticed that

Leonard was unusually interested in what she had to say. Typically, he was dismissive of her concern for the patients, often abruptly bringing their discussions to an end before she was finished. She was wary of his interest, but tested its limits. "I would like to examine the patients on the third floor. We can't be too careful, as ye say."

"I agree it is wise. Perhaps you should also check in on the few inmates still housed in the shed." It was most unusual for Leonard to draw attention to the fact that there were patients in the small timber annex. Martha vehemently disapproved of its use and usually only found out patients were there if she could hear them crying through the crumbling walls or one of the other inmates told her. "I've told Mr. Morrissey to give you his full cooperation." Leonard informed her that he was finished in the asylum for the night and that she could make a full report to him in the morning.

"He wants ye to know she's not here," Daniel told her as they climbed the stairs to the third floor. "He knew ye'd find out Felicity went missin' and he wanted to make sure ye didn't suspect she had been taken back here."

Martha nodded in agreement. "Aye, ye're right, I think. Still, we're here and we may as well check to be sure.

They made quick work of checking the cells on the third floor. Martha was surprised to find Andrew Faulkner looking well rested and at peace. "Ye look well, Mr. Faulkner."

"Thank you, Dr. Quinn. I'm feeling much better." He could not keep the smile from his face. "I've slept soundly these last two nights."

"That's wonderful news. What's changed?"

"I did what Mrs. Awalte asked me to do. I took note of every little detail in my dream." Andrew's voice filled with relief as he continued. "It wasn't my fault. Thomas pushed me out of the way as we charged up the hill!" Martha was pleased, but confused because she had never heard what specifically about his nightmare had been so distressing, but he told his story and everything became clear. Andrew thought he had stumbled and, in falling, cleared a path for the rebel bullet that was meant for him to hit Thomas. He hadn't realized that Thomas had pushed him aside and saved his life.

"He saved me! Thomas saved me." Tears were streaming down the young man's face. "How can I ever thank him?"

Martha had to dry her own eyes before she could reply. "Mrs. Awalte told ye he was still by yer side. Just tell him. He'll hear ye."

"'Tis a wonderful gift to be able to give a soldier," Daniel told her as they were walking out to the shed. He had been blessed to receive absolution from Ian through Felicity and knew first-hand how life-changing it had been.

"Aye, Mrs. Awalte is a blessing to us here. She has taught me how to help these poor souls in ways I hadn't thought possible.

As they exited the building and made their way along the dirt path to the shed, Daniel suddenly put out the lantern and pushed Martha behind the bushes between the outbuildings. Motioning for her to stay quiet, he pointed off in the distance, toward the Keeper's quarters, where they saw someone briskly descend the stairs. "Who could that be?" Daniel whispered, watching as the man made his way toward the street.

Just then, they saw another person exit the Keeper's quarters. This person, a woman, did not leave the porch. The shadowy figure turned toward the building and looked as though he was speaking to the woman on the porch. "That's Leonard," Daniel said as they crept along the row of bushes in an effort to get close enough to the Keeper to hear what he was saying.

"I've barely enough time to meet him as it is and you are delaying me with this nonsense! Just do it and return to your quarters. Nobody will be the wiser." He turned away from Mrs. Boswell, but she must have said something because he turned back. "It is bad enough that I must go off and deal with Kraus' incompetence, Henrietta. Do not also make me suffer yours."

Without another word, Leonard hurried in the direction of the road. He had paid good money to secure a packet boat and a team of mules to travel the canal through the night. The appearance of Mrs. Quinn and her nephew at the asylum late in the evening could only mean trouble. Leonard would not see his bed until Kraus and his captive were safely on their way. To himself, he muttered, "Idiots, the lot of them."

"C'mon, there's no time to check the shed," Daniel whispered. "He'll be off to meet Kraus."

"Go on ahead and I'll catch up. I'll check the shed just to be sure," Martha cautioned. At first Daniel was reluctant to leave her, but his worry over Felicity forced him to acknowledge that his aunt was more than capable of taking care of herself and after a reassuring nod from her, he was off. Leonard took off on foot, avoiding the ruckus that would result from entering the stable at such a late hour to tack up his horse, oblivious to Daniel following close behind.

Martha made her way toward the shed in eerie silence. No longer having the lantern to light her way, she stepped carefully along the dirt path. The typical moaning and occasional screaming that could be heard coming from the unfortunate occupants of that wretched place was conspicuously absent. Not even the creaking of the cots could be heard. There was nobody there, Martha suspected it as she opened the door and strained to see in the dark down the short hallway. Every cell door was ajar and it did not take her long to check them all and confirm her suspicions.

Why would Leonard direct her to the shed if there were no patients there? The answer became clear as the last cell door slammed shut behind her, leaving Martha on the wrong side of a locked door. "Who's there? Let me out of here!" She called out as loud as she could, but there was no answer. Why would there be? Countless patients had shouted that very command over the years and had been ignored by the staff and the other inmates. She listened as footsteps made their way swiftly back in the direction of the asylum.

Could it have been Leonard who doubled back and shut her in? If it had been, surely Daniel would have followed and seen what he was up to. She was nearly sick with thoughts of Daniel injured or worse after having been discovered by the nefarious Keeper. "I mustn't panic." She spoke the words aloud as calmly as she could. Martha took a deep breath and tried to silence her mind. She focused on Daniel trying to connect with his energy as Alva had taught her to. Finally, she heaved a sigh of relief. He was fine, she was certain of it.

Someone had locked her in, but who? Martha focused on the noises she had heard after the door slammed shut. The efficient clacking of wooden boot heels on the floor, the swish of skirts as the door closed. Martha had heard Henrietta Boswell make her way up and down the corridors of the asylum a thousand times and never realized how distinct her sounds were compared to the soft shoe shuffle of the inmates. Realizing who had locked her in the shed was of little consequence since she was still stuck in a cell and there was very little chance of getting out until morning when the men would be about the grounds doing their chores. Still, she would have a few things to say to Mrs. Boswell come morning.

It was difficult to say how much time had passed, ten minutes, maybe twenty, but she heard someone walking on the dirt path along the back side of the shed. She had never been grateful for the flimsy walls of the dilapidated old asylum annex until now. "Is someone there? 'Tis Dr. Quinn, please help me!"

"Dr. Quinn, whatever are ye doin' in here?" The voice of Big Mike became louder as he entered the annex.

"I'm down here, Mr. Kinney. Can ye fetch the keys? They should be hangin' by the door." There was a moment of panic as she spoke those words. Had Mrs. Boswell taken the keys? Martha heaved a sigh of relief when she heard the clang of the iron keys as Big Mike lifted the ring off the hook.

Martha gave the old man a hearty embrace when he opened the door. "Whatever are ye doin' outside at this time of night?" she asked him.

"Well, I started to feel a wee tickle in my own throat and I thought as long as ye're still here, ye might take a look. I saw out the window that yer trap was parked in the yard, so I thought I could catch ye before ye left."

It was more likely that he just couldn't sleep and wanted the company. Kinney had resided at the poorhouse long enough to know how to sneak about after hours, but Martha could hardly chastise the old man for doing so now. She held the lantern up to his face as if to examine him. He was a kind old man and she wanted to respect his request for help, but she desperately wanted to get down to the wharf. "Aye, well, ye are a wee bit peaky. Off to yer bed and I'll stop by with a tonic in the mornin'."

"I thank ye, ma'am." Kinney gave a brief bow and walked her back to her trap. "Straight back to bed with ye now!" Martha watched the man walk off and then hurried on her way.

The clip-clop of hooves on the paved street echoed in the night as she made her way down Main Street and Martha worried that Leonard might hear her coming. She concluded that he would be well into the

Canal District by now and would not likely hear her over the boisterous district nightlife. As the trap crossed Seneca Street, an overwhelming sense of urgency struck her. Her men were in danger; that much she knew. But she feared she would not get there in time. Martha urged her horse on and approached Canal Street at a full gallop, the trap swaying dangerously.

Piano music and laughter filled the air as Martha slowed down and turned the trap into an alley by the distillery just before the slip. Her horse had barely come to a stop when she jumped out. Martha stayed close to the side of the brick warehouse as she made her way carefully toward the bridge. The moon provided enough light for her to see Mason Leonard approaching from the other side of the distillery. He was completely unaware of the three men crouched on the bridge above him, but had they seen him? She didn't dare make any attempt to communicate with them for fear of alerting Leonard to their presence. Overcome with a sense of helplessness, she could only wait and watch.

So preoccupied with the appearance of Mason Leonard, Martha hadn't seen the small packet boat at the entrance to the slip. Apparently, it took Leonard by surprise too, because he turned abruptly and walked quickly toward the mouth of the slip. Kraus angled the boat toward the distillery, getting close enough for Leonard to jump aboard. The two men looked as though they were arguing, but she was too close to the street noise to hear them. There didn't appear to be any sign of Felicity topside, but it was really too dark for her to tell.

Kraus and Leonard were nose to nose in a heated exchange when they passed under the bridge and didn't see the three men who descended from above. There was shouting and then a splash. Someone had fallen into the slip, but under the shadow of the bridge, she couldn't see who. Looking onto the boat, she could see two men trying to subdue a third. Judging by his size, the third man was Kraus. There was a lot of grunting and then finally the sickening sound of fist meeting bone. Kraus fell over. Whether unconscious or dead, Martha did not know.

"Get Felicity," Michael told his son. "I'll take care of him." Daniel disappeared below while his father pulled Kraus off to the side and began looking for some rope to bind his hands and feet. Better the man be restrained, Michael thought, in case he should regain consciousness before they got Felicity safely on to the pier.

With Kraus out of the way, Michael grabbed a length of rope to secure the boat to the dock. Martha ran out to help him, but her attention was diverted by the skirmish in the water. Two men had actually fallen into the slip. She knew one of them had to be her husband, which meant that the other was Mason Leonard. One man, she couldn't tell who, was struggling to gain control of the other who was trying his hardest to push his aggressor under the water. "Help him, Michael," she screamed.

Stumbling over Kraus' slumped form, Michael leaped toward the bow and jumped into the slip. He swam to the men, one of whom now had the other completely under water. Michael made to grab the assailant from behind, but he proved to be much stronger than he looked. It took precious minutes to wrestle the man away, but by the time he did, the other had not come up for air. Michael punched Leonard in the face as hard as he could and didn't wait to see if the blow had rendered him unconscious before he dove under in search of Johnny. Michael barely registered the sound of Leonard swimming away as he broke the surface only long enough to take a deep breath and descend again.

Daniel had come topside with Felicity in his arms. Looking toward the crowd that had gathered on the dock, he shouted, "Don't let him get away!" as Leonard tried to climb out of the water.

"Where is he?" Martha screamed. "Where's Johnny?" She ran along the dock for a better look.

Martha was scanning the water's surface, frantically searching for her husband. Her attention was only diverted by Daniel, who was struggling to get Felicity on to the dock. She was groggy from the laudanum, but with the help of a few bystanders, he was able to get her off the boat. With Felicity safe, he dove into the water to help his father.

The minutes it took for both men to pass above and below the water's surface in search of her husband seemed to pass at excruciating intervals. Finally, they both appeared with Johnny in tow. Daniel propelled himself up on the dock and then reached down into the water to help his father pull Johnny's lifeless body out of the water.

"Hurry! Lay him here," Michael ordered, pointing in front of him.

Martha stood by stunned while Michael began the process of raising and lowering Johnny's arms in an effort to expel the water from his lungs.

"'Tis not workin'!" Daniel cried.

Michael placed his mouth over Johnny's, trying in vain to breathe air back into the man's chest. For the next few minutes, Michael alternated breathing into his mouth and raising and lowering his arms, but it was no use. Johnny was dead.

"No! Don't stop," Martha screamed at him. "Don't stop!" She threw herself on the ground, sobbing over her husband's lifeless body.

Chapter Twenty-Three

"I think we're done here." Maude could hear Charlotte's voice coming from outside the horrific scene by the Commercial Slip. "Come back now, Maude." She boarded the waiting train. Was it always just sitting there? Maude couldn't recall. At the station she rode the escalator up through the periods of the train station's history, quicker this time, and came back to the present. The whole journey must have taken a long time, because it was getting dark outside. Charlotte looked at her watch. It was after just after eight o'clock.

Maude opened her tear-filled eyes but it was a while before she was able to speak. The room remained quiet while she attempted to process all that had been revealed. When she was finally in control of her emotions enough to speak, her voice was shaky. "Johnny died trying to rescue Felicity." Saying those words took all the air from her lungs. There was no point in trying to hold back the tears now and she began to sob.

"I'm sorry. I know it seems foolish to be this upset over the death of a total stranger who died so long ago," Maude said, more to herself than to Charlotte.

"Oh, dear, he wasn't a total stranger; He was your husband. Of course you'd grieve his loss again." Charlotte offered her a tissue and Maude had to resist the urge to lean into the old woman's arms and cry her eyes out.

Instead, she blew her nose, wiped her eyes and took a deep breath. Although she tried to sound like she had pulled it together, her voice still quavering when she spoke. "As illuminating as this has been, it doesn't tell me how exactly Mason Leonard ended up in the Willard Asylum." She blew her nose a second time before continuing. "Obviously he survived falling into the slip. Do you think this was the scandal his death notice referred to?"

"I would say so," Charlotte agreed. "Is there anything else in those files that might confirm our suspicions?"

Maude thought for a moment. "Wait a minute! There were some municipal reports in Mason Leonard's file. If he was fired, it would have been recorded there."

Without another word, Maude turned on the computer and clicked open the PDF labeled 1870 and began scrolling through the Keeper's Report for that year. "Here we go!" She moved aside so that Charlotte could also read the testimony from the trial that ended in the termination of Mason Leonard as the Keeper of the Insane Asylum.

"What a scandal, indeed," Charlotte commented after she had read the report.

"Yes," Maude agreed. "It is interesting that Leonard did not accuse Martha and Mrs. Awalte of letting that girl escape."

"I imagine it would only have made the Keeper look worse in the long run," Charlotte suggested. She scanned the page again. "It was Michael's testimony that put the nail in his coffin, so to speak," Charlotte pointed out.

"I think you're right, and it may well have been Leonard's rant about educating women and allowing them into medical school that resulted in his committal. It almost looks as if he blamed Michael for everything that went wrong."

"You must try and see this in nineteenth-century terms, dear," Charlotte explained. "Martha defied his authority every chance she got, and most egregiously by helping that young girl to escape the asylum. He could not openly accuse her without making himself look incompetent. To his mind, she was to blame for everything that went wrong in his life but he could hardly say so. Ultimately I think it drove him mad."

"I guess I can see that, but that still doesn't tell me... Oh shit!" For the second time Maude felt all of the air leave her lungs and it took a moment before she could finish her thought. "Mason Leonard was responsible for Johnny's death. He deliberately drowned him. Could that mean that somehow Don is in danger?"

Maude didn't wait for a response and instead dumped the contents of her purse, frantically looking for her phone. The seconds it took for the phone to come to life seemed to drag on. Finally, it began chirping, indicating that she had missed several phone calls and a text from her husband. She did not have the patience to manage voicemail, so with trembling fingers, she fumbled through the menu until she found Don's message.

> *"Christine just called in a state of panic because she can't seem to reach you. She blurted out something about Lester Northrup and that Basil had double-crossed her. I'm pretty sure she is heading to the marina down on the outer harbor. I think she is planning on confronting both of them. What does Lester have to do with this and why is Christine involved? Okay, strike that last question. This could be the time her taste for intrigue comes back to bite her, so I'm going to take a ride and see if I can find her. If I'm not home when you get here, we'll both either be in jail or in the ER. Ha, you know I'm just kidding. Call me if you know what this is all about. Love ya!"*

Maude pushed the redial button and waited for Don to pick up. She tried twice more and it went to voicemail each time. She looked at the time stamp on the text message and then at the clock on her phone. It was just after 9:30 and he had sent the message just ten minutes ago. Don would not have his phone accessible if he was driving.

Maude read the text again and wondered why Christine would be heading to a marina on the outer harbor, and then it hit her like a blow to the chest, a palpable feeling of dread like she'd had that day on the river when they had come to the spot near the lakeside restaurant undergoing remodeling. That restaurant was part of the marina on the outer harbor. "Shit! Shit! Shit!! That girl has completely lost her mind!" Maude stood and began throwing things back into her purse. "I have to get back to Buffalo. It's happening again!"

"Slow down, dear, and tell me what's going on."

For a moment, Maude was speechless, unable to articulate the panicked thoughts rampaging through her mind. "Charlotte, it *is* happening again. I'm sure of it. Everything has led to this moment, my connection to the skeletons, Frederika Kaiser's journal, all of the dreams and visions have led me to this moment."

As the words were coming out of her mouth she was putting the pieces together. Once it became clear in her mind, Maude was able to see that her connection to the past had been gradual, allowing her to accept what was happening to her with the understanding of each separate event. She became even more certain as she relayed Don's message that Christine was planning to break up the meeting between Lester Northrup and her jewel thief, Basil Hewitt. "If I don't get back to Buffalo, Don could die just like Johnny did, trying to save Christine!"

"Surely she'll call the police," Charlotte suggested.

"Actually, I'm not so sure," Maude admitted. "She would be afraid of incriminating herself. It was her idea to call in a known jewel thief in the first place. Knowing Christine, she'll have some stupid romantic notion that it is her responsibility to make this right." With keys in hand, Maude made to leave.

Charlotte rose and cut her off at the door. "Dear, we are sixty miles from the city and it is dark. You are in no shape to get behind the wheel. I'll drive and you call the police."

"Call the police and tell them what? I just had a past life regression and I think my husband is in danger at the hands of my nemesis, who seems to have followed me into this life from the past?"

It sounded so ridiculous that Maude actually sat down to reconsider her next move. "Is this for real?"

She hadn't really directed the question to Charlotte and so was taken aback by the answer that followed. "Yes, I think it is, but we don't have much time, so let's get moving."

It wasn't until they were in the car and pulling out of Lily Dale that Maude had the courage to ask Charlotte to elaborate. "What aren't you telling me?"

"I know this is frustrating for you to hear, but I have told you all I know. My guides are telling me that you are heading into a dangerous situation and that I am supposed to be with you. Beyond that, I really do not know."

They were silent for most of the trip and Maude had to resist calling Don's phone as many times as it took to get him to answer it. Charlotte didn't speak until they merged on to the Niagara Thruway. "What exit, dear?"

They had made it back to the city in forty-five minutes and Maude thanked all of the gods she could think of for Charlotte's lead foot. "Get off at Louisiana and head toward Fuhrman Boulevard." Maude tried to comfort herself with the notion that the place where they were headed was a mile or so away from the Commercial Slip and maybe that small alteration could change the outcome of this event. It was a tiny hope to cling to and she wouldn't dash it by asking Charlotte if a small variance in the location could actually make a difference.

There were no streetlights on Fuhrman Boulevard as Charlotte wound her way toward the waterfront. The large lot appeared empty but for Don's truck parked close to the street. "Maybe nobody's here," Charlotte suggested.

"Turn off your lights and pull over by that truck," Maude instructed. "I can't see from here if anyone is in it."

Charlotte maneuvered the SUV toward the driver's side of Don's truck so it wouldn't be seen. Christine's small Volkswagen had been obscured by the larger Chevy. It was evident when they pulled up that nobody was sitting in either vehicle. Maude laid her hand on each hood and could feel the heat generated from the engines. "They haven't been here long," she remarked.

"I really think you should call the police, dear."

"I don't see any other cars. Let's just take a look out back by the patio. Maybe they're doing the same." It did briefly occur to Maude that she was leading a little old lady into a potentially very dangerous situation.

"Don't even think about asking me to wait in the car," Charlotte warned. "I'm not about to let you go out there alone."

The two women walked as quietly as they could across the large gravel parking lot. The smell of treated lumber filled the night air as they rounded the newly rebuilt patio behind the building. It seemed odd that none of the external lights were on. Only the sound of water lapping up on the boats moored behind the restaurant could be heard as Maude strained her ears to detect any sign of human activity. She looked out toward the water. The security gate that kept the public out of the private marina looked to be closed, but the boats were too far away to see clearly in the dark if anyone was on them.

"Let's just check out the marina and then we'll go," Maude suggested. "Both of their cars are in the lot, so Don and Christine have to be here someplace."

With the exception of a few park benches, the terrain between the back patio of the restaurant and the marina was wide open. In daylight, they would be easily seen. Charlotte hesitated, weighing the odds of making it to the gate of the marina undetected by whoever else was lurking about. "Have you thought about what we'll do if we find trouble down there?"

It was a bit late to be asking that question, but Charlotte did anyway and she was grateful that it gave Maude pause for thought. "I'd call the police but I honestly don't know what to tell them."

"My dear, your husband's and your friend's cars are both parked in the lot of an establishment that is not yet open for business and they are nowhere to be found. I think that is reason to call the police."

"I guess when you put it that way, we should call the police," Maude agreed, reaching into her back pocket for the phone.

"Nobody will be calling the police." Lester's voice was startlingly close and Maude realized that while she was coming up with rationalizations for why they were not in danger, he had been coming around the building with his gun drawn. "Now, you two come on over here with me."

He was standing right in front of them and Maude was certain he would use the weapon he held in his hand if they tried to make a run for it. She glanced to the side to find Charlotte already making her way carefully to the path where Lester stood with her hands up in front of her. "Take it easy, Lester, we are just in the wrong place." Maude did her best to keep her voice even. "We were supposed to meet Don for a drink. I must have misunderstood his directions." She looked at the gun in his outstretched hand. "Whatever you are doing is your own business if you just let us be on our way." It was worth a try, but Maude knew that Lester wasn't having any of it.

"Like hell you're in the wrong place!" Lester could not help but laugh. "I figured you would show up eventually. You've stood in my way before, but not today. I'll be damned if I'll spend a single minute locked in a cell this time!"

He wore such a look of disgust, and Maude felt as if the ground beneath her was moving. The way he looked directly at her, as if they shared a secret, gave her chills. "You know." It wasn't a question, but a realization. Charlotte was right: Lester was fully aware of his connection to Maude in their past lives.

"Damned right I know. I was labeled a murderer! They had me declared insane. Me!" His eyes were wild with rage. "I spent my final years in an asylum because of you. I was punished for your incompetence, but not this time. In this life you'll get what's coming to you!" Lester shook the gun in her direction. "This time it will be you who goes to jail!" He took his keycard and opened the gate, making sure to leave it propped open for Basil Hewitt.

Several thoughts went through Maude's head as they made their way along the dock. Oddly enough she had questions for Lester. Although this was hardly the time to ask them, she did anyway, and was mildly surprised when he actually answered them. "When did you know?"

"I didn't at first. Dawn did, the minute she laid eyes on you. That's why she left. She wanted nothing to do with me after she found out about you!" The wound left by his wife's departure was still raw and his voice trembled with anger. "It hit me just after I met you that she was right, and then it all came back to me, everything you did. Dawn told me you and I had unfinished business, but I'll take care of that tonight and then it will be you that gets locked up!"

That last statement angered her to the point where any fear of him disappeared. "You're the one pointing a gun at me. Just how do you figure it will be me who ends up in jail?"

"Oh, that's easy. An anonymous tip will put the old lady's P.I. on your tail. He'll put it together that three of your clients had jewelry stolen just after visiting your shop."

Maude knew that her clients would never believe she had stolen from them and told him so.

"The incriminating evidence, however, is in your shop." He had finally gotten the better of her and made no effort to keep the smug condescension from his voice. "It won't be difficult to find when the police search it." He shook the gun again in her direction. "As much as I'm looking forward to seeing you hauled away in cuffs, it will have to wait until I've completed my business. Keep moving!"

There were enough holes in Lester's feeble plan to frame her for the thefts to give Maude confidence that he'd never get away with it, but she wasn't foolish enough to tell him that. Glancing to her side, it looked as if Charlotte was holding up okay. They needed to find out the end game here. Surely, Lester hadn't actually expected to find her here at the marina. Now that she was there, and with a frail looking old woman in tow, how would he alter his plan?

It was dark and there appeared to be no other people at the marina. Their proximity to the water frightened Maude and she desperately tried to push thoughts of Johnny's struggles in the slip out of her mind. Did Lester have a boat that he was driving them toward? It seemed likely that she and Charlotte would be stashed below so that Lester could complete his transaction with Basil Hewitt. Maybe they could scream for help, but would Basil come to their rescue or just take the jewels and run?

"Turn here," Northrup commanded. With the point of his gun, Lester nudged Maude in the back, pushing her toward a large sailboat on their left.

As Maude turned toward the boat she caught the familiar scent of Don's aftershave. No sooner had she made the connection than did he leap off the end of the boat and tackle Lester. The gun went off and the two bodies fell into the water.

"Don!" Maude screamed for her husband, her head spinning as history repeated itself before her eyes. Both men went under right after they hit the water.

Maude stood at the edge of the dock waiting for her husband to break the surface.

"Go after him!" Charlotte shouted.

"Don!" Maude called out again as she jumped into the water.

She broke the surface and immediately went back under, although she could see nothing below the murky lake water in the dark. Gasping for air, she heard sirens. Someone had called the police. Thank God.

"Over there!" Maude looked up and Charlotte was pointing toward the dock. Without hesitation, she went under again and swam beneath the dock.

There was a disturbance in the water that Maude could feel rather than see, like someone was frantically kicking arms and legs. She swam closer and a panicked hand grabbed on to her arm. At first she tried to shake it off, but the she realized that one of the men who had fallen into the water had pinned the other to the pylon of the dock. He was unconscious and the other man was stuck beneath him. She pulled as hard as she could, giving the man underneath the room to get free.

She did not know if the man she set free was Lester or Don, so she grabbed the arm of the unconscious man and struggled to get to the surface. It became more difficult to tow the unconscious man and she realized that the other man was grabbing for his arm. Whether he was trying to help or hinder her, Maude did not know, but when all three of them broke the surface, only two of them gasped for air.

"He's been shot." It was Don who spoke. Thank God, it was Don! "We need to get him out of the water." They swam to the dock, towing Lester along between the two of them, and managed to push him out of the water. By the time they pulled themselves out of the lake the police had arrived. Charlotte was speaking to one pair of officers while the other two ran towards Lester.

"I think it's too late," Don told them. "His gun went off when I tackled him. We hit the water and sunk like two stones. I couldn't get him off of me."

"You could have been killed," Maude was unable to control the panic in her voice. "Dear God, you might have died trying to save me." Her voice broke and the sobs came uncontrollably.

"Hey, take it easy. I'm fine." Don held Maude in his arms, mindful that the police were hovering above them and would require their statements.

"You don't understand. You were supposed to die. Johnny died." Maude's voice broke over those last two words. "This whole thing happened before, in Martha's past, and Johnny died."

"It's okay, I'm fine. I'm right here." Don held her tighter. "It's alright. I'm not Johnny."

Maude was still for a moment, finally she leaned back so she could see his face. After a long look, she said, "Actually, I think you are."

Chapter Twenty-Four

A great deal transpired after Lester Northrup was taken to the morgue. Maude and Don were examined by the EMT's on the scene and found unharmed by their exploits in the water. They all went to the precinct and gave statements to the police, who confirmed the theft of Mrs. Houston's jewelry as well as the others. Most of the pieces were found on Lester's boat. Each of Maude's clients was notified of the recovery of the stolen items. Mrs. Houston had assured the police that it was not necessary for them to accompany her to The Antique Lamp Company and Gift Emporium to search for her two rings that weren't among the jewelry on Lester's boat. She trusted Maude would find them in the morning and keep them safe until she could collect them.

"I don't think I'm up to driving you all the way back to Lily Dale in the middle of the night," Maude told Charlotte. "Would you mind if I brought you back to our house for tonight?"

"That's kind of you dear. I think we could all use a good night's sleep." Charlotte agreed.

The ride back to Main and Chippewa was largely silent as each woman considered the events that had transpired that evening. Finally, Charlotte spoke. "You are right about your husband."

Maude had been so lost in her thoughts that it took her a minute to leave them behind and focus on what Charlotte had just said. "Right about what?"

"I have known for a while now that Don was also your husband in the life in which you were Martha. I struggled with the decision of whether or not to tell you. Ultimately, my guides said you were not yet ready to know. I guess now you are. I am sorry for keeping it from you."

Oddly enough, Maude focused on the phrase "in the life in which you were Martha" and took a moment to ponder whether she wanted to ask questions about her lives before Martha. Ultimately she decided against it. The revelations from one past life were enough. "Charlotte, you have been so gracious in your willingness to help me sort out all of this. I can hardly hold it against you if your reasons for not telling me were in my best interest." She took in a deep breath, blew it out slowly and then was silent for a minute. "I do feel compelled to ask you what it all means."

"I have asked Spirit that myself. What I can tell you is that each time we enter a new physical body we bring the experiences from our past lives with us. We are attempting to learn from our past mistakes and resolve issues that may have been following us across many lives. Each time we resolve something we become free to continue on the journey we have set out for ourselves."

"So, I was right before when I said that all of this was focused toward helping me save Don this time around?" Maude had to fight back tears every time she realized that her beloved husband could have been killed. "Do you think we are soulmates? I mean, has Don, or some version of him, been with me through all of my lives?"

"I can tell you this: Martha was devastated after Johnny's death." It came as no surprise that Charlotte did not answer the question directly. "I felt it in her and I feel it in you. His death changed things for her and left her unable to continue on the path she was following."

Maude considered that for a moment and then was afraid to ask her next question, but ultimately the need to know helped her find the courage. "What would have happened if I hadn't gotten there on time?" The tears came again. "What would have happened if he had died again?"

"I do not know, dear, and it is best that you not think about that. You did get there on time and you were able to save him. You will be able to continue on the path you have chosen, a path, I believe, you are supposed to travel together."

Maude did not have the energy to ask what the old woman meant by her last remark as she parked her car in the alley behind the shop. They continued into the apartment in silence.

After Maude saw Charlotte settled in the guest bedroom, she found Don in the kitchen. He nodded toward the bottle of whiskey and the generous portions already poured for each of them. "I assumed you would not be ready for bed just yet," he told her as he held out one of the tumblers.

"You are a wise man, Don Travers." Maude took a long sip before she continued. "Thanks. I know it hardly seems like enough, but I have to say it anyway." The gratitude was directed at her husband, God, her spirit guides and the universe in general. There were so many reasons that she was grateful to have Don seated across from her, too many to mention.

"Perhaps it is I who should be thanking you." Don swirled the amber liquid around in his glass, wanting to ask some questions but not quite ready for the answers. "Help me to understand all of this."

Maude knew that he wasn't just referring to what had transpired this evening. Her trip to Lily Dale earlier in the afternoon had helped illuminate this unique connection to the past and Don knew that somehow he was intertwined in all of it. "I will, but I need to understand some things first. Tell me how you ended up on Lester's boat. How did you know which one was his?"

"I got here and saw Christine's car, but it didn't look like anyone else was here. I got out of my truck and heard arguing, so I followed the voices." Don paused for a drink. "I found Christine and her jewel thief on the back patio."

What were they arguing about?"

"Basil was insisting he hadn't tried to double cross Mrs. Houston and Christine looked as if she was ready to believe him. For the record, I wasn't buyin' it. Anyway, by then I had called the police and I advised both of them to get the hell out of there before they arrived."

"What about Lester? Wasn't the whole idea for Basil to meet with Lester and confirm he had Mrs. Houston's jewelry?"

"Basil Hewitt seemed to think under the circumstances that it would be enough for the police to find the stolen jewelry on Lester's boat. I'm sure he was looking to avoid the police and I certainly didn't want Christine to have to answer any questions, so I told them to be on their way. They must have circled around the bar just when you were approaching from the other side. If you had been a few minutes earlier, you would have run into them."

"The police will want to talk to Christine. What do you think she will tell them about Basil?"

"Christine may love a good drama, but she is not foolish enough to lie to the police," Don speculated. "Besides I doubt that is his real name anyway. If he is indeed an international jewel thief, I'm guessing he can disappear for a while."

Maude smiled. "She will be heartbroken." Her expression faded as she considered the rest of the evening's events. "So, the boat..."

"That was easier than I thought. I looked at the names. His was called *Darling Dawn*." He grew serious as he added, "I must say, I didn't expect to see him herding you at gunpoint."

Tears began to well up in Maude's eyes. "Don, you could have been killed. You should have been killed."

"Maybe, but I wasn't. Are you ready to tell me about your trip to Lily Dale and why you dragged poor Charlotte all the way back to Buffalo and into a very dangerous situation?"

Maude drained her glass, poured herself another, and then began telling her husband what she had learned from the files Abby had given her and from the past life regression. The first shimmers of dawn could be seen from the kitchen window by the time she was finished. "I think everything I have experienced during the past two years was leading up to this. I think I was supposed to save your life."

Don had listened carefully without interruption. He took a few moments to consider everything he had been told before he responded. "So, if I understand you correctly, I was Johnny in my past life."

"I think so." With more confidence, she added, "Charlotte told me you were."

"Hmph." The response was so typical of Don. He would not argue or ask questions. He believed it if she believed it. "I guess this makes us soulmates, which is pretty great, I think."

Maude smiled. "Yeah, it is pretty great."

Don leaned in and kissed his wife. It was a kiss that held the devotion of past lives and present, as well as the promise of life and love through the remainder of time.

Epilogue

Fall 1871

Martha heard the sound of the front door close and then soft shoes on the hardwood floors traveling toward the back porch. She lowered her stocking feet, which had been curled up underneath her, and used them to propel the porch swing gently back and forth while she waited for Alva to make her way outside. *Thank God for her!* Martha made sure she acknowledged that thought every single day, for what would have become of her had Alva not suggested that they move to Cassadaga and join the other Spiritualists in the picturesque lakeside community? There were enough year-round residents in the area between Cassadaga and nearby Laona that her skills as a physician were of use. Between Martha and Alva, they saw to the spiritual and physical health of their neighbors and protected those who caught the interest of Constable Schaeffer.

The members of the Laona Free Association had been meeting regularly in the summer months in a grove on Willard Alden's farm. What started out as daylong picnics turned into weeklong camp sessions where members came to discuss everything from religion to the enfranchisement of women and to organize their rapidly growing movement. However, Martha wasn't fooling herself or anyone else. She came hoping to hone her gifts for the sole purpose of reaching out to Johnny on the other side. Sadly, it was a goal she had yet to achieve. Martha spent long hours in the Leolyn Woods in silent contemplation, hoping Johnny would reach out from the other side. So far as she was able to determine, he had yet to make contact.

Alva opened the screen door and extended her hand toward Martha. "You have a letter."

Martha nodded, accepting the envelope, but setting it facedown beside her. "Do ye miss yer children?" It had been over a year since Johnny's death and she had not been back to Buffalo since shortly after the funeral. While Martha had exchanged letters often with her son Robert, they had not seen each other since she left the city.

"Of course I do. Any mother would, but they are grown with families of their own." Alva had two daughters and a son, all of whom lived in Buffalo. Her eldest daughter, Barbara, had recently finished medical school and had taken Martha's place at the asylum. Jennifer and Douglas took over the healing practice when their mother moved to Cassadaga. Jennifer had her mother's gift of clairvoyance and Douglas produced and sold the many botanical remedies Alva had devised with the help of her spirit guide. "It is my own fault that they have little to do with me. They wanted for nothing when they were young and as a result are unable to manage their own finances." Even before she met Martha, Alva's three children had little contact with her. Each of their quarrels with her occurred on separate occasions and each over a sum of money that was lent to them by their mother and had not yet been paid back. The last straw came when Barbara tried to have her own mother committed to the insane asylum in an effort to gain control of the considerable fortune that Alva had amassed over the past two decades. Even though her eldest daughter eventually gave up the attempt to have her mother declared insane, Alva knew it was time to leave Buffalo and force her adult children to make their way without her help or interference. "If Johan were still alive, he would play the role of peacemaker. He always did when they were young, but he is not here and it is not in my nature to chase after them."

Martha rose from the swing, leaving it gliding back and forth in her wake with the letter now precariously balanced on the edge of the seat. "'Tis a fine afternoon. Will ye join me for a bit? I'll make some tea." Indeed it was. The sun was shining, the lake was shimmering and a gentle breeze made the back porch much more comfortable than the house.

Alva reached out and stopped the swing, gesturing for Martha to sit back down. "Read your letter and I'll put on the kettle."

There was always a bit of guilt associated with reading a letter from home and, were it not for Alva's insistence, Martha would put it off for as long as she was able. "Aye, thank ye." After a deep breath and a long sigh, she opened the letter.

Martha Quinn
Cassadaga, New York

September 3, 1871

Dearest Mother,

I hope this letter finds you well. I'm sure you have noticed by now that there is a second letter included here from Daniel. Although it pains me to do so, I'll let him share what I know you'll agree is joyous news. There is much to tell you. Most of it shall leave you in better spirits than this letter found you, I hope, but there is some sad news and I do you no favor by saving it for the end. Charlie has passed. The only consolation I can offer with this grievous news is that he passed peacefully in his sleep last week. As you well know, our hearts were broken and we will dearly miss him. He is at peace next to his beloved Karin at St. Joseph's Cemetery, should you desire to return to Buffalo and pay your respects.

It is my hope that I raise your spirits, which must certainly have fallen with this last report, with the news that Auntie Ciara and Uncle Michael have purchased the house on Linwood Avenue. I know that you consider the house mine, nevertheless, I shall have the proceeds from the sale sent to your bank in Cassadaga. The shop has attained such success that we have opened another further down Main Street, which I alone manage. I have greater need of peace of mind where your well-being is concerned than I do of coin and I hope you will indulge without argument my wish that you keep the money from the sale of the house.

I am unsure how often you hear from your sisters, my aunties, so I will divulge without fear of breaking any confidences that Auntie Patricia and Uncle Rolland are moving to Albany. Mary Karin is in blessed expectation of her third child and Auntie dearly wishes to be closer to her grandchildren. It is their intention to depart by month's end. Perhaps you would consider a trip to Buffalo to see them off.

That is all the news I have to share. Know that Gertrude and the boys are well and send their love. We all miss you terribly and pray that you will find the strength to return to Buffalo, even for a short while, so that we may all assure ourselves that you are well. Should you need anything, you have only to ask. God Bless.

Your devoted son,

Robert

P.S. Rudolph wishes you to know that he was in the top of his class in spelling. It is my belief that he is eager for you to hear of this accomplishment in light of the fact that his older brother, Frederick, struggles with that very subject. Rudolph says he will make a demonstration of his superior skills in a letter to you in the near future!

Martha Quinn
Spiritualist Camp
Lily Dale, New York

September 3, 1871

Dearest Auntie,

As of the writing of this letter Felicity and I are well and hope it finds you the same. I will not waste time and space with further pleasantries as undoubtedly my cousin has informed you that we have news that I know you will be eager and pleased to hear. Felicity and I are expecting our first child in the spring and it is our hope that this child will be brought into the world among the Free Thinkers and raised in the absence of suspicion and fear. As the Spiritualist community continues to grow in Cassadaga, we feel that each of our chosen professions will be needed. It is my intention to set up offices there and once again practice law. As you know, Felicity is a teacher and feels in her heart that she could be of use in helping the children both with their common schooling and their spiritual education. The extraordinary sensibilities that allow her to communicate without the advantage of hearing the spoken word will be an advantage in furthering the education of these gifted children.

We want you to be secure in the knowledge that we relocate to Cassadaga in the hopes of improving our own well-being and prospects in a way that we cannot here in the city, among like-minded people. We have no plans to intrude upon the life that you have made for yourself, although it is our dearest hope that this news brings you joy and that you will welcome us into your new world. I'll be traveling to Cassadaga this month to secure a plot of land and arrange for the construction of our new home. Please write back as soon as you are able so that I may know whether or not you would welcome a visit while I'm there. God bless.

Your loving nephew,

Daniel.

A smile spread slowly across her face as Martha folded the sheets and returned them to the envelope. "Good news, I see," Alva speculated as she returned with the tea tray.

"Aye," Martha agreed. "We're to have company soon."

Now it was Alva's turn to smile. "I knew they'd come!"

Acknowledgements

To my husband, Bob, and my son, Charlie, I thank you for taking care of yourselves, the dogs, the house and the business when I needed you to.

My novels are inspired by my scholarly work and so I thank Drs. Joyce E. Sirianni and Douglas Perrelli for inviting me to join the Erie County Poorhouse Cemetery Project. It has been such a pleasure to work on this project. I have learned so much from the both of them and their friendship has inspired each of my books.

There were several historians who were incredibly generous in giving me both their time and their detailed knowledge of various aspects of Buffalo's history. Jennifer Liber Raines from the Western New York Genealogical Society is without a doubt the most gifted researcher I know. She provided me with countless municipal reports and period newspaper articles that helped me to understand where the Erie County Poorhouse and Insane Asylum existed in the public stream of consciousness. She also tracked down much of the secondary source data for the treatment of the insane in Buffalo.

Cynthia Van Ness and her staff from the Buffalo History Museum provided me with enormously helpful primary and secondary source data including microfilm of the Erie County Poorhouse Inmate Records, period maps, the City of Buffalo Directories, information on the 116th Regiment New York Volunteer Infantry and images and details on prisoner carriages used in Buffalo.

Charles Alaimo from the Buffalo and Erie County Public Library helped me navigate period maps of the city so that my characters could move about on foot, horseback or by carriage as they would have in Buffalo during the nineteenth century.

Douglas Platt from the Museum of disABILITY History in Buffalo, New York, helped me to understand details of American Sign Language that were very helpful to writing the scenes in which dialogue takes place between a hearing character and a deaf character. I am also grateful to the Museum of disABILITY History for their general support and their commitment to preserving institutional cemeteries in New York State.

Ron Nagy from the Lily Dale Museum and Amanda Shepp from the Marion H. Skidmore Library, in Lily Dale, New York, provided me with period newspaper articles and other primary and secondary source material on the history of Lily Dale and Modern Spiritualism.

Linda Lohr from the History of Medicine Library at the University at Buffalo was a tremendous help in tracking down articles from the Buffalo Medical and Surgical Journal and other historical references relating to medicine, medical care in Buffalo and the diagnosis and treatment of insanity during the nineteenth century.

I am so grateful to Cydney A. Kelley, Attorney at Law, for taking time out of her very busy day to help me understand all of the many documents associated with Antoinette Matteson's will. The character of Alva Awalte is based on Matteson and the will provided valuable insight that helped bring this character to life.

I have four wonderful friends who helped me sort out how to treat heal abscesses in horses during the nineteenth century. Many thanks to Heather Allen, DVM, James Albert, DVM, Nancy Tatarek, Ph.D. and Lisa Guerrera.

There is a real antique lamp shop located on Hertel Avenue in Buffalo, New York, called The Antique Lamp Company and Gift Emporium. John and Sue Tobin, the owners of this wonderful establishment, were very gracious and accommodating in answering all of my questions about their business and about the retail items mentioned in this book. I am also grateful for their continued support.

Thanks to my readers, Bob Higgins, Casilda G. Lucas, Jacqueline Lunger, Jenna Orlikowski, Betty Lou Johnson, Jerry Scharf and Christine Hicks for helping me with everything from inner senses and local history to spelling and grammar.

About the Author

Rosanne Higgins was born in Enfield, Connecticut, however spent her youth in Buffalo, New York. She studied the Asylum Movement in the nineteenth century and its impact on disease specific mortality. This research focused on the Erie, Niagara, and Monroe County Poorhouses in Western New York. That research earned her a Ph.D. in Anthropology in 1998 and lead to the publication of her research. Her desire to tell another side of 'The Poorhouse Story' that would be accessible to more than just the scholarly community resulted in the *Orphans and Inmates* series, which chronicles fictional accounts of poorhouse residents based on historical data.

www.rosannehiggins.com/blog.html

www.facebook.com/pages/Orphans-and-Inmates/516800631758088